Fire ♥ Me

A Tale of scheming, Dreaming, and Looking for Love in All the wrong places

LIBBY MALIN

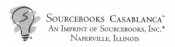
SOURCEBOOKS CASABLANCA™
AN IMPRINT OF SOURCEBOOKS, INC.®
NAPERVILLE, ILLINOIS

Published by Sourcebooks Casablanca, an imprint of Sourcebooks, Inc.
P.O. Box 4410, Naperville, Illinois 60567–4410
(630) 961–3900
FAX: (630) 961–2168
www.sourcebooks.com

Library of Congress Cataloging-in-Publication Data

Malin, Libby.
Fire me : a tale of scheming, dreaming, and looking for love in all the wrong places / Libby Malin.
p. cm.
1. Work environment—Fiction. 2. Corporate culture—Fiction. 3. Sex in the workplace—Fiction. I. Title.
PS3613.A4358F57 2009
813.'6—dc22

                                2008043078

          Printed and bound in the United States of America.
                VP 10 9 8 7 6 5 4 3 2 1

To Leslie
With much love and gratitude

Chapter 1

From Mitch Burnham's book *Use It or Lose It*:

> *Think of your employees as children. You might let them sit behind the wheel, but you'd never give them the keys to the Maserati. Sure, let them pretend if it makes them feel good. But in the end, there's only one driver and it's not one of the kids.*

Monday, 7:02 a.m.

SOMETIMES ANNE WYATT WISHED she could feed parts of her life into a shredder.

She stood staring out at the crystal blue sky from her seventh-floor, Crystal City, Virginia, apartment, fingers warming around a Burnham Group mug, thoughts jammed in first gear as they outstripped her ability to process them all. Her short, reddish hair was still damp from the shower and she wore one navy pump but couldn't find the other.

Should I call my brother to apologize for getting angry with him last night? Should I give up on Lean Cuisine and start eating regular frozen meals? Should I have handed in my resignation earlier when I first got word I'd landed the California job? Should I start drinking decaf or will I get a headache? Am I spending too much time with Rob when I know the relationship's not going anywhere? Should I forget about finding the other shoe and just change my outfit entirely?

Her thoughts danced and fluttered like the blossoms outside her window, eventually landing gently on the argument with her brother. Her brother was in the military and headed out for deployment overseas.

Her cat meowed gently from the short hall to the bedroom.

"Maisie, don't you think I should be able to suppress minor irritations at a time like this?" she asked without turning to look at her. She took the cat's silence as a yes.

But no, no, she had to jump in with verbal fists flying and rhetorical arrows zinging. She came from a family of fighters, after all. Her father had been a full-bird colonel and his father a general. Her mother had been an Army nurse.

Anne had not followed their path but had spent most of her young adulthood carving out a road that led in the opposite direction, away from rigidity and structure toward freedom and flexibility. She'd pursued a degree in the arts.

But she was Corporate Girl now, having forsaken flowing skirts, velvety jackets, and dangly earrings. Sometimes she wondered if her previous life had been a dream, or if she'd really wanted that life, or merely wanted to rebel or… or what?

It didn't matter anyway. She might be a responsible contributor to society now, but in her brother's eyes she would always be… Irresponsible Anne. She wished she were.

I should call Jack and smooth things over, but that's tantamount to surrender. Surely he'll lose what little respect he has for me if he senses I'm waving the white flag.

Noticing a smudge on the flat pane of glass, she quickly retrieved a bottle of window cleaner and square of paper towel. Here, at least, was a problem she could quickly solve. She'd become fastidious about her apartment lately, since she was going to need to sublet it. As she rubbed the glass, she admired the lush green landscape of spring, the earth so thick with new growth it looked like you could scoop it up with a spoon. She stepped back to admire her work just as a flash of deep blue broke away from the paler blue sky.

Bluebird of happiness—an omen! She smiled. *What message do you have for me?*

Bump! Splat! Bluebird of happiness ran into transparently clean window.

Ohmygod. She dropped the window cleaner as if it were a smoking gun.

Get out of here, Anne, before you slay any more harbingers of spring. She hustled to her bedroom, searching for that other shoe and rehearsing her speech.

"I'm resigning, Mr. Burnham, because…"

Kenneth Wright Montgomery III growled to himself as he threw drawings and pencils into a large leather portfolio. *Simple enough to get going early, Ken. Just means waking up when the alarm goes off the first time.*

Let's go, man!

As he closed the portfolio, a corner of heavy paper stopped him. *Okay, no go.* He pulled out a sketch to right it, but spent a few seconds smiling at the beginnings of a pencil drawing of his coworker, Anne Wyatt. If he could just find the time, he'd capture those big eyes perfectly…

He shook his head, repositioning the drawing before zipping up the bag.

He'd be lucky if he had time to think, let alone sketch at the office today. The workload was preposterously heavy, and his boss was a mercurial maniac who changed his mind about graphic designs as often as Britney Spears changed hairstyles. But it paid extremely well and that was all he was interested in right now.

Ken was all about the "right now" right now. *Let's go, let's go!*

He stepped forward, catching a glimpse of himself in the mirror by the door. His thick hair dampened his blue oxford shirt. His dark hair wouldn't take so long to dry, of course, if he'd cut it. Not likely. Then he'd really look like his father. He straightened his blue and gold tie and reached for the doorknob. And stopped cold, remembering.

Okay, no go.

Today was "Pizzazz Day" at the Burnham Group. Staff members had been exhorted to wear something unique, crazy, fun, even weird. A blue blazer, tan Dockers, and varsity-striped tie didn't exactly shout: "Here stands a creative man."

He growled again and rushed back into his bedroom, hangers screeching on a desperate hunt for the Wild Outfit. Shirts, suits, blazers, neatly pressed pants—*no go, no go, no go, dammit!*

Finally, his gaze lit on a bright, lime green tie with a Santa design. Okay, that would have to do, something that expressed his "inner child." He yanked off the old and threw on the new.

Let's go, let's go, let's freakin' go!

But as he hurried to the foyer of his Silver Spring, Maryland, one bedroom, his toe caught on a stray piece of parquet tile. *No. Go!* He'd have to call the landlord to get that fixed. Damned if he'd lose his security deposit. Every extra bit of cash he made now was going toward "The Escape Plan." Escape the corporate world. Escape his father's clutches. Escape... oh hell, other stuff he couldn't think of now.

He'd come to the conclusion, after working for his father's financial services business in Baltimore for two years, then for an arts consortium in DC for another five, and now for the Burnham Group for a scant six months, that he had to approach life the same way he approached painting and drawing. He couldn't just stare at the canvas, waiting and imagining. He had to make the first stroke and let it both limit and free him at the same time. He had to make choices.

Okay, here was a choice—he'd call the landlord later. *Let's get going!*

He grabbed his portfolio, opened the door, and raced to the elevator, stepping on just before the doors glided closed. A business-suited woman nodded a quick hello.

"Morning," he said, leaning his portfolio against the wall while he finished knotting his tie. Triggered by the motion, the tie burst into cheerful electronic song. They zoomed to the lobby to the tune of "Santa Claus Is Coming to Town."

Chapter 2

From Anne Wyatt's ghostwritten foreword to Mitch Burnham's book *The Action Alternative*:

> *How do we know when to jump on an opportunity and when to let it pass by? This question is at the core of life, not just of business. There are no easy choices. There are only choices.*

7:25 a.m.

AT THE BURNHAM GROUP'S K Street office in DC, Anne threw her purse into her lower-right drawer, booted up her computer, and craned her head over the top of her cubicle to see if Mitch's office door was open yet. Nope. Closed tight as a vault. So much for coming in at the crack of dawn to talk to him. He was usually in early, but maybe killing that bluebird of happiness at her apartment had given Anne bad karma.

She blew out a sigh of frustration. She'd awakened gloriously joyful, about to embark on a major new step, one that would kick-start her drifting life into purposeful gear. "Mr. Burnham, I'm leaving because..." She mouthed the words to herself, smoothing the hem of her lime green shell. Hmm... was it "pizzazzy" enough?

They'd had dress-down days and dress-up days. They'd had company-color days (gold and teal) and they'd had "against the grain" days where they were told to dress against type. (Lenny in accounting had been so convincing as a female hooker that he had been propositioned twice on the metro on the way in and nearly arrested on the way home.) And they'd had what Mitch called "business blah" days where they dressed in neutral colors and bland clothes, the purpose of which was to demonstrate how demoralizing such a monochromatic palette can be on the psyche.

It had disturbed Anne that she'd had so many outfits to choose from for that particular exercise.

Mitch Burnham was many things, but he would never be described as bland. Famous for his theories on quality-improvement techniques, he walked the talk, using his "team" as guinea pigs. At a recent consulting gig for a Cincinnati theater company, Mitch had been impressed with how "vibrantly" the troupe dressed and acted. He thought it helped them stay in touch with their inner muse, their creative energy. Thus, Pizzazz Day was born.

He'd even written an article about "putting the pizzazz back in the team" for the Burnham Report, the pricey, twice-monthly subscription newsletter Anne edited. "Forget casual Fridays," he wrote— or rather, Anne had written for him—"tan Dockers and high-end blue jeans have just become another business uniform. If you want your workers to feel and act extraordinary, you have to encourage them to look that way, to think creatively from the moment they wake up and wonder what they'll wear to the office."

Anne had had a lot of meetings with Mitch, drafting that article, fun meetings where he let her push back while he challenged her assumptions. Won't this seem kind of juvenile to some folks? she'd asked. And he'd stared at her through his eyelashes, those long, sexy eyelashes that shaded his hypnotic eyes.

Damn but it's unfair for him to have eyelashes like that when all I've got are short, stubby ones that require a mascara hair weave before they even show up.

"Doesn't matter if it seems juvenile, Anne," he'd said in that smooth, low voice that always held mirth when his ideas were being questioned. "It's not what they think when they're given the order. It's what they feel when they're carrying it out."

Mitch was proving his point about Pizzazz Day. The employees at the Burnham Group would be the first to try it out.

Poor Lenny. When he first saw the memo, he thought it said "Pizza Day."

The soft whoosh of the elevator around the corner had Anne peering over the edge of the cubicle again. A strong male voice cut through the near-silent hum of the office ventilation system. At its sound, her heart started to flutter and her palms tingled. Her eyelash-challenged eyes opened wide. Mitch did that to her. From the first moment she'd met him, when his rugged face crinkled into a wide smile that seemed to communicate it was his lucky day now that he'd found her, she'd been under his spell.

"—but what did they say two months ago, Lenny?"

Shooting completely upright, Anne moistened her lips and smoothed her short hair. Nerves pinpricked her fingers so she shook them while taking a deep breath. She could do this.

And so, Mitch, I couldn't turn down this offer, and I'll be submitting my letter of resignation immediately. Dead bluebirds or not.

No, not "will be submitting." Too weak. "Am submitting." No—"will submit." *No, no, no. I submit my resignation. And don't forget to say "Mr. Burnham." It's always Mr. Burnham in the office, never "Mitch."*

This was nuts. She tried to blow out her nerves by taking a deep, cleansing breath—just as they'd done in the Yoga Business Dynamics class Mitch had forced them all to take. Poor Lenny hadn't fared too well in that one either, come to think of it. He'd sprained his right wrist.

Anne stepped forward to catch Mitch's attention as he entered the area, but he was deep in conversation on his cell phone. When he was focused on something, he willed the rest of the world away. Oddly enough, Anne found this attribute more charming than irritating. It made his focus on her so damned exhilarating.

"But what about the quarterlies? I saw those reports myself, dammit. The subscriptions are up by nearly twenty percent if you count the bonus numbers…" He noticed her. His big, angular head nodded in her direction and the faintest smile played at his lips.

He might be in his fifties, but Mitch had the muscular, well-toned body of a man twenty years his junior. His graying hair was a wavy cascade from his high forehead to his shirt collar. And with his usual panache, he'd chosen a vintage blue-and-tan paisley Nehru jacket for his "pizzazz" outfit. Paired with faded jeans, it looked more hot than cool. Anne was struck, as always, by how easily he managed to hit just the right note.

And she got that nervous girl-crush sensation she always seemed to feel around him, where the most important thing in her world at that moment became making him like her, respect her, yes, even want her.

She opened her mouth to speak—*Mr. Burnham,* she heard herself say as she followed him, but it came out in a thin, little-girl voice that made her sound like she was about to ask for money for the ice-cream man. He looked at her outfit and raised his eyebrows. Not enough pizzazz. *Rats.*

"I…"

He shook his head and pointed to the phone, then dashed into his office, shutting the door with a soft kick of his heel.

A long exhale escaped her. Biting her lip, she stood alone outside his door. No pizzazz here. And she had been looking forward to this little *tête-à-tête.* Maybe that's why she was so damn nervous about it. She had all these expectations of how it would go, of how he'd beg her to stay, tell her how valuable she was. And now she couldn't even get his attention enough to set the stage, let alone begin the performance.

Disappointed in herself and him, she returned to her desk, giving herself a pep talk along the way. So what if Mitch was a sexy—and now single—hunk with gazillions in his bank account? So what if he regularly lunched with *Forbes* 500 CEOs, golfed with the president, appeared on CNBC's business shows, and could melt the faint-hearted with his penetrating glare? She was Anne Wyatt, Daughter of Warriors. *You'd think I was just hired, for crying out loud, when I've been working here for four—okay, three and a half—freaking years.*

It's not Mitch that rattled her, she consoled herself. No, not any longer. It was spring. When she was a kid, spring always made her feel like her skin didn't fit. Like something amazing was about to happen, just out of sight or around the corner.

Nothing is coming, Anne Wyatt, she lectured herself, unless you talk to Mitch before he walls himself up for the day in meetings, on phone calls, and in do-not-disturb-me work that will occupy him until the next millennium. If she was going to hand in her resignation face-to-face, she'd have to scoot in before the cone of silence descended.

"I resign," she said into the quiet office, pleased with the simple, active-voice construction. "No, I quit." Much better. The staccato of those one-syllable words conveyed strength, forcefulness. Mitch would like that. Action, Mitch preached, is almost always better than inaction. A mistake made while doing something can turn out better than a mistake made by hesitating and taking no action. That gem of wisdom had appeared in his book *The Action Alternative: Why Doing Something Is Better Than Doing Nothing.* Anne had helped write the foreword to the second edition.

Over the past twenty years Mitch had written a dozen mega-bestselling books about how to make businesses operate smarter, leaner, faster, better, and more profitably. With titles like *Use It or Lose It, The Twelve-minute Management Plan, The Team Theory of Business Success,* and *The Mitch Principles,* they skyrocketed to mega sales when various CEO buddies of his touted them on talk shows and in magazine interviews.

The Burnham Group was the physical manifestation of all his advice—it now did international consulting, produced quarterly reports on business productivity, published a twice-monthly, twenty-four page newsletter (Anne's main project), scheduled lectures for Mitch around the world, and coordinated the latest program, the Burnham Business Adventure Series, a selection of outdoor survival-type camps for management teams that needed to work on "trust" issues.

The camps, in fact, were what had led Mitch to take his company public a year ago when he needed the investment dollars to expand. It had been a nightmare ever since, however, with "bean counters" hovering over everything and pesky board meetings that left him dour and irritable, looking like he needed more than an infusion of pizzazz to buck him up. In fact, he looked oddly vulnerable after many of these meetings. He talked to Lenny a lot now.

The elevator slid open again and Ken, the new graphic designer, stepped off.

That Ken. He was a good-looking guy but kept to himself. And why did he insist on bringing his portfolio to work with him every day? It made him look like he was still job hunting, waiting for the opportunity to bolt. Maybe she would talk to him about that, offer him some collegial advice.

"Good morning," he said before vanishing into the coffee room.

She just nodded a hello.

Since all was lost as far as seeing Mitch alone right now, she settled in, flicking on her computer and clipping her cell phone to her waist after noting a missed call from her friend Louise.

Like all the cubicles in the center of the administrative floor, Anne's was small and spare. Three of them were all in a row on this side of the floor—Ken on her right and Sheila, another communications assistant, on her left.

When she first came to work here, they'd had an open floor arrangement—no cubicles, just desks in odd configurations. It was supposed to engender a sense of excitement and spirit, but actually led to irritation and disgruntlement—it was too noisy and disorganized. Over time, it began to evolve into jerry-rigged cubicles as some creative types began bringing in bamboo screens and framed curtains. The room started to look like a colorful but shabby third-world alleyway.

Right before he took the company public, Mitch sent around a memo. He would be giving them all a gift to celebrate the change in company configuration—spanking new Softone work modules designed to mute office noise and enhance privacy. The next day the screens disappeared and the cubicles went up. And the day after that, the new board of directors came through for a tour.

Anne had tried to dress up her cubicle with some personal touches, but she wondered sometimes if that had been a mistake— sort of like photos on a prison wall, more a reminder of what she was missing than what she had. Above her utilitarian desk she'd tacked a calendar with pictures of California, a gift from Louise. In the corner was a plant stand overflowing with dying greenery, and on top of her bookcase were photos of her family, her cat, and a snapshot of Anne in front of a small but very selective art gallery in Carmel. A low filing cabinet was topped with Burnham Group brochures, reports, and press releases, all in perfectly aligned stacks.

Picking lint from her jacket, she stared at her navy shoes, which made her feel like a librarian on her way out on a date. Remembering Mitch's disdainful glance at her pizzazz-challenged outfit, she opened her bottom desk drawer and pulled out a pair of walking shoes, substituting those for the blue heels. They were bright white and clunky but at least they stood out. She'd hardly worn them. She'd bought them three years ago when she thought she'd have time to exercise on her lunch hour. Fat chance. Between deadlines and meetings with Mitch, she was lucky if she had time for lunch on her lunch hour.

And so, Mr. Burnham, I am leaving the Burnham Group because I really want to eat lunch.

All right, so some of those missed lunches hadn't been because of work.

Just one more thing to feed into the shredder.

Chapter 3

From Mitch Burnham's book *All Management Is Crisis Management*:

> *Business isn't beanbag. It's a fight-to-the-death struggle in the arena. You're either the lion or supper. Those are the only "market niches" you need to keep your focus on. Lion. Or supper.*

7:39 a.m.

KEN SIPPED AT HIS mug of tea—no more caffeine for him or he'd be as wired as a tree in an electric storm—and smoothly moved his mouse around a design of the Burnham Group Annual Report. For the fiftieth time since coming here, he reminded himself how lucky he was to get the job on such short notice. He'd left his last position rather precipitously. He glanced with longing at the portfolio stowed under his desk.

Was his coworker Anne talking to herself?

He'd heard her muttering when he came in that morning and they'd nodded their hellos. He thought he'd caught the boss's name a few times in her mumblings. *Good for you, Anne. Tell off that pompous ass who runs this place. I'll be rooting for you.*

He'd wanted to come in early today, but he'd overslept and traffic was slow. He made a mental note to get up earlier tomorrow to either work from home first or come in while it was quiet. He had this plan. Sometimes, like this morning when the Santa Claus tie sprang to life, he felt foolish and ungrateful for wanting a change so badly. As jobs go, he could do worse. He *had* done worse.

He looked at his portfolio again. His business plan wasn't the only thing beckoning to him. Nudging the leather case with his toe, he brought it to the side and unzipped it, pulling out an unfinished sketch like a spy glancing at secret codes.

It was the drawing of Anne. So far, he'd roughed in only the shape of her face and hair, but had spent an inordinate amount of time on her eyes. He was thinking of calling it "Dryad Observed," after the wood nymphs that silently watched the world. Anne was like that, quiet and watchful, her face as smooth as a still summer sky—but just as changeable. He'd seen her transform from grim to gregarious in an instant, from mask-like serenity to hilarity, her face shifting into wide eyes and a broad smile when touched by humor or surprise. He was trying to capture in his drawing the very second the change occurred, but so far that look eluded him. He worked from memory, stolen moments, and a photograph of her in her cubicle.

This drawing was an exception to how he normally approached his art. He usually was looking for ways to enhance or "explode" a scene, thinking how playing up the lighting on a landscape could make it appear dreamlike, or how using muted grays on a happy scene would bring out an undercurrent of poignancy. But with this drawing of Anne—just getting her right would be intriguing enough. He didn't need to add his spin on the image.

He'd considered asking Anne out, but ditched the idea when he'd heard her on the phone with somebody named Rob. It sounded like a relationship.

Ken Montgomery had few rules but this was one of them—don't poach. Not good for the poacher. Not good for the poachee.

Before he had a chance to look up again, his phone rang, echoing the ring of Anne's phone. Simultaneously, but to different callers, they both said, "Hello."

The airy voice of real estate agent and business counselor Cyndi Rogers greeted him. After friendly greetings, she got right to the point.

"The places I've scouted out for you have rents that are double what you want to pay, Ken," she said in a voice that was as cheerful as a sun-drenched nursery. Cyndi could be giving you a diagnosis of terminal illness and she'd still use the same perky voice.

He flipped a pencil onto his desk, leaning back in his chair while he ran his fingers through his hair. He could barely afford the figures he'd already provided her.

"What if we look outside of Georgetown?" he asked, grimacing. Georgetown was the best place for what he wanted to do. Great foot traffic, great demographic, everything he needed.

"Well, some of these are on the fringe as it is. I could try Dupont Circle, some of the areas that haven't yet been gentrified. Or Northeast, near Catholic University. But you're probably not going to find much else substantially below these."

He waited for her to offer more of a plan, realizing after a few seconds that she wouldn't. Cyndi's voice might paint bright colors, but when it came to facing facts, she was a realist working mostly with dark charcoals and amber shadows. He would have to pose the tough questions, the answers to which would be obvious before the breath left his mouth.

"I take it you wouldn't recommend any lower-rent districts?"

"Not for what you want to do. You might as well—"

"—take the money and burn it." Despite his frustration, he smiled. He'd heard her offer that advice so many times he'd begun to wonder what a pile of cash would look like consumed by dancing flames.

He picked up the pencil and turned it round and round in his hand, trying to think of something to say that would get him where he wanted to be in as short a time as possible.

His father would know what to do. He'd whisper orders with the confidence of royalty and have a dozen minions scouring the landscape, making the perfect deal, strong-arming business partners into cowering to his will, or sweet-talking them with promises of good things to come. His father and uncle might have inherited their financial services firm from a long list of Montgomerys before them, but neither shrank from using the power the firm had accumulated.

All Ken had to do was call him, ask him for the seed money…

Maybe he'd work a little harder. Maybe he'd stay a little longer at the Burnham Group. It wasn't that bad a job, certainly not for the short notice he'd had to find one. Who was he to complain? He had the means to realize his dream, he just wouldn't get it instantly. *Suck it up, man.*

Cyndi filled his silence with a muffled "thanks" to someone in her office. A few seconds later, she spoke.

"Ken, this is your lucky day," she said in a five-thousand-watt voice. "A storefront on the edge of Georgetown is coming open in the next twenty-four. Can you break away to see it with me today? It looks good on paper—it's sure to be snatched up fast."

He sat up straight, grabbing the pencil tight. "Can we do it over lunch?"

"I'll see what I can set up."

The husky, no-nonsense voice of Jack, Anne's brother, crackled over the phone and her heart zoomed into third gear. He never called her at work. And he never, never, ever called her first after an argument. That military training ain't for softies.

Anne had experienced only once the unexpected "Firebell in the Night" phone call announcing doom and gloom, but it was enough to send her heart racing and mind careening through a thousand deadly scenarios whenever a family member called at an unusual time. When her mother had called at two in the morning a year ago to say her dad had passed away, she'd been dreaming of angels singing. She liked to think that's because they were, considering he was marching through the Gates.

Although it wasn't night, when she heard Jack's voice on the other end of the line, she had the same panicked reaction. She sat upright and gripped the phone like a life preserver.

"Mom okay?" she blurted out.

"She's fine as far as I know," he said. "Deployment's been moved up, that's all."

That's all? "When?" Her pulse rate throbbed wildly, her skin buzzed with tension, her heart had dropped to below sea level. And then a horrible, horrible thought arrived on the wings of the dead bluebird—*at least Dad isn't alive to worry about Jack's deployment.* And then another horrible thought spawned of the first one—*maybe that's why Dad died, because Jack is going away and Dad would be heartbroken if... No, no, mustn't think that way.*

"In about a week."

"You're kidding! I thought you had a couple of months—"

"It's been in the works for awhile, Anne. I told you about it, remember?" He didn't hide his impatience.

"I need a favor," he said, cutting to the chase.

A favor? Despite her worry, reflexive sibling rivalry kicked in and she narrowed her eyes. Their argument the night before had started because Jack wouldn't do *her* a favor. She'd asked him if she could keep her car parked in front of his Virginia home until she got settled in her new job in San Francisco, and he'd said no. Okay, so he hadn't really said no. He just hadn't immediately agreed. He'd hemmed and hawed and told her he was afraid if he said yes, she'd just end up leaving the car there forever and he'd be stuck with having to deal with it.

"What, me irresponsible?" she'd protested. And then he'd launched into the litany. "Well," he'd said, "you do have this history…"

There was the time in middle school when you let an older friend drive and wreck the car when we were stationed in Georgia.

There was the time when you thought hitchhiking was safe in Arlington and Dad had to ground you.

And then, of course, there was California. So many things to choose from there—like the year she maxed out her credit card (Mom bailed her out) or the January her landlord locked her out of the apartment because she'd failed to pay the rent (well, it wasn't just her; others shared the flat).

Ah yes, California. Her Great Rebellion. Dreaming her way to a bachelor's degree in art history and working odd jobs after graduation as she waited for life and fame to find her. Her most stable period was working for the art gallery in the photo.

Jack thought he'd rescued her from aimless drifting when she came back East by introducing her to someone who knew Mitch and voilà—just the kind of job an artistic type with a talent for word-smithing would enjoy. "Job" being the key word in that sentence.

"What do you want?" she asked, clipped and to the point. She was about to add something snotty like, "I don't mind doing you a favor even if you won't do one for me," when he launched into his request.

"I want you to tell Mom about my deployment."

"What?!"

"Marie and I have a lot to do before then."

Her stomach flipped over. *Lot to do*—she knew what that meant. It meant making sure his will and life insurance were up-to-date and that his wife Marie understood their finances, that the military had the correct "next of kin" listed for… the unthinkable. Their Dad used to help the men and women under his care with all this stuff whenever they were being deployed.

But what's with Jack avoiding telling their mother? She was used to this sort of thing. What did he think she'd do—burst into tears?

But of course. She had been distracted and melancholy ever since Dad's death. And big, brave Jack might be able to crawl under barbed wire, jump out of airplanes, and attack in the face of an onslaught of fire, but he couldn't stomach seeing a woman cry.

Come to think of it, that wasn't high on Anne's happy list either. When Anne had told her mother about her new job with a children's hospital on the West Coast, her mother had immediately said, "That's going to be quite a commute." And then when Anne had talked about how much she'd longed to return to the Golden State, her mother had become all weepy and distant, sniffling her way through the obligatory "I'm so proud of you" sentiments and then asking Anne what her boyfriend Rob thought of all this. Translation: When are you getting married and settling down near here?

Aw geez. She and Rob were friends, not boyfriend/girlfriend.

The guilts, the guilts. They washed over her like a tsunami, swamping her bad, pulling her under. It must have been guilt-sale day at the Karma Warehouse. First the bird, now this.

"Tell her not to worry about anything," Jack said, his voice changing to Army-standard-issue bluster. "You know *I'll* be all right. I'm not stupid."

Ah yes. Only the stupid are killed.

"Tell her Marie's going to come visit her with little Jason as soon as I take off—for a long visit."

"She'll love that."

"She loves Marie. But Marie's not you."

So they were back to this—Anne, the one who had not married and borne children. Lately, her mother had become more blunt with her questions. She'd even asked Anne a couple of weeks ago if she ever thought she was getting too old to have kids. Too old! She was only twenty-nine!

"Has she done anything about going back to work part-time?" Anne changed the subject.

"She's talked about it. That's all." Their mother stopped working when they were born, went back part-time after they settled in the DC area when Anne was finishing high school, then quit when their father fell ill. "I think she likes being 'retired.' She has her gardening club and church and her friends." He paused. "And you. She loves going shopping with you," he reminded her.

"Yeah, well…" Anne thought of the times they'd bonded over racks of fresh-smelling cotton, linen, and leather. "I won't be able to do that as much with my new job," she said softly.

"Oh yeah." His voice became solemn and disapproving. "When does that start?"

"In six weeks. I'm handing in my notice today."

"What's Rob think of it?"

"Are you and Mom sharing notes?" For crying out loud, she and Rob were just… friends. Just ships passing in the night. They were both so busy they barely saw each other, and they'd been going out for only six months, anyway. She wasn't even sure you could call it "going out." Rob felt more like a good buddy than someone with whom she could be romantically involved. No wonder she hesitated to mention a guy's name around her family.

She continued, "She asked me the same thing when I told her about the job."

"Well, he is your boyfriend. How long you been seeing each other?"

"He's a friend. Not a *boy*friend."

"Whatever. You talk about marriage?" Just like Jack to get to the point. She envisioned Rob standing before Jack like a new recruit. *Are you going to marry my sister, you scumbag rat bastard? Yes, sir! No, sir!*

"It's too early for that!" No, not too early. Just not in the cards at all. She suddenly felt like she was talking to her father. He'd had this way of zeroing in on her deepest worries, fears, or transgressions, and laying them out on the table to analyze and discuss. When Corey Daigler, a science geek with few friends, had asked Anne to the prom her senior year and she'd fretted about it for days, her Dad was the one to say, "You don't want to go with him because you think people will think you're a loser. You don't have the courage to stand up to what people think about you. Admit it to yourself." He had been right, of course. Admitting it didn't give her the courage to go with the poor fellow, though. But it did push her into turning him down right away instead of stringing him along until someone else asked her.

"Too early?" Jack repeated with skepticism. "You can't tell me it hasn't crossed your mind—either for a thumbs-up or a thumbs-down."

Grrr…

"I'm not rushing to the altar myself, you know. I could ask him. This is the twenty-first century, after all."

"So how come you haven't?" he parried.

"Haven't what?" she stalled.

"Asked him to marry you—this being the twenty-first century and all."

She could have sworn she heard him chuckling.

"Because I'm not sure I want to be married. I'm still young."

"What kind of relationship you gonna have if you're three thousand miles away anyway?" he continued.

None, she wanted to shout. *None at all! She was a loser, okay? She admitted it. Happy now, Jack?*

"Rob works for a congressman from northern California, you numbskull," she retorted in her best "so there" voice. "We'll see each other plenty when he's traveling with his boss. He helped me get my job—put in a word for me, remember?" She'd been flattered that Rob asked the congressman to mention her to someone on the hospital board.

"Hey—why not ask Rob to keep your car for you? Doesn't he own some townhouse in Silver Spring?"

"Falls Church. He rents it."

"You could get him to look after your car for you."

"It's too small. He gets only two parking spots," she said in a taut voice. *Outmaneuvered again.*

"How many cars does he have?"

One, only one. But I won't tell Jack that. Hell no.

"His brother visits him a lot from Sacramento."

"So his brother has to park somewhere else. Big deal."

"Look, I have to go, Jack."

"Don't forget—talk to Mom."

"Will do."

"I'll call you before I leave."

"I'll come see you."

After hanging up the phone, she noticed that the office was starting to fill up. She smelled coffee brewing and heard welcome chatter and hellos. She heard nothing from either of her cubicle neighbors, but sometimes Ken was so quiet she didn't notice he was there. She wondered if he wore an invisible cloak. For all she knew, he could still be in his cubicle, unseen by human eyes. She peered over the edge. Nope, he was gone. He must have gotten up while she was on the phone.

His leather portfolio was sticking out, though, and from it, a corner of drawing paper teased. Better not leave that there. It clearly was personal work. She'd be doing him a favor by putting it back, right? She crept around to push it into place—okay, so maybe she took a quick look at it first, but her intentions were good.

Blush flamed her cheeks—it was a drawing of her!

Did Ken Montgomery—silent Ken Montgomery—have a crush on her?

No. Couldn't be. She'd heard him on the phone with a "Cindy" more than once, talking in that sometimes funny, sometimes angry tone that only intimates shared. Surely he wasn't carrying the torch for l'il ol' Annie?

Hurrying back to her desk, she smiled at the prospect. *And why not, Anne Wyatt? It's not like you're leftovers at the Girlfriend Buffet. You're smart, good looking (in a quirky kind of way), available (sort of), and… a catch. Poor Ken. Here he is, lighting the flame, when it's blowing out to the West Coast in short order.*

A pang of regret pinched her heart. Ken, with long, artistic fingers and curved face, dancing eyes, and thick hair, would have been nice to get to know. Maybe he could have been the one…

Whoa, rewind!

She wasn't looking for a husband. That was her mother's dream, Jack's dream. It wasn't necessarily hers. She had other dreams. Dreams like… like… like… dropping decaf, looking up the calorie count on frozen foods, buying more pizzazzy clothes.

Mental headshake. She gave herself the "pep talk"—she was charting her own course, living her own life, with a great career and a great future. She didn't need a husband. Or children. She didn't. Nope. Really.

Really.

I swear.

Really really really.

For the love of God, will you drop it?

She looked over at Mitch's still-closed door and was irritated for coming in early only to watch His Royal Highness retreat behind the moat. Jack's questions, Ken's drawing, Mitch's unavailability all conspired to swirl her feelings around again like those wind-tossed blossoms she'd watched from her window. Ah yes, there was a sweet memory—killing the bluebird.

She sighed.

I'm almost thirty frigging years old and I don't really know what I want, despite all those mental pep talks.

Shouldn't you have it figured out by now? Her brother's voice—or was it her father's?—echoed in her brain, demanding answers.

I wanna.

I wanna.

I wanna… what?

Dunno. Be happy. Be loved. Get five minutes with my boss so I can quit.

Buy that shredder.

Before she had time for more existential musings, Robin Dewitt, Mitch's secretary, came around the corner. Robin's hair was unapologetically L'Oréal blonde and she wore tight clothes and flashy jewelry more suitable for a woman ten to twenty years younger. In Anne's mind's eye, Robin was always cracking gum. Robin had been Mitch's secretary and gal Friday since the beginning of time. Anne learned early that you might cross Mitch if you had the courage, but if you were smart, you never dared take on Robin. His loyalty to her was as great as his loyalty to his wife. Scratch that—greater than his loyalty to his wife, who was, after all, now his "ex."

Today Robin's pizzazz outfit included a white leather miniskirt and skintight red bustier, enough gold-tone jewelry to start an Avon franchise, and shoes with heels so spiky she probably had to get a permit to buy them.

It occurred to Anne that Robin might have worn this outfit before, on non-pizzazz days.

"Oh good, you're both here. Staff meeting in his office."

Both here? Anne turned toward Ken's cubicle and darned if he hadn't appeared out of nowhere. He looked good, she noticed, sizing him up afresh after viewing his sketch of her. Strong jawline, bright eyes, that artsy long hair…

Ken stood, holding up his mug, his electric green tie blinking wildly. The lights around a morbidly obese Santa seemed to be triggered by movement. She looked him over for clues to… something.

Was the tie a sincere effort to accommodate Pizzazz Day or a joke? Who was Ken anyway?

"I'm going cold turkey with caffeine," she barked, thinking he was offering her coffee, and regretting her snappy tone as soon as the words left her lips. She saw him look at her as if taken aback and she wanted to apologize. But for what? For letting her mixed-up feelings bubble over into rudeness.

It wasn't Ken's fault that her brother was shipping out and she'd argued with him. It wasn't Ken's fault that she felt guilty about quitting her job, moving to California, and leaving her mother alone. It wasn't his fault that this day that started with such promise was already feeling odd and off-pitch.

And it certainly wasn't his fault that she'd have to make an appointment to announce her resignation to the boss, a man who both inspired and excited her, who made her go all wobbly inside even after nearly four years on the job and countless hours of intense work together.

A man who, two years ago, was her lover.

Chapter 4

From Mitch Burnham's book *The Twelve-minute Management Plan*:

> *Business isn't personal. Not even firing someone is personal. Don't waste time worrying about how the team "feels."*

7:51 a.m.

GESTURING TOWARD THE OPEN entranceway, Ken nodded for Anne to take the lead. She had looked at him so oddly a moment ago he'd wondered if he'd offended her. He really should get to know her better. Even if she was in a relationship, there was no harm in being friends. And maybe if he spent more time with her, he'd get that sketch of her right. He was sure it would be a magnificent piece, something he could showcase once he was in his own place.

He looked at his watch. The last thing he needed this morning was to be cooped up in a meaningless, meandering staff meeting where everyone shared news of their projects. Or worse, "look at me" events where Mitch Burnham—Mr. Burnham to all of them—proselytized about some new idea he'd pulled out of his... brain while yachting on the Potomac with heads of state.

Ken sank into a chair near the credenza, staring out the windows of Mitch's spacious corner office with its view of downtown Washington.

The windows stretched from wall to wall, creating a portrait of spring light that Ken's fingers itched to capture. He thought of the budding trees and fresh grass outside his apartment, and of the cherry trees about to bloom near the Jefferson Memorial. There was a special tint of green to spring on the Atlantic seaboard, something with more yellows in it, maybe just a hint of cyan, but only a muted drop. Spring was all about the bright shades bubbling beneath the surface ready to burst out. He'd need weeks to get such a painting right, to make it more than just a good re-creation of what he saw. Painting wasn't photography.

Spring in DC reminded him of Paris, where he'd spent his junior year of college. Small streets were covered with canopies of blossoming trees, fountains gurgled, and flocks of gaily plumed tourists roamed the parks. It made you feel like you could just reach up and pluck possibilities from the sky. How he longed to have the time to watch it unfold, to think about its attributes, to put paint to canvas.

"Lenny, shouldn't you be able to hit a few buttons and reconfigure everything?" Mitch growled into the phone, keeping everyone cooling their heels while he took yet another call from accounting.

That poor soul Lenny. Seemed like Mitch Burnham was meeting with him a lot lately and Lenny was looking even more nervous than usual. A smile twitched at Ken's mouth as he remembered a barbecue at Lenny's condo right after Mitch had hired Ken. Lenny had grilled outside on an unseasonably warm fall day, putting his hibachi on a brand new resin table.

Jeez, did that smell when it melted.

Ken's smile faded as he remembered the rest of the story. Mitch Burnham, imported beer in one hand, ice pitcher in the other, dousing the flames with an exaggerated casualness designed to amplify what a cool guy he was. Damned if he didn't get under Ken's skin. Good thing he wasn't planning on staying here long.

Ken glanced at Anne who sat quietly across the room, observing all around her, her eyes not registering her opinions. He wondered what stirred beneath those depths and if she found Mitch Burnham's antics as ridiculous as he did. She reminded him of spring with all its possibilities. What in her was yearning to burst free?

She sensed his gaze and turned her head toward his, a faint smile lifting the corners of her mouth, her eyes lighting up with warmth and recognition. There it was—that moment he'd wanted to freeze on canvas! If only he could rush back and grab his pencils.

Instead, he stared at her, trying to memorize it. He stared so long, in fact, that he saw her face turn crimson from his attention.

Maybe he *would* ask her out to lunch some time soon after all.

My God, Anne thought, he *does* have a crush on me. How sweet.

She didn't know much about Ken except that his last job had been with a small, nonprofit arts consortium. Washington was awash in nonprofits, everything from political think tanks to advocacy groups to issue-oriented organizations that ran public relations campaigns for this cause or that one, usually started by former congressmen or White House staffers whose careers had waned but who still felt they had something to give back. She tried to remember the one Ken had worked for but could recall only that it had been small but run by someone—an arts patron?—who had a reputation for panache.

Mitch was winding up his phone call. She sat up straight and reminded herself not to call him Mitch. That had been Rule Number One of their relationship. Everyone—except maybe Lenny—called him Mr. Burnham.

Robin, coffee mug in hand, whispered to Anne and Sheila: "I don't have any idea what this is about," before heading to her position leaning against the credenza by the windows.

Sheila, the other communications assistant, was a petite, no-nonsense woman who, like Ken, hardly spoke except for business.

They never quite clicked as a social circle, thought Anne as she waited, never approached the camaraderie she felt as a college student or even in the dead-end jobs she held after that. It didn't matter. They still managed to work well together. One of Mitch's tenets, in fact, was "Friendly, not friends." In other words, the goal was to maintain friendly interactions with your colleagues, but not necessarily bosom-buddy relationships.

And so, Mr. Burnham, I'd like to work where I can make friends…

Robin cleared her throat, cueing them that the meeting should begin soon. In her hand was a steno pad and pen, ready to take notes. But Mitch lingered on the phone for a few more "uh-huhs" and "rights."

"When did he call this meeting?" Anne whispered to Sheila. "Did I miss something?"

"It's a last-minute thing," Sheila said. "Shouldn't take long. He has an appointment in a quarter hour. Chairman of the board."

How did Sheila know what his schedule was?

Sheila Baker sat in a leather armchair directly in front of Mitch's desk. She wore a bright tangerine halter dress that had the unfortunate effect of making her tan skin look jaundiced. Maybe it was intentional? Nothing like fear of infectious diseases to put a little pizzazz in the day. Her dark hair was pulled back so tightly into a bun that Anne inwardly cringed at the pain she was sure it inflicted on Sheila's scalp. She sat quietly, her lips pursed and her hands crossed in her lap. Was she meditating?

Sheila, Anne reflected, was the type of woman who could eat a double-stuffed taco in a white suit and not get a drop on herself.

Whenever Sheila looked over copy Anne had written, she wrote annoying little notes in the margin. "Didn't you mean to say…," they began, with a word substitution that was spot-on, if lacking in color. It's not that Sheila didn't have smarts. It was that Anne always got the impression Sheila thought her smarts were a few notches higher than they actually were.

Sheila reminded Anne too much of people she went to college with, people who *always* thought they knew more than Anne did, when in fact they knew more only *some of the time.* There's a difference. A big difference. For these reasons, Anne's relationship with Sheila was... well, friendly, but not friends. Mitch would be proud.

Nonetheless, Sheila's bright dress made Anne self-conscious about her own attire, especially her walking shoes. She crossed her feet under her chair. Maybe the shoes were a bad idea. They made her feel dorky, not pizzazzy.

The door opened and Greg Peterson skulked in and stood in the back. A tall, skinny man, Greg was all dark clothing and weird looks, his hair pulled back in a tiny ponytail, and his face always one day short of a good shave. His official title was web coordinator, but he was supposed to work under Anne and Ken on other projects as well.

In fact, Mitch had hired Greg because he also had graphics experience. So everyone figured he'd be able to pitch in on design. It had never happened. Greg's time was consumed with Internet tasks, and even though Anne was no expert in that field, she wondered sometimes if Greg really needed so much time to post material to the corporate website. Whatever the case, he spent his days holed up in a tiny, dark office that used to be a closet, staring at his computer screen and letting out a high-pitched, cackling laugh from time to time. Anne didn't like going near there. Greg's clothing today was no different than on other days. But then again, Greg was a "didn't get the memo" kind of guy.

Slowly, slowly, Mitch turned in his chair to face the group.

Does he realize how predictable he is? Ken had seen Mitch's "bad news" act before and could plot it out like cels in a cartoon. First, the look of worry.

Mitch's high brow furrowed, his mouth turned down in a grimace, and he swallowed as if tasting bile. Mitch Burnham was a dramatic man—he believed it inspired productivity and loyalty if a leader was viewed as larger than life—a characteristic that at first had impressed artistic Ken, then repelled him as he realized how studied Mitch's act was.

Okay, now the hands before the face...

Elbows on his armrests, Mitch placed his fingers before his face, steeple style...

Now, the sigh...

... and let out a long, melodramatic breath.

And finally, the silence before the storm...

His eyes half-closed, Mitch didn't speak for a few seconds, the better to heighten their anxiety. Ken couldn't help himself. He yawned and looked at his watch. Maybe if he spoke up now about a "meeting," he could get the news and be on his way...

As Anne watched Mitch pose, she wondered again what he would say when she tendered her resignation. A frisson of anticipation coursed through her. She knew he'd ask her to stay—that was a given. But he might even *implore* her not to leave. She smiled. She'd like to have someone implore her, just once in her life.

She'd done good work for the company. The same creativity that fed her artistic pursuits drove her to excellence under his tutelage. Art was nothing if not communication, after all. She'd won three publication awards for the Burnham Group. She'd garnered great publicity for Mitch and even came up with moneymaking ideas. His last book included a dedication to her.

Well, not really a dedication, but an acknowledgment. In the list of people he thanked for their tireless work and continual inspiration, he'd included Anne's name.

Yes, he might very well implore me to stay, talking about how I inspire him and how losing me will break his heart...

Anticipation morphed into something else, something less pleasant as a memory began its relentless stride toward the forefront of her thoughts. When she'd ended their affair, Mitch hadn't begged her to stay. He hadn't come close to that glorious moment of imploring she anticipated now. He'd merely looked mournful, like a big puppy dog that had lost a savory treat. What were his exact words? "You're breaking my heart—you know that, don't you?" Was it sincere? She'd thought so at the time. But sometimes when she remembered it, it seemed... less genuine.

What did it matter how Mitch had felt when she'd ended it? The important thing was that she had extricated herself from a difficult situation.

As she studied him now, she forgave herself this folly. Mitch, after all, was a hard man not to like. Women swooned over him all the time. His name was linked with supermodels and celebrities regularly on "Page Six" now that he was single again. When she and Mitch had been involved, he was on his second marriage. Since then, he had reconnected with his wife, then separated again, and was now officially divorced.

But his attractiveness made it all the more exciting when he chose you, Anne thought, looking at his rugged face and crystal eyes. After all, he could have anyone—obscure princesses or well-known movie stars. And it wasn't just the people he could have. It was the things. His Watergate apartment was decorated with the expensive side of sensible chic—the five-figure redos for each room. Original African artwork, a French masterpiece, Tuscan antiques, and a spa-like bathroom where the Jacuzzi comfortably held two and included a misty view of the Potomac River. In many ways, it was harder to part with that Jacuzzi than with Mitch.

When a man had the ability to acquire such exquisite things, you felt exquisite when he wanted to acquire you.

Anne sighed and glanced at Ken who was checking his watch for the third time. He really needs to be more careful. First, the personal portfolio at work, and now, a not-so-disguised impatience with the boss in an important meeting. Was he trying to get fired or something? She looked back at Mitch and wondered for the thousandth time what she had been thinking getting involved with her boss.

Flip the shredder switch on the way out the door, won't you please?

"You're probably wondering why I called you here," Mitch Burnham said softly, not looking at any one of them in particular.

Thank God, he's getting started at last. Ken sat up straighter, hoping attentiveness would somehow move things along.

Mitch stood and walked to the window, where he stared toward the Capitol. "We've had some bad news." He put his hands in his pockets and rocked on his heels. "Quarterly earnings were not as high as I'd hoped. And that puts a real crimp in our stock price—something I have to consider now that we've gone public."

This was new. Mitch was using the inclusive "we" when he usually used "I." One of his tenets was not to shy away from sounding like a leader, to do away with any fake sense of shared leadership and unequivocally let your employees know who's boss. It was another of the things Ken had initially admired about the man—how he refused to go with the touchy-feely, *I'm okay–you're okay* brand of management.

Mitch turned back to the group. The worry lines were gone and his face was now just sad. "So that leaves us with two choices. Either we cut salaries or we cut staff."

Cut staff? Dammit to hell. Just my luck.

Ken needed this job. Just for a little while longer, at least. He shook his head. He had the least seniority. So he'd be the one to go. Why was Mitch doing this in front of everyone? Was this some new technique he'd come up with—publicly humiliate the staffer who is to be let go?

Ken moved in his chair. He would not allow Mitch to shame him in front of the group. He'd quit before that happened.

Ken opened his mouth to speak but Mitch rambled on.

"Cut salaries or cut staff…" Mitch said, first holding up one hand and then the other. "Both scenarios would break my heart—you know that, don't you?"

It took a few seconds to register.

As soon as Mitch said, "cut staff," Anne had squirmed in her chair, ready to jump to the rescue by handing in her resignation here and now, in front of the team, saving them from a layoff. *No need to cut anyone, sir, because I'm leaving!*

Why did she imagine herself in a cape saying those words?

But before she had a chance to play her superhero-of-the-office role, Mitch's words crept up on her, washing slowly through her psyche like a deadening paralysis gripping her from toe to head.

All the analyses of the breakup moment she'd done in the past? They were swept away, useless reports brushed off a desk as the Blinding Realization hit her. Mitch had not regretted the demise of their affair at all. He'd not mourned it. He'd not even wept a single rhetorical tear.

Oh, deep down, she'd known—when she broke up with him, he was probably relieved. She just couldn't face that utter ego deflation at the time. She'd enjoyed the glow of his attention too much to believe he'd not found parting as difficult as she had.

She looked at him with fresh eyes. Why, he might even be relieved to hear she was leaving now. No grand "imploring" was in her future. She'd be lucky if the door didn't hit her on the way out.

Her mouth fell open, shocked and saddened. To use those same words again, the words that she'd embroidered on her heart as the last memento of a failed love affair—it was as if he were holding up for ridicule a sentimental treasure he'd discovered in her closet of girlish dreams. Her face warmed. Maybe this was what that dead bluebird had portended. Humiliation. Her leg began to twitch.

You're breaking my heart—you know that, don't you?

A misty September afternoon in the Marriott penthouse suite downtown. They had been listening to the soft pelt of rain on the window as blue shadows crept into the room and their hearts.

I'm going to give it a go with Glynda, for the kid's sake. You do understand, don't you? Things don't have to change. It's up to you… You're breaking my heart—you know that, don't you?

Those words were tattooed on the soft underbelly of her heart, the painful spot where scars never really healed. They were wrapped away in acid-free tissue in the memory box of crushed dreams. *Yes, yes, I admit it! I was a fool!* But to have Mitch utter those words again, here, in a cold office, with his adoring team around him like cult members ready for the Kool-Aid… It was too much.

Her leg twitched faster. Blush warmed her face.

She wanted to leave the room and hide. Or maybe upchuck. All this time she'd thought…

She'd thought that at least she'd be the one who stayed in his memory, the one whose image appeared in his mind when a special song played, or a whiff of her perfume blew by or…

She studied him now. Mitch was anything but sentimental. No one broke his heart. It was made up of genetically altered rejuvenating tissue.

She loosened her jacket and took a quivering breath. She gripped the sides of her chair.

You're leaving. Count to ten. You're leaving. C'mon, c'mon, c'mon. Suck it up. Soldier on. Be a warrior, Anne, daughter of warriors.

The room was so hushed, it was as if everyone was holding their breath.

"I am not going to cut salaries."

A sigh of relief.

Masterful. Make us think you're doing us a favor by cutting staff. Hadn't he done the same thing to me before we broke up? Hadn't he said, "I can't be the one to end it"? He knew I was smart enough to get the implication. If it was going to end, I'd have to do it. God damn you, Mitch Burnham. May you roast in hell.

She stared intently at Mitch, willing her gaze to bore a hole through his perfect Nehru jacket into his imperfect heart. Maybe it would ignite some pilot light that could inflame it with human warmth.

But his eyes were blue ice and, for the first time, she noticed how they didn't smile when his mouth did. They remained the same—sparkling crystals reflecting only what the beholder wanted to see. What had she wanted to see?

"Now normally, I would make my decision based on seniority." He shook his head ruefully and returned to his desk.

Suddenly, she was afraid she'd burst out crying. She really wanted that shredder now. She wanted to feed every single second of her tawdry affair with Mitch Burnham through the shredder while she screamed curses at him. She bit the inside of her lip instead, waiting for the moment when she felt in control of herself so she could speak.

"But seniority doesn't tell the full story, does it?" He looked directly at Ken. "How long you've been on the job doesn't mean you're the most valuable employee. And how short a time you've been here doesn't mean you're the least useful either." He clasped his hands in front of him and stretched them forward. The room was eerily silent. And Anne felt like a volcano about to explode. She opened her mouth to speak, to tell him to cut the crap, she was leaving, but Greg jumped in first.

"Uh, Mitch, a question." Greg was the only one who ever dared call Burnham "Mitch" in the office. Everyone turned to face him.

"How many staff, uh, will you be letting go?"

Mitch smiled. "Only one of the communications team, I'm happy to say. Other departments will face bigger losses."

❖ ❖ ❖

Ken's grip on the armrest relaxed. So he wasn't the automatic layoff. Then who was? And why drag it out like this? My God, Anne Wyatt looked upset. Poor gal. She probably was afraid it was her. He gave her a quick look, trying to communicate his sympathy and encouragement, but she was so wrapped up in her worry she didn't notice. He'd have to say a word or two to her. She did excellent work. She wasn't likely to be a candidate for the pink slip.

"I spent a bad weekend going over files and performance reviews and trying to make a decision," Mitch continued, his voice slow and weary. Good Lord, it even seemed to Ken that Mitch had suddenly incorporated a drawl into it to slow it down and increase tension. "And I thought that wasn't fair. It wasn't fair to come in from a great weekend and have your boss give you the axe. Other department heads can handle it that way, but we've all worked so closely together... I wanted to do something fairer." His face brightened.

"And besides, you're all so equally great," he said softly, "that I couldn't come to any conclusions."

"So you're not letting anyone go, after all?" Anne spit out. Damn but her voice sounded high pitched and whiny. She really *was* rattled. "Because if you have to let someone go, I can..."

"Just a minute, Anne," Mitch said, holding up his hand. In his Nehru jacket, the gesture made him look like a Hindu god, probably the effect he was aiming for, thought Ken cynically. "We have a lot of projects on the burner, a lot of deadlines to meet, a lot of team activities. There's the Annual Report, the employee newsletter, the brochure copy for our new adventure team-building camps, the sales pitch demos, the video presentations for our conferences, the..." He looked at each employee as he spoke of their projects.

"We get the picture," Anne said, not hiding her irritation. "We've got a lot to do."

Ken's mouth opened as he tried to think of something to deflect attention from Anne, who was obviously so shaken by this announcement that she was letting her guard down. Mitch was glaring at her and if she wasn't careful, he'd shift course and let her go on the spot.

"I think what Anne means is we're all eager to finish our assignments," Ken said. If he expected a reward for such chivalry, he was disappointed. Anne just glowered at him with the same venom she seemed to be directing at Mitch.

Mitch moved on. "So I thought the fairest way to handle this, since you're all equally qualified, is to let you hash it out…"

Hash it out?

"… and at the end of the day, we'll gather in the boardroom and I'll let you know then who is going to be let go."

Oh my God. The man expected them to vote someone off the island. Ken couldn't help it. He unsuccessfully tried to abort a laugh, morphing it into a cough instead.

"You okay?" asked Robin.

Ken nodded and cleared his throat. "So we'll be making the decision?" he asked, making his voice sound serious.

Mitch shook his head.

"No, Ken. I'll ultimately be the one to decide." He looped his hands behind his head and smiled. "It will be an intense day. It will get the adrenaline pumping. Who knows what ideas you'll come up with by the end of it? There's nothing like pressure to bring you to the top of your game. The pressure doesn't get much heavier than this."

So Mitch was going to have them all "run a race," with the swiftest hanging tight to their livelihoods while he got to watch everybody panting and sweating to the finish line. *Yes, that's far more humane than just getting a pink slip the old-fashioned way.*

Ken studied him. The man was enjoying himself, dammit. He was probably already thinking of how he'd write this up for an article in the Burnham Report, or maybe his nationally syndicated column, or even a book.

Anne's leg twitched like a sapling in a hurricane. She kept opening her mouth, trying to get a word in, but Mitch was purposefully
avoiding eye contact with her so as not to give her a chance. She
knew how outrageous this was, just like Ken, and she was having a
hard time stomaching it. *Just get through this meeting, Anne, and run
the race.*

But then his eyes lit on Sheila, the serene, no-nonsense woman
who shared some of Anne's responsibilities. Both of them were
surely the most vulnerable because they had duplicate skill sets.
Ken, on the other hand, was unique, the only graphic designer on
the island.

Not island. Office. God almighty, this was already getting to him.

Mitch once again held out his hand to hold at bay any questions
as he continued talking about how fair it would be, how they'd all get
to show off their skills since there was so much work to be done, and
how even the loser wouldn't walk away empty-handed because...

"... the one who's let go gets a full severance package, of course."

"Severance?" Sheila's voice, strong and low, cut over his.

"Yes, Sheila. As you know, the Burnham Group is extremely
generous with severance. Former employees are still ambassadors for
the company, after all. To refresh your memory—" He gazed around
the room. "It's six weeks' pay for every year worked. So that could
be a tidy sum—in addition to whatever the value is of your accumulated leave, of course." Smiling benevolently, he nodded at her. "I've
always believed in fair compensation. You know that."

Yes, he'd spelled that out in one of his earliest books, one Ken
had actually read. It created a sensation in the business world—a
management guru arguing for higher salaries and more benefits even
for the lowliest employees. It made him both a folk hero and a re-
spected expert at the same time.

A helluva lotta good severance will do me, Ken thought, since
I've been here such a short...

As if reading his mind, Mitch looked at Ken and said, "Your severance, Ken, while less than those who've been here longer, is still a good sum. We'd count you as a one-year employee, despite the fact you've been here only a few months."

Ken did the mental calculations. Okay, not bad. Six weeks' pay plus his four weeks of vacation (he'd argued for more time off and Mitch had acquiesced) and unused sick leave… it wasn't a stash but it was fair enough.

"Anne," Mitch said softly, turning to her. "Did you want to ask me something?"

"I just wanted to say that I would like to announce…" She mumbled and then stalled, sitting there with her mouth hanging open as if she couldn't bring herself to say what she was really thinking. Ken could fill in the blanks, though. She probably wanted to say that this was crazy and unfair and exploitive. He envisioned her standing on Mitch's desk, Norma Rae style, placard in hand, urging them all to resist. She was a fighter. He'd seen her go head-to-head with salesmen and pesky reporters trying to get dirt instead of news.

"Uh… I would like to talk to you about…"

"How the severance pay works?" Mitch interrupted. "It's simple. At the end of the day whoever leaves will go straight to accounting and I'll have Lenny cut the check immediately. There will be no time lag, no difficult waiting period. Don't worry."

Money. That's what was stopping Anne from announcing right there that she was leaving. Money.

The cash register rang in her head. If she quit, she would get nothing. If she got fired, she'd get—

Enough to go on a cruise, invest in stock, buy a new car… Ideas paraded across her mind with price tags on them that she could afford if she only snagged this prize.

I will not quit, Mitch Burnham. I will force you to fire me.

With a growing sense of satisfaction, she already started to envision the scene in which Mitch had to give her the bad news. He would, of course, be bewildered that she, of everyone, would come in last. Perhaps he'd even feel a bit betrayed by her bad performance and have a hard time actually uttering the words. Oh yes, it would be something else entirely to have to push her away when he was such a master of manipulating women into thinking they were leaving him. And what would she do?

She could see herself smiling and patting his hand. *That's okay, Mitch, darling. A leader's gotta do what a leader's gotta do. What did you say in* Business as Warfare? *Don't expect every good decision to make you feel good. Wasn't that it?* She'd smile benevolently, like the queen staying an execution, and from somewhere in the background violins would swell and they'd all be decked out in black and white like an old Bette Davis movie. *Don't feel bad, Mitch. I've learned so much here. I'll make do somehow. I'll soldier on. Are the lights dimming or is my eyesight failing?*

She looked now at Mitch's serene eyes. *You'll be one who has to make the hard choice. Surely firing me will give you a twinge or two. Surely you will suffer just a little, tiny bit at least. A pinprick or so. A sting. A bite.*

She wanted him to suffer, even if it created only a ripple over the placid blue lake of those still, silent eyes.

Chapter 5

From Mitch Burnham's book *The Action Alternative*:

The successful manager creates an atmosphere that encourages workers to push the envelope even to the point of embarrassment. It's not their dignity you're after. It's their productivity...

8:10 a.m.

"ROBIN, WHAT'S MY SCHEDULE?" Mitch asked his secretary. "I want to fit in time to talk to everyone individually today."

Robin peered at him over her half-glasses. "You have that press conference at noon and the meeting with Cal at four," she said.

While she talked, he reached for his teal Burnham Group mug and took a long sip of coffee.

A long sip was abruptly interrupted by a gag, followed by a Ricky Ricardo–like spray of java onto his once-pristine desk blotter.

"My God!" Hand at his throat, he looked at Robin. She straightened, grabbing the mug from his outstretched hand. While she took a sip, Mitch tugged at his shirt collar and wiped the coffee off his lips.

Should someone be doing the Heimlich maneuver? Ken looked around. Before Ken could leap to his feet to help, Mitch, the unflappable, coughed, looking as if he'd sucked on three lemons when he'd expected sugar cane. He waved his hand at everyone to indicate all was well.

"What the…" Robin's eyes squeezed shut and her mouth puckered. "I didn't make the coffee this morning, sir," she said meekly.

Greg, who had a mug in his hand, sipped and smiled broadly. "Wow. Cool."

"Did somebody put something in it?" Mitch looked around the room as if a conspirator had tried to poison him in anticipation of his one-day-until-the-guillotine scheme. Ken looked around, too, searching faces. He just saw confusion and fear. *Of course they're afraid. Who wants to start off this day with a black mark?*

"Mr. Burnham, I made the cof—" Anne began, standing slowly.

Poor Anne. So sweet and honest. Even in the face of Mitch's wrath, she takes her lumps. Now Mitch would check off a box next to her name, and this one unfortunate incident—a small, inconsequential mistake in the scheme of things—would color his opinion throughout the day.

It didn't have to be that way. Ken shot to his feet.

"I made it this morning," Ken said. "I wanted to do something… special."

"No, I made it, Mitch! I like it this way!" To prove her point, Anne grabbed Sheila's untouched mug and gulped down a mouthful. Ken suppressed a smile as she swallowed and coughed.

"Does someone know the number for Poison Control?" Robin asked.

Mitch was looking at Anne oddly, his mouth ajar and his eyes squinting. She'd called him Mitch. Another black mark for her. She stepped forward as if proud of herself, as if owning up to her mistake was as important as not getting fired. Despite his worry for her, Ken couldn't help admiring her action. She was choosing the riskiest moment to rebel. Something in him cheered her on.

As she stepped forward, Mitch's gaze went to her shoes and his lip curled up in disgust. Anne's walking shoes probably weren't pizzazzy enough. Yet another black mark!

"Mr. Burnham," Ken said, trying to divert his attention, "let's just throw the coffee out and I'll make a new pot." Burnham's gaze zeroed on Ken with a look of disdain. Maybe Mitch didn't approve of guys making the coffee. For all his equality talk, Mitch liked macho.

A movement swiped by the corner of his eye. Sheila. She was standing, too.

"Anne's just covering for me. I made the coffee. Old family recipe." Sheila tugged at the top of her halter dress, while Ken stared, confused. Why had Sheila picked today to win the Miss Congeniality Award? And was she color-blind? That dress's shade was appalling, offending his painter's eye.

Then Sheila turned to Ken, as if in slo-mo, and... smiled at him, her perfect white teeth gleaming, her eyes twinkling. He'd hardly ever seen her smile, so focused was she on the tasks at hand. He'd not given her a second glance. Now he did. That halter dress did nothing for the ruddy tone of her skin, but it did a heck of a lot for the curves under it. Was she batting her eyelashes at him?

Anne looked from Sheila to Ken and back again. Was Sheila trying to save Ken because she was "sweet on him," to use her mother's antiquated phraseology? Ken and Sheila? Both were quiet and private. Both hid their feelings with Vulcan-like skill. Both were bright. Maybe they'd had some secret thing going on under Ken's invisible cape. Maybe this was a regular *Melrose Place* and Anne hadn't noticed it because she was so absorbed in pleasing Mitch and perfecting her clueless-worker-bee talents. She glanced at Robin, the office gossip-meister, but the secretary wasn't even raising her eyebrows.

"Look," Ken was saying in that straightforward, reasonable voice of his, "I came in early and I made the coffee. I don't usually do it. I put some of that coffee-flavoring stuff in it to make it special. I guess I put too much. End of story."

Robin again sipped at the offending brew and managed to speak without choking, her voice tight and thin. "You know, it's not all that bad, sir. Sort of like espresso, kicked up a notch."

Mitch's game face returned, the earlier fear and rage vanishing. Like an addict, Anne craved the rage, though, and was about to lay claim to the coffee offense once again when Mitch spoke first. "Came in early, eh, Ken? That's a good sign. You always were a go-getter." And so it began. Ken got a good-boy mark. Anne wouldn't rain on that parade.

Before Mitch could say more, his phone rang and Robin rushed to answer it.

"Ron Crane again," she whispered to Mitch with the receiver pressed into her breasts. Ron was chairman of the board.

"Good." He took the phone from her with one hand, while wagging his other in the air to signify the meeting was over.

Like students who'd just been smacked on the knuckles, they paraded single file out of the room, in shocked silence. Greg was the only chipper one among them.

"Uh, you know what? I just remembered—I think I made this coffee today. Don't usually do it and I forgot!" He looked at all their faces and grinned, happy to have solved his own personal mystery.

8:14 a.m.

How do you begin a day of trying to earn black marks from your boss? Anne wasn't normally a "look at me, look at me" kind of gal. This strategy would take her far outside her comfort zone. Maybe the thing to do was simply to make a list of her projects and, under each one, another list of how to screw them up.

A to-do list for foul-ups. She could handle that.

She returned to her desk energized and yet strangely discomfited. She had a day stretching before her during which her sole occupation would be to earn her boss's wrath. What could be more fun than that? So why wasn't she feeling fun-filled and joyous?

She looked over at Ken as he slid back into his chair.

Something pricked her heart, sending a twinge of unwanted sadness to her brain.

Sheila and Ken—the thought again sped through her mind, whisking by the Accept-reality troopers who never quite caught up with her dreams. No, not Sheila and Ken. Not when she had thought…

Thought what? That Ken might be good date material? If so, she should have acted on it sooner. She glanced over at Sheila's cubicle. Who would have thought Sheila was so fast in the snag-a-man arena? Maybe Anne was slowing down in her dotage.

Stop it! You're only twenty-nine, not a hundred and nine!

Still, Anne could have sent out the thousand Shy-girl Flirting signals every young woman learns at puberty (and is sworn to secrecy to protect), but she'd stopped herself and forced her actions into the business like mode that suited the office. Obviously, that had been a mistake.

Sigh. But today, mistakes were her friend. Big, fat, juicy mistakes. She sat at her desk drumming her fingers, ready to jump in and bollix things up but stalled by swirling jitters. To calm her nerves, she played a game of Minesweeper, turning the volume up high so that the exploding mines could be heard far and wide. Oooh… she looked forward to a game or two of FreeCell, too, and solitaire! Lots and lots of solitaire! She loved seeing how the cards all fell and shattered like crystals when you won.

Trouble was, Mitch had to see her playing these games for it to count.

She smiled as she remembered Mitch's face when he feared the coffee was poisoned. He'd looked like a cartoon version of himself—hair askew, face pale, eyes wide. Even his perfect jacket had seemed a little silly at that moment. With his face a mask of worry, the jacket merely made him look like an older guy trying to stay young by dressing hip. The tiniest shudder rattled Anne's shoulders. That's what had her feeling unsettled—in that instant she'd seen him as he really was, not the image he so successfully projected to her and the world. Why didn't these scales fall from her eyes earlier? Why was she developmentally delayed in the relationship department?

Pages flipped by in the photo album of her memories of Mitch, as she re-examined her mental image of him, looking for what she saw today. But her memory had put up a gauzy filter and she didn't know how to uninstall it. She saw Mitch grinning, champagne flute raised toward the sun, as he stood on the deck of his sailboat *Excelsior* on the Potomac. She saw him intently reviewing a speech Anne had written, as she anticipated his fulsome praise. She saw him smiling suavely as he glided her around a dance floor at a Washington banquet.

What kind of fool was she?

A man like Mitch Burnham doesn't make commitments to a woman like Anne Wyatt. Anne Wyatt is freckled and skinny. Anne Wyatt is no pleasure princess. She's a lonely, artsy type with dreams instead of burning ambition. Anne Wyatt is...

...referring to herself in the third person. Isn't that a sign of schizophrenia?

She shook her head to clear it and got down to business. Forget the to-do list. Action, not planning, was what she needed. Ack— wasn't that from *The Action Alternative?* No matter. She'd hoist Mitch on his own petard today. Just as soon as she figured out what a "petard" was.

As part of her normal morning routine, she usually spent a few minutes checking personal email to see if there was anything from Mom or Jack.

This time when she opened that program, she saw a half-dozen spam messages, some with attachments. Okay. No time like the present to get started on a new task. So she did the responsible thing.

She opened them.

She opened them, she forwarded them, she went to links embedded within them. Her mouse scurried into the goblin-infested world of the Internet Inferno. Only ill-begotten and evil creatures lurked in these depths, things with names like Worm, Mydoom, Trojan, and Spybot.

Anne Wyatt offered them all an engraved invitation—The Burnham Group welcomes you to its shores.

Along the way, she learned how she could enlarge her... male organ... and view women cavorting for her pleasure. She happily responded to most humble gentlemen from Lagos and Russia who wanted her help with bank transactions. She excitedly emailed a grateful message to the many lottery organizations telling her she'd won. She clicked on the links in messages telling her that her PayPal accounts had been compromised. And she eagerly went to any website an email suggested she visit.

Her computer made a funny clicking noise when she was finished.

Ken poked his head up.

"Something wrong?" he asked, pointing at the tower.

"Nope. All's well." She gave him a quick thumbs-up, then turned back to her work.

But Ken was still standing, and it was clear he had something to say.

"You were quite brave in there," he said, gesturing toward Mitch's office.

"Huh?" she said/thought at the same time.

"The way you tried to take the blame for the coffee... saving someone else."

She snorted. "Yeah, Greg." Poor Greg. He was the most vulnerable of the lot of them. "But I didn't do anything you didn't do. You were willing to take the blame, too. You did, in fact."

As she smiled broadly at Ken, she saw the strangest look pass over his face—his eyes softening, his mouth slightly ajar, as if he was witnessing a rare event. Did she really smile so infrequently?

Then she remembered the drawing. Maybe that's why he'd risen to his feet to claim the coffee mistake—not to impress Sheila, but to show Anne he had guts… and chivalry, too.

"Ken, do you have lunch plans?" she blurted out. And why not?—a nice long lunch would be a good way to cinch the campaign she was launching.

"Uh…" He hesitated.

Oh no, she'd miscalculated. Perhaps that wasn't her face gracing the pages of his portfolio but some doppelgänger with whom he was secretly in love.

"That's okay," she said, before he could reject her outright.

"No, it's just that…" He frowned. "I have an appointment." He seemed genuinely disappointed, which gave her the courage to suggest an alternative.

"Hey, how about breakfast tomorrow?" she asked him. Tomorrow, if she were successful, she'd be flush with cash and free as a bird. *(But not that bluebird!)* She deserved a celebration. "There's a French bakery just the other side of the river—"

"LaBonne's," he filled in, the frown completely gone now.

"I treat myself there every once in a while." Her gaze shifted past him to the windows at the end of the room with their glimpse of blue sky. "I'll stop there and then we can meet at the Tidal Basin," she offered. "Maybe catch some cherry blossoms."

"All right."

They set a time and place and Anne went back to her work, or rather, lack of it.

Ken eventually turned and sank below the cubicle wall. In a few seconds, she heard him typing, and a wet blanket of regret draped around her soul. She'd be leading him on by going out with him, even for a casual date. No future in long-distance affairs. Sniffing the air, she smelled his aftershave. It was something with sandalwood in it. Sandalwood was a question mark of scents—it made her want to know more. Had he always worn it or did he put it on just today?

Anne's phone rang and she considered not answering it but figured that wouldn't earn her any black marks if Mitch or Robin didn't see. So she picked it up only to hear the perky voice of Kathie-Rose Kimball, the blue-eyed, blonde news babe of a national cable news show.

"Why, hello there, Anne. How are you?" Kathie-Rose asked in a drippy drawl. It always amazed Anne how Kathie-Rose was able to turn off that drawl as soon as the cameras started rolling. Before Anne had a chance to answer, Kathie-Rose went on, "I just called to say I might be late for that noon press conference. Can you shoot me a press release early? You have my email and fax, right?"

"Right," Anne said. Mitch would be disappointed, which sent a bolt of satisfaction through Anne. He had asked Anne specifically if Kathie-Rose was on the invite list when she'd put this press conference together. He was only announcing the opening of a new adventure team-building camp, but as usual, it would be done in grand Mitch style with a good visual for the cameras. In this case, he'd make the announcement in a canoe with the CEO of MicroBeers, an up-and-coming company, at a Potomac River marina. After the announcement, Mitch and the CEO would paddle off toward the white water. Just the kind of image Mitch liked to project, and Anne knew he'd love having a gorgeous newswoman there to drool all over him. The whole event had been tricky to arrange and, frankly, Anne was not looking forward to finishing all the logistics.

She brightened. She was not looking forward to it, so she wouldn't do it.

"Hey, Kathie-Rose, that's okay," Anne said, straightening in her chair. "I'm going to have to postpone it anyway. You beat me to the punch."

"If you do it this afternoon, I'm free. That would be terrific. I'd love to see Mitch."

Hmm... this afternoon. Robin said Mitch was meeting Cal, a major investor, this afternoon, too. He'd want time to prepare for that.

"Okay. Three o'clock," Anne told Kathie-Rose. And, if Anne was going to spoil Mitch's fun by moving the press conference to a time that was inconvenient for him, why not spoil it even more by moving it to the office with its lack of great visuals? "Here, at the Burnham Group conference room."

"Thanks, honey. I'll be there."

This was fun.

After Anne hung up, she pulled up her press list and broadcast emailed everyone on it, telling them the new time and location. Oops—she forgot to notify Mitch. What a shame.

After she finished, she stood and stretched. She looked into Ken's cubicle, half expecting to see nothing because she hadn't heard anything coming from his space while she was on the phone with Kathie-Rose. Maybe he had his magic cape on. She wished she had one too.

But he was there, intently working, his tan arm stretched out on his desk, his long fingers gliding his mouse around the screen, dragging a headline on the Annual Report to a corner of a page. Ken's work was superlative. It didn't overpower the message yet at the same time made a statement all its own. Elegant, but not intrusive.

The way he worked was elegant, too, she realized as she spied on him. He was sure of his decisions, not hesitating when he shifted a color or downsized a font, just as swiftly changing it again if it wasn't what he expected. His approach to design work was what Anne would describe as "muscular"—beautiful, but strong. And his work method was the same.

She now realized that in the past, whenever she'd thought of how good Ken was, she had immediately chalked it up to Mitch's skill in recognizing talent more than to Ken's actual artistic abilities. She always shifted her admiration for Ken's work into admiration for Mitch's sure eye and nurturing attitude. After all, Mitch plucked her from an artistic background and helped her turn her natural communications skills into a business asset. She figured he'd done the same with Ken—steering him from unfettered artistic endeavors to channeled business art.

Now Anne looked at Ken's design with fresh vision, as something that belonged only to Ken, not to Mitch. And, for some reason, it triggered a little shiver.

She squinted at Ken, trying to see him through her eyes alone, not through her previous veneration of Mitch. He was a strong, confident artist and not bad looking to boot.

His long, thick hair fell in waves around his temple. Occasionally, he finger-combed it back. Anne smiled—she pictured him as a boy with his mother running after him, as her mother had done for Jack, to brush his hair off his face. His tan neck was smooth and graceful against the pale blue of his shirt. And that sandalwood scent teased at her senses.

All of a sudden, she wanted to hug him and tell him she was sorry.

I'm sorry I never noticed you before except in the reflection of Mitch's mirror. I'm sorry I disregarded you because I am such a dunderhead.

He turned to look for a paper and sucked in his breath when he noticed Anne staring.

"I…" he said. His face flushed to a warm umber that only accented the brightness of his brown eyes. "Did you want something, Anne? I mean, can I get you something?"

She was afraid. Afraid she'd blow it, this chance at a connection.

Damn she hated being scared. Where was the off switch for that?

"Uh… just wanted to say… I'm looking forward to tomorrow. It can be a picnic." She sounded pathetic and childish. She squared her shoulders and retreated to more comfortable turf—business talk. "I'll have Mitch's message for that this morning." She pointed to the Annual Report.

He nodded and smiled. And she noticed that, unlike with Mitch, Ken's eyes smiled too.

Chapter 6

Review of Mitch Burnham's book *The Twelve-minute Management Plan* on Amazon.com:

> *Hogwash for the Gullible—One star. Twelve minutes is a long time for some guys, I guess, but Mitch Burnham proves in this latest bit of hokum that even 720 seconds is too long to spend with a boring and arrogant salesman whose main product is himself. If you want to figure out how to treat your employees, save your money. You don't need this or any other Burnham Baloney Book. You need the Golden Rule—treat them right, and they'll do right by you... by Anonymous Reader, Crystal City, VA.*

8:46 a.m.

AFTER ANNE SETTLED BACK to work, Ken couldn't concentrate. He itched to pick up a pencil and draw her. This is why he needed to open his own place! He needed the freedom to create whenever he felt like it, instead of fitting it in around brochure and Annual Report designs. By the time he had the time to get back to that drawing, the inspiration would be gone.

Or rather, the woman who inspired the inspiration would be. Maybe he needed to just give up on that picture. If he were leaving the Burnham Group, he'd be out of her sphere anyway. She had asked him to lunch, though, and quickly rescheduled to breakfast when he couldn't make it. Maybe she really wasn't in a relationship. He shouldn't jump to conclusions.

As he turned his attention back to his computer screen, his cell phone vibrated in his pocket. He did a quick glance at the number—the Arts Consortium where he used to work. After a moment of hesitation, he strode away from his cubicle into the relative privacy of the hallway.

"Ken? This is Bethany Forester. How are you?"

"Fine," he answered curtly. Bethany was the gal Friday in that office, doing everything from typing to scheduling to chauffeuring for the boss, Felicia Lanagan, artist-turned-arts-advocate and head of the multimillion-dollar consortium whose mission was to promote struggling artists and underwrite worthy projects. Since leaving the Consortium, Ken could have been quite happy if he never crossed its path again, and especially if he never heard Felicia's name one more time.

"Felicia sends her regards," Bethany went on. "She asked me to call you to see if you were coming to the Spring Gala. We didn't get an RSVP."

He resisted the urge to sarcastically reply, "That's because I didn't send one." Bethany wasn't to blame for his rift with Felicia.

"I can't make it," he said instead, keeping his voice free of emotion. "Other plans."

"Oh, too bad. I was hoping to catch up with you!" Bethany was a great gabber, always eager to talk about anything from the weather to great art. "Felicia's still not filled your job," Bethany cooed. "Personally, I think you're irreplaceable."

"Well…"

"You liking the Burnham Group?"

"It's great."

She laughed. "That doesn't sound like a ringing endorsement!"

"No, it is great," he said, but couldn't keep the flatness out of his voice. Damn. Bethany was a good soul. He tried to be more cheerful. "How are things there?"

"Oh, same old, same old. We're still trying to find enough funding for the summer festival."

Ken nodded to a coworker walking by and stepped into the coffee room, grimacing at the odor of Greg's experimental coffee. Hadn't someone dumped that out?

"I thought that was wrapped up before I left," he said to Bethany.

"Not that I know of. Hey, that reminds me—you said you'd stop by sometime and show me how to access the photo files and all. And I've got to do up a piece for Felicia by the end of the week using the shots of Heilgan's sculptures."

He sighed. Bethany was smart, but not as computer savvy as she needed to be for the job. He'd meant to go help her out with this a week ago, but got sidetracked by an appointment with Cyndi. He looked at his watch. It would take him under ten minutes to get over there, and he had to pick up some paper samples at a printer nearby anyway.

"Felicia in yet?"

"Nope. Just talked to her on the phone. But hey, I could tell her if you were going to stop by—"

"No, don't. I might be able to come in. Not sure. If I do, I can't stay long."

They wrapped up the conversation, and Ken rushed back to his desk. It would be good to get this out of the way, he thought. Besides, it made him look busy to be running off to a printing press, emphasizing the unique position he held at Burnham.

As he clicked his way to save his document, he noticed Anne was slapping her hand on her desk to the rhythm of a country song on the radio turned up to decibel-shattering levels. What on earth was going on with her?

She smiled at him as he left, waving her fingers in the air. "To-morrow morning," she mouthed. Or maybe she actually said it. The radio was too loud to tell for sure.

Anne sang along with Big and Rich on the radio as she typed up reviews of Mitch's books and posted them on Amazon.com and BN.com. Maybe she'd even have time to hit some other book-selling websites in the afternoon, coming up with more reviews using different pseudonyms throughout the day. She was particularly proud of her idea to use Kathie-Rose's name for one.

When Anne first came up with this idea, she'd nearly nixed it—first, Mitch might not notice it right away; and second, when he did, he'd be suspicious. But then it came to her how to draw his attention to the reviews while providing an explanation at the same time. She hastily scribbled a note to Mitch, sending it off to his email:

"Oh no! I asked several friends and relatives to read your books and post reviews. I had no idea this would happen!" She thoughtfully provided links to every blasted review she wrote.

That done, she looked around for more work to undo. Getting fired wasn't as easy as she'd thought. She couldn't just screw up. She had to screw up in a noticeable way and have reasonable explanations for each gaffe.

"Anne, do you have a moment?" Sheila yelled. Anne turned to see her standing in the entrance to her cubicle.

"Sure." Anne swirled around completely. Looking at Sheila's outfit, Anne suddenly felt schoolmarmish in hers. *Dressing inappropriately—that should rank high on the bad-vibe list. But how does one dress incorrectly for the office when the office is smack in the middle of Pizzazz Day? Must solve that one.* If only she'd kept some of her college clothes.

"Do you have the employee newsletter file?" Sheila asked, arms crossed and lips pursed. Anne could tell the radio was bothering her, but Sheila said nothing about it.

"Uh… yeah."

"I have some time so I could handle it for you," she shouted, holding out her hand as if expecting the file to jump into it like a trained dog.

"It's not that much to do, really," Anne said. She wasn't lying. It didn't take a lot of skill or talent for Anne to handle the employee newsletter. It was just a piece of cheerleading fluff that took her a mere few hours every week to put together. This was the project Mitch had trained Anne to do—and when she picked it up quickly and impressed him with her writing skills, he was appropriately appreciative. His appreciation, in fact, fed her admiration of him. It had been a vicious cycle, she could now see all too clearly.

Sheila grimaced. "I wanted to help. I had some ideas…"

It dawned on Anne that Sheila was eager to get a box checked off, too, just like Ken. Who was Anne to stand in the way of such ambition? She had no need for show-off projects today. She could afford to be charitable. She reached into her desk's standing file and pulled out the bulging folder, then slipped in a computer CD on which the latest draft was stored.

"Here you go," Anne told her, handing over the bunch. "Have at it."

Sheila tilted her head to one side and lifted one side of her mouth in a half smile. "Thanks." When she turned to leave, her tangerine dress flared out in a silky swirl. It was frightening to think Sheila had worn that in the real world.

Hmm… but maybe Anne should steal a page from Sheila's book and look for something cringe inducing. She'd do it on her lunch break, yet another thing to add to her mental to-do list.

As Big and Rich ended their wild-West lament and an ad for erectile dysfunction meds came on the radio, Anne's gaze lit on some scribbled notes in her in-box. Written on a cocktail napkin, those were Mitch's bullet-points on language that absolutely must be incorporated into a speech he was scheduled to deliver at an appearance before the National Press Club later in the week. Anne was supposed to have a draft in his box by the end of the day.

She felt a sneeze coming on and used the napkin in lieu of a tissue. She threw away the napkin and rang up Robin.

"Robin, is he available?"

"You're joking, right?"

"Would you give him a message?"

"I live to give him messages."

"Tell him I lost his notes on the Press Club speech."

Without missing a beat, she said, "Will do."

Inspiration struck Anne. "Tell him I'll make something up anyway."

"Sounds good."

She hung up and turned back to her computer. Despite odd whirring and clacking noises, it was running well enough to let her zoom through the Internet's byways. She quickly found what she was looking for—the website of management guru Peter Jasmine, Mitch's archenemy.

While Mitch was aggressive and self-taught, Peter was pop psychology motivational science. He had a PhD in something called "Workforce Efficiency Neural Mechanics" and had poked fun at Mitch's techniques on numerous occasions. Anne remembered one well—last year, Peter had delivered a speech to the National Association of Chambers of Commerce in which he derided "snake oil salesmen who advise you to take your teams on survival adventures more suitable for reality television than a serious business endeavor."

That had led Mitch to retaliate by referring to Peter obliquely as "the teddy bear in the boardroom who wants you to learn to cuddle each other's 'inner child.'" Peter's most famous team-building exercise was the "Revelatory Sharing," in which he urged business leaders to make sure they knew their employees' motivations and thought patterns. He'd even gone so far as to promote an exercise where employees were encouraged to bring stuffed animals to work that represented their deepest natures. Stuffed-animal sales spiked when his book *The Soft Approach to Hardcore Success* went into a third printing.

At last, Anne found what she was searching for: the Chamber of Commerce speech. It was on Peter's website, right next to his picture. Come to think of it, the guy looked a little like a teddy bear, with round spectacles and a pudgy body decked out in business regalia.

She copied the speech and was about to paste it into an MS Word file, but her computer kept telling her that file was "corrupted." She suppressed a giggle and used an alternative program instead, quickly tinkering with some words here and there to make the speech sound like Mitch. And then she emailed it to him, confident that he would recognize the words of his archrival even from a quick skim. Man, but that felt good. Not only would he hate the speech, she was sure to infect his personal computer with the virus-loaded attachment.

As the radio station segued into an "uninterrupted thirty minutes of your favorite Dixie Chicks songs," Anne decided it was time to visit Lenny in accounting. She had an idea, a really devilish one that tickled the back of her brain into convulsive laughter.

But as she passed the copying machine in the hallway near the elevators, she was sidetracked. Someone had tacked a bright orange sign over it: "Don't use any plastic or plastic-coated papers. They jam the machine!!!! Sue in Finance." Poor Sue. She was an assistant's assistant in Lenny's office and handled a lot of grunt work. Anne wondered if she was on the cut list in her department.

But Anne couldn't worry about that now. In fact, she might be helping Sue make a case for staying, just to fix the problem Anne was about to create. Plastic-coated papers? She had some of those in her desk.

She detoured back to her cubicle and rummaged through her drawer for those sheets. Drumming her fingers on her desk, she tried to figure out what would lead folks to her as the culprit of a copy machine jam fest. Personal stuff, that's what.

Her fingers on fire, she typed out a quick invite to a Spring Fling party at her apartment with her name in big fat letters. She printed ten copies of this—one for each copy machine—and headed for Machine Number One, plastic sheets in one hand, invite in the other.

It took her a few seconds to load a couple of plastic sheets into the paper tray, but then she was ready! Her invite on the glass plate, she hit the green copy button and...

And what a display! The machine whirred and purred like a toy train stuck in neutral. Then a pungent smell fouled the air—the plastic sheet had melted around the gears. No wonder Sue used all those exclamation points. This was more than just a jam. It qualified for a hazmat cleanup. Leaving her invite on the copying plate, Anne headed for the other machines on this floor to work her magic.

When she was done with those, it was off to the elevator and down a floor, humming as she went, merrily putrefying the air and bollixing up the works at each trusty machine. Sue, Anne noticed, had been a veritable Kilroy. Her exclamation point–decorated notes adorned the walls above each machine. *I'm really doing you a favor, sweetie. Lenny won't want to handle getting these machines fixed. He'll delegate it to you, making you invaluable.* Anne dusted her hands together at the end of this task and headed back to her original programming.

She headed through hallways and by cubicles until she came to Lenny's corner office. Lenny was more than the office accountant. He was CFO and Mitch's guy Friday—tall, skinny, balding, and wearing thick eyeglasses that looked like they belonged on Mr. Magoo.

When she knocked on his open door and entered, she had to stifle a laugh.

For Pizzazz Day, Lenny had chosen leather. Black leather pants, biker jacket, embossed boots—even a pair of leather gloves sat on the edge of his cluttered desk. Lenny really got into this stuff. Sometimes it scared her how much he got into it.

"Hi, Anne," he said, turning from his computer.

"Hey, Lenny. Great duds." Anne pointed to his pants. "I'm writing some stuff for the Annual Report. What's this I hear about quarterly earnings being down?"

Lenny looked behind Anne as if expecting to see a spy. She closed the door and stood in front of his desk, accidentally knocking over a couple of spreadsheets. Poor Lenny—he had one of those big desks that looked a lot like tables. No drawers for files and papers. Like Mitch's desk, except Lenny's was always full of materials. When she picked up the papers, she pretended to be reading them, deciphering their prophecies. "Come on, Len, I gotta know so I know what to write."

"Well," he began, looking at his fingers, "you know things aren't good."

"Yeah. Mitch is letting people go."

Lenny cringed. "I hate sending out pink slips. There are good people here, good people." He shook his head, then became resolute. "But if productivity increases, things should stabilize."

"Productivity?"

"Increased quality with no increase in cost."

"Aha."

"Doing the right thing. Doing it well…" he recited from the speeches they'd all heard Mitch give on the subject. His voice became serene, swami-like. Whoa—had she ever sounded like that? She gave her head and shoulders a quick shake.

"Doing it lean," she finished for him all the same. She tapped her finger on her chin. "Mitch's take-home—it's seven figures now, right?" She had no idea what Mitch's income was, but she could guess from his lavish lifestyle that his salary was the equivalent of Jack Sprat's wife.

Lenny nodded. "Just about. We're really a small business, you know. Of course, with his royalties and bonuses, he's well into seven figures."

"So if he cut his salary, he'd be increasing productivity by cutting costs while maintaining quality?"

Lenny let out a quick seal-bark laugh. "That's a good one, Anne, a CEO cutting his own salary."

She beamed him a smile. "Well, you know Mitch—always doing the unexpected."

Lenny's straight eyebrows lifted like an elevator. Before he had a chance to say more, she thanked him and left. As she exited, she noticed him tugging at the crotch of his leather pants.

Ken raced from the metro exit to the brownstone near Dupont Circle where the Arts Consortium was located. He'd already picked up the paper samples he needed but now was in a hurry to get this favor over with, the offer which he now regretted.

When he pushed open the heavy door, Bethany smiled from behind her receptionist's wall, standing quickly to greet him.

"I thought you might not come!" Her voice echoed in the open gallery and she leaned over to kiss him on the cheek, her frizzy hair tickling his face. She suggested letting other coworkers know he was there, but he shook his head.

"Can't stay long," he said, rushing around to her computer. She moved aside so he could sit in her chair.

If he'd harbored a single doubt about leaving his old job, he was now rid of it. As soon as he'd stepped over the threshold and smelled the mix of musty plaster, oils, and Felicia's expensive, designer perfume, he'd felt a cold snap of relief that he no longer had to face this every day.

"Well, you certainly are the whiz," Bethany said over his shoulder as he zoomed through program after program, bringing up the files she needed. "But not very talkative."

He gave her a quick shrug. He was in a hurry.

"You didn't sound too happy about your job," Bethany continued.

"It's all right."

"Just all right? I thought you were going to some big new opportunity when you left here."

He knew she was fishing for gossip, but he had neither the time nor inclination to give her any. The past was best left in the past. He kept his concentration on the task at hand.

"Didn't you want to set up your own place?" she probed.

"I'll get there eventually." He renamed a file so it would be easier for her to open, and moved it to her desktop. "Just taking me a little longer to stockpile the cash."

As he said these last words, a soft rustle behind him caught his attention. But he didn't need to turn his head to know who was there. The heavy scent of a bouquet of blooms preceded her. Felicia. Damn. Bethany had said she was out. He whirled around and stood, ready to leave.

She smiled when she saw him, a grin as brittle as the woman herself. Tall and slender, with nearly coal black hair as straight as a poker flowing down her back, Felicia Lanagan looked more like a sophisticated doyenne than a small nonprofit's CEO. She wore a tailored pantsuit of luminescent black silk and Audrey Hepburn ballet slippers. In her hands she clasped dark-framed reading glasses. Beside her stood an older man who she quickly introduced as Arthur Howard. Ken recognized the name—a retired financier, prominent philanthropist, and art lover. A new prey.

Ken attempted to make his farewells along with Mr. Howard—
really must be going as well, so nice to see you, Beth, Felicia—but Felicia
would have none of it. With a voice of lace-covered steel, she stopped
him at the door, insisting he stay because she had a "question or two"
to ask him.

Once Arthur was gone, though, she turned to Bethany.

"Would you be a dear and run across to the drugstore to fetch
me a cola? I have a dreadful headache." Her voice carried a hint of
her native city—London.

Bethany was out in a flash and there he was, in the one position
he'd wanted most to avoid, alone with Felicia.

"You're looking a little ragged," Felicia said, eyeing his Santa
Claus tie.

He glanced down but offered no explanations. "Look, I just came
over to help out Bethany. I have to get back—appointment."

She smiled, as if aware he was lying but signaling she didn't
care. "Bethany has many talents, but higher-level computer skills are
not among them." She moved closer to where he stood and for one
horrible moment he thought she was actually going to kiss him. Really kiss him, not the air kisses everyone in this field used in lieu of
handshakes. Good Lord, she couldn't still think…

When he stepped back, she laughed, then flicked a piece of lint
from his collar.

"Look," she said. "I heard you telling Bethany you're stockpiling
money to open your own place. You know I support that, Ken. I
think you're a marvelous artist, top drawer."

He said nothing.

She dropped her smile as quickly as a cloud blows across the sun.
"Arthur could help you." She gestured toward the door where Arthur
had just left. "I'd be happy to set something up, darling. Don't let
pride make you foolish."

9:13 a.m.

"You know Mitch—always doing the unexpected." Anne repeated the words she'd used on Lenny, but this time they were in a whispered conversation with a reporter from CNBC. Someone had turned her radio off by the time she came back upstairs and she'd yet to flip it back on.

The reporter was incredulous. "So you're saying he's cutting his salary? Is this a gimmick, Anne—something to get in the headlines?"

"Of course it will be to get in the headlines, Darren. But that's the point. He wants to set an example for other CEOs. He looks at it this way—"

She searched for a Mitch-like metaphor, feeling simultaneously proud and frightened when she came up with one in a nanosecond.

"—executive salaries are giant ticks sucking the blood from the body of corporate America." Anne spoke slowly so Darren could type what she was saying. She knew he was typing even though she'd told him all this was "off the record." Darren had "come across" this story in the first place because she had "accidentally" faxed a memo on this topic to him when she was faxing out a routine press release. Wouldn't you know it? Of all the reporters in her spreadsheet list, she ended up making a mistake like this with Darren the Unscrupulous. She'd asked him to hold the story until it was official, but he wouldn't commit. That Darren. He was a coy one.

"In order for the companies to be re-energized, the tick has to stop sucking," she continued. "The bloodletting must cease. The CEO's salary is the tick," she explained, just in case he didn't get it. "Mitch thinks all CEOs should follow his example. He's thinking of putting a proclamation up on the company website, daring others to sign."

Oh yes, Mitch would put up that proclamation. Anne made a mental note to get Greg working on that after her phone call.

She heard Darren snicker as he typed. "That's good, Anne. Really good."

"You know Mitch," she said, "always at the forefront. He expects the parade to catch up to him."

At the end of their conversation, she reminded Darren how this was all "on background" and it had been a mistake for him to see the memo and wouldn't he be a sweetheart and hold it just this once? After she got off the phone she wondered precisely how long he'd wrestle with his conscience before violating her request to keep the story quiet. A half hour? Naw, more like five minutes. He probably had getting past his conscience on speed dial.

She stood, stretching as she did so. Sheila wasn't in her cubicle and Ken wasn't back from his errand. His neat desk held a perfectly aligned stack of papers related to the Annual Report. She had to get Mitch's message to Ken or he wouldn't be able to finish a draft of that project. She really didn't want to sabotage Ken today. She would get on it as soon as she finished the task at hand, Mitch's proclamation to the world that CEO salaries had to stop ballooning out of control while the proletariat labored in the fields for peanuts. She sat back down and got to it.

The words flowed effortlessly from mind to fingers to screen:

"Whereas American business is a constantly evolving paradigm (Mitch hated that word) that requires fresh ideas, innovative innovations (how's that for prose that sings?), new approaches, and bold strokes to survive, I, Mitch Burnham of the Burnham Group, proudly proclaim this date as the beginning of a new revolution...

"As CEO of the Burnham Group, I have long made more money than Croesus. My salary, like those of other CEOs, is a double-digit multiplier of the average salary of those in my employ...

"I proudly proclaim that I will cut my salary to a modest yet fair amount, slightly above the salary earned by the best-paid employee in my business (that would be Lenny)...

"I proudly (there's that word again) challenge all CEOs to do the same, to cut their salaries to amounts more in line with what their average workers take home and to stop sucking the lifeblood from their companies and their stockholders by padding their own bank accounts and feathering their own nests (nothing like clichés to spice up a business communiqué)…"

She emailed this to Greg with a quick note: "This goes on the first page of the website." She neglected to tell him to hold it until she gave an "okay to launch" directive. She knew that Greg prioritized his work by what he found most interesting. Anne's guess was that he'd find this tantalizing enough to push it to the top of his to-do pile.

After finishing this grand task, she looked around again. Still no Ken or Sheila. Darn. She felt like gabbing. She also felt like snacking. Normally she'd run to the vending machines downstairs and get herself a bag of pretzels to quell the morning hunger pangs. But today that wouldn't do. So she picked up the phone and called the local Bonne Buns bakery, ordering pastries and cinnamon buns for the entire office. That would be a nice treat to nail down the image of Mitch's generosity.

"Send the bill to Mitch Burnham's account—today," she purred into the receiver.

That accomplished, she took off for the hallway leading to Mitch's office.

9:32 a.m.

Robin was away from her desk and Mitch's door was closed. Anne could hear him talking on the phone, though, and from the sound of his voice, it wasn't a business call. He was laughing in that soft, sexy chuckle of his that Anne swore he must practice. A new favorite, as Alison Krauss would sing. Who could it be—the just-graduated daughter of a U.S. senator, or the just-separated starlet wife of a box-office hunk? Mitch had been photographed with both in the past year.

Anne wondered, as she tapped her foot waiting for his conversation to end, why he'd taken up with her. She wasn't powerful, or even attached to anyone powerful. Having Anne Wyatt's name turn up with his in a column meant nothing.

But here was another sad clue to how little she'd meant to him—her name or photo never had turned up in a column with his. They didn't go to that many public functions together and she'd always assumed she was too nondescript for columnists to notice anyway. At the time, she thought of her absence from society gossip pages as a badge of honor. Her relationship with Mitch was so special that he didn't want it splashed across broadsheets in 10-point Times New Roman.

The events they had attended together were glittery enough that the only thing that counted to Anne was "the moment," the reality of being on his arm, being seen with him, being loved by an important man.

Loved? No, she didn't think he'd ever loved her, or even knew what it meant to really love. Did she? Or was that just one more thing she'd been playing at for years?

It had been easy for a man like Mitch to bewitch a girl like her at that vulnerable point in her life. She had stepped into his universe from the impoverished world of a dreamy artist, fresh from a Bohemian lifestyle in Monterey, California, where dressing up meant putting on shoes instead of sandals.

She shook her head, stirring up another memory of a similar glittering night out with her father at the Turkish embassy. In Washington, it wasn't unusual for embassies to donate their space for fundraising galas, and this one had been a Boys and Girls Club benefit. Anne was a teenager at the time—that was when her Dad had just traded in his uniform for the business suit of a defense-contracting consultant, and he had to schmooze occasionally. He hated it and she herself wasn't quite self-confident enough to feel at ease in the champagne-and-caviar crowd, but it somehow had made the night better that they'd bonded over their mutual discomfort. Mom hadn't been available that night, so he'd asked Anne. Begged her, really. He'd called from work and kind of sheepishly worked up to it. *Didn't your mom mention this to you? Aw, gee, Annie, I'd really appreciate it… you can wear your prom dress or something. Are you sure Mom didn't say anything?*

It was one of those moments where she suddenly saw her parent as vulnerable, a human just like her, afraid things wouldn't go the right way. It scared her for a few minutes. But she'd agreed to go and she'd worn a long cotton dress, something retro-hippie. Not her prom dress—she'd had a feeling that would look like she was trying too hard to seem older.

She'd pulled her shoulder-length hair back, Renoir-painting style, with a blue satin ribbon. It was her senior year and she'd already been accepted into the Monterey College of Art and Design. She was beginning to feel the passage of time, the long good-byes that initiate you into adulthood.

That night *was* a good-bye of sorts. Her father danced with her. He waltzed her around the room, smiling like a man with a wonderful secret. To her embarrassment, he reminded her of how she used to dance on the toes of his shoes when she was little.

"You used to get mad at me," she chided him. "You told me I was scuffing your shoes." His spitting-clean military shoes, so shiny you could do your hair in their reflection.

"Oh, Anne, that was only when I had my uniform on. You remember all the other times, don't you?"

And then she did remember, but in her still-childish mind, those times had been clouded by the few occasions he'd gruffly told her to "scram." She'd lumped them all together, viewing his willingness to dance with her as capricious, never sure her joy would be reflected in his.

Anne's eyes misted as she remembered.

That night of dancing with her father was like paradise, something she'd wandered away from and never rediscovered.

Man, she missed him. Why do they have to get so interesting so late in life, huh?

There'd been no unease the night she went to the Turkish embassy with Mitch, though, for an opera function. She'd been working at the Burnham Group for three months, and they'd shared a drink or two already after a few long days. They'd shared secret jokes and private smiles, too. The kind that carry but one message—*we're different, you and I, we're not like "them." We're special. And it's lonely, here, isn't it, in this special world of ours? Come stay with me.*

They'd both known it was the ramp-up to an affair. Who doesn't know? It was spring, just like now, with everything—even the air—alight with possibilities.

Everyone else had left for the day and he'd sat alone in his office, staring out the windows, toying with an envelope on his desk. Anne had stopped in to wish him good night (She'd waited until the floor was clear because she cherished those private moments—she was hoping he'd ask her for a drink, even thinking that perhaps they'd move on to a "next step."). He'd looked up when she entered the room.

"What's that?" she'd said, pointing to the envelope. "Something you forgot to have me do?"

"This?" His left lip twisted up into a rueful smile. "This is a lonely evening."

A shaft of sympathy pierced her. He explained how he'd agreed to make a presentation on behalf of the Burnham Group, but he didn't feel like going alone. He looked at her and sheepishly asked, "You wouldn't happen to have an evening frock suitable for a thing like this, would you?" And before she could answer, he'd waved the air and said, "No, you probably have plans. I shouldn't ask."

An evening frock? It was part of his charm. It fed the fantasy—he, the dashing suitor, Anne, the blushing innocent. Of course she went. He arranged to pick her up at seven thirty. Before that, with heart racing, she'd run at marathon speed to Nordstrom in town, used up a week's salary buying an outrageously expensive black silk-and-chiffon dress that would have made Coco Chanel proud, a new pair of black evening shoes designed to put a podiatrist's children through college, a wispy wrap, and a satin clutch.

And yes, the evening ended the way she had imagined. In the limo on the way home, he leaned over and kissed her. In a throaty voice, he asked her if she wanted to stop by his place for a nightcap.

When Mitch's wife divorced him, she got a sizable settlement. When Anne broke up with him, she just kept the outfit she'd bought for their first evening out, an outfit she had not worn since.

As Anne stood in front of Robin's empty desk, she resolved to give that dress to Goodwill. *Or some organization that provides clothes for poor people who need evening attire. In Washington, there must be one.*

Damn. She needed to get into Mitch's office and get his TV turned on so he'd see the CNBC report as soon as it aired. Where was Robin? If she were around Anne could just have her do it. She looked at Robin's desk. A pack of cigarettes sat open on its flat surface. Smoke break.

Hmmm… why not? She grabbed a cigarette and lit it, coughing on her first drag. As she did so, she heard the elevators ding in the distance and the voice of a deliveryman asking where he should put the cinnamon buns. Ah yes, the buns. She wrote a note for Robin: "Thought we deserved a break. Ordered five-dozen pastries and twelve-dozen cinnamon buns from Bonne Buns. Charged them to Mitch's expense account."

Then she grabbed the knob of Mitch's door and burst into his office. It startled him so much he jumped in his seat. His new lover must have been jabbering away, though, because he said nothing.

Letting the cigarette hang from the corner of her mouth as if she were a sailor on leave, Anne picked up the remote from the credenza and clicked on Mitch's flat-screen plasma set, zipping from the Travel channel to CNBC faster than you could say "Damn you." She took a long drag from the cigarette and blew smoke in the room toward Mitch. At his bewildered stare, she smiled and said, "Pizzazz Day," before shrugging her shoulders and marching out, leaving the door wide open.

Chapter 7

Review of Mitch Burnham's book *Use It or Lose It* on
Amazon.com:

> *Does what Sominex can't do—One star*
>
> *Get out the NoDoz before cracking open this
> so-called book. It's a downer for sure, even if you're
> into this kind of how-to for the business-hopeless crowd.
> Successful CEO Mitch Burnham proves in this book
> what people probably already know from countless work
> experiences of their own. Bosses don't have to be nice
> people... Henrietta B., Tuscaloosa*

9:41 a.m.

STEAMED AND IMPATIENT, KEN stood in the arched underground
platform waiting for a Red Line metro to take him back to the office.
Just his luck—the next train wasn't coming for another fifteen minutes, according to the flashing electronic sign. He couldn't wait. He
raced from the area, sprinting up the dead-still escalator. He'd have
to fork over the cash for a cab ride. That was two today, dammit, and
he was trying to be frugal. For the millionth time since graduating
from college seven years ago, he thought of how hard it was to go
from pampered only child of a moneyed family to artistic nobody
living on a shoestring budget. As a boy, he'd gone to private schools,
vacationed on St. Barth with his parents, skied the Alps at sixteen,

had a sports car given to him for his eighteenth birthday, studied at Yale and the Sorbonne, and could have kept a harbor-view condo all his own after getting his sheepskin if he'd only... sold out and stayed in business with his father.

Oh, his dad wasn't a martinet about it. There were no fiats about what to study in college, only serious suggestions. (Now, however, Ken was glad he'd taken financial-management and accounting courses, but he'd not tell his dad.) There were no ultimatums, no "drop the art study or we stop subsidizing you" threats. But at the end of the college slog, his dad had made it crystal clear—he was willing to launch Ken in a lifestyle to which he'd grown accustomed, but only if he tried out the business for a while. Sure, he did it out of love. He truly believed his son had an eye and skill for the good deal. He thought Ken could "do his art stuff" on the side.

Well, I showed him, Ken thought after snagging a taxi and settling in for the ride to the Burnham Group.

He'd actually given in to his persuasive father—and his more subtle but equally convincing uncle—and worked for Montgomery Financial in Baltimore for more than a year. Not a day had gone by during that time that he hadn't felt called back to creating things, where he found himself increasingly distracted, sitting in his office staring out at the harbor, seeing each view as scenes waiting to jump onto a canvas, wondering if he could fit in the time in the evening to finish an oil and acrylic he'd not even started. Distraction eventually melded into slacking, and slacking into making a near-ruinous mistake on a client's account.

He looked out at the blur of DC life going by, confident people streaming to important jobs, in power suits and cool attitudes. His father's attitude after Ken's mistake shifted from indulgent to angry, and their first big argument erupted. For years, they'd both hidden their fears and resentments under the thin scrim of upper-class politeness. His father blurted out that he'd "humored" Ken's artistic endeavors because Ken's mother had insisted he have a chance to find his way. Ken had hurled back that he'd always assumed his father was just patronizing him, and he had taken the job only so he could live comfortably while putting together enough pieces for a showing on his own. His father had countered with the coup de grâce—all right, where are those pieces; how many have you done; let me show them to some friends of mine in the gallery business.

He'd called Ken's bluff. Ken had not finished a single new piece since graduating from college. He'd frittered away nearly two years… just being comfortable, partying, enjoying the luxury he couldn't bring himself to sacrifice on the altar of fine art.

The things he'd said to his father in that moment—Ken wished now he could take them back. It took several months before they talked again. By that time, Ken had moved out of the condo, found a place in DC, and landed the job at the Arts Consortium. He'd felt vindicated when he'd landed that job as Felicia's assistant. How little he'd known.

As these grim thoughts soured his mood, his phone rang. Cyndi. She was calling to confirm the look-see of the Georgetown space. At least things were looking up, he thought, as he closed the phone following the call.

"This okay?" The taxi driver pulled to an open spot at the curb, a half block from the Burnham Group.

"Fine, just fine." Ken dug into his pockets and paid the man, giving him a generous tip. Some habits were hard to break.

"Hey, Anne, there are cinnamon rolls in the coffee room!" A secretary smiled and pointed toward the combination supply closet/coffee room from whence the homey odor of cinnamon and sugar emanated. She had a big, gooey one on a napkin in her hand. Very nice, Anne thought to herself. Workers would probably glop up their desks and papers with the food she'd ordered.

She made a quick detour into the coffee room and grabbed one for herself, licking the sweet, melting icing as she walked.

On the way back to her cubicle, she wandered by a room where a meeting was taking place. For a second she stood stock still, eyes wide, holding her breath. She was supposed to be there! The sales team was looking at several ad presentations for the Burnham Report, the adventure camps, and various other Burnham Group products and services. They were tasked to review them all and then hash out new advertising ideas and the scope of a new program. Damn.

No, not damn. Hip hip hooray. In fact, guilt quickly morphed to disappointment as Anne realized how good she would have felt planning to miss the meeting instead of missing it by accident.

No matter. She relaxed and blew smoke inside the room, holding up the cinnamon bun with her other hand.

"Hey—I ordered these for everybody! Take a break—they're in the coffee room."

She left, humming that song about feeling like today to herself, catching the stunned looks of the sales team, including the marketing director, as she sailed by. She saw Sheila at the table with them. So that's where she'd been all this time. Once out of eyesight, Anne said, loud enough for them to hear, "Thank God I skipped *that* boring powwow!"

This serendipitous snafu gave her an idea. She rushed back to her desk and phoned the advertising company that handled most of the Burnham Group's stuff, reaching the sales representative after three rings.

"Terese," Anne cooed into the phone at the sound of the woman's voice, "this is Anne Wyatt at Burnham. Look, you know that Hawaiian adventure team-building camp ad we're running in *Forbes?* Is it too late to change it? We need all the insurance disclaimers set in larger type. Yeah. Really big. Maybe 20-point boldface. It's okay if it takes up most of the page… In fact, put a headline on it: 'Read This First.'"

The "insurance disclaimer" was language the office carrier forced them to put in ads the way pharmaceutical companies were required to list every possible side effect to any drug. In Burnham's case, the disclaimers included things like "The Burnham Group is not responsible for any accidents, injury—psychological or physical, property destruction, theft, or death of the participants. All participants must sign a waiver before coming to the camp and must have written proof of insurance coverage, including life and disability programs."

"Oh, Terese, would you add something in there about us not being responsible for lava burns, too? And fax it directly to Mitch's attention when it's pasted up today—tell him I directed the changes. Uh huh."

As soon as Anne hung up the phone, it blinked with a message. A few clicks later, Anne listened to the voice of Robin, who must have returned from her smoke break, telling Anne to send her the minutes to the last meeting where they'd discussed the Annual Report. In the background, Anne could hear the CNBC reporter, Darren, going on the air. It wouldn't be long now.

Anne phoned Robin back but her line was busy, so she left a chipper message on the secretary's voice mail. "Was I supposed to do the minutes for that, Robin? Tell Mitch I forgot, will you?"

The cigarette was beginning to make Anne feel a little queasy so she looked around for something to stub it into. She'd smoked only a little in college, and then only to look "cool." She couldn't find an ashtray in their smoke-free environment, so she dropped it into her Burnham Group mug and heard it hiss into oblivion.

She turned the radio back on. Switching from country to rock, she stopped when she heard Jack Johnson singing "Bubble Toes."

She turned this way up. Once he hit the "la da da da dahs," she knew everyone would be hearing that as a tape loop in their heads for the rest of the day.

Standing, she tapped her fingers on her desk wondering what to do next, impatient to have Mitch start discovering all these wonderful mistakes she was making. She was in a different zone, feeling energized and alert in ways she'd hardly experienced before. In fact, she felt downright pizzazzy.

Just yesterday, she would have been happy to have accomplished so much at this early hour, but now she felt the day slipping away from her even though it was only early morning. She used to move from task to task with efficiency and speed, glad to be able to finish jobs with a quality touch, eager for Mitch's praise. Now she was searching the horizon for ways to mess up things she'd previously taken pride in accomplishing. It troubled her that she wasn't more bothered by this—shouldn't she feel a sense of regret over being able to so quickly jettison years of work?

Maybe. Maybe she'd feel regret later. Maybe that had been part of her problem all along—her regret switch had a delay button.

Her gaze fell on Sheila's empty cubicle. On her desk was a copy of the galleys for a Burnham Special Report, one of the quarterly booklets they sent to premium-plus subscribers and camp alumni. This one was on "Managing the Difficult Employee." How appropriate.

There are few documents one can really harm in this day of saved computer files. But marked-up galleys fall into the "one of a kind" category. Sheila's notes were handwritten in the margins, and Anne knew from her work patterns that she wouldn't have made a copy of the document until she had finished her editing.

If there was one thing Anne could count on, it was Sheila. She wouldn't keep a foul-up by Anne Wyatt quiet, especially something like this that would create extra work for her.

Anne grabbed the document, looking to and fro as if someone would stop her. Ken still wasn't around. That was disturbing. If Mitch noticed his absence, he could be in trouble. Before proceeding with her own foul-up, Anne decided to cover Ken's. She hastily scrawled a note and left it on his desk: "Meeting with Annual Report printer. Be back soon. Ken."

Satisfied she'd done what she could to keep him out of hot water, Anne carried the galleys to the shredder and fed the report through page by page.

The shredder at last—an almost erotic shiver rattled her as she watched the pages disappear. This is how she'd feel if she could shred all the nasty parts of her own life, starting with the Mitch affair.

No, no, it wasn't just Mitch she wanted to tear up. It was a host of other stupid mistakes. The years she spent in California after graduating from college probably qualified. Living in an apartment near Salinas, barely getting by. What made her think she could make a go of it as a struggling artist? She was not the artist type. She was buttoned down. Look at her pizzazz outfit. Navy blue slacks and lime green shell? That wasn't pizzazz. That was JC Penney. Her family just humored her until Dad got sick. What were they thinking?

Lump in throat time. Dad getting sick was what lured her home. But if she'd realized sooner how little time he had, maybe she'd have come home…

Whirrrr, click. The shredder was finished.

She collected the confettied pieces and took them back to her desk. She made a fainthearted stab at taping some of it together, then wrote a note, which she clipped to the remains and placed on Sheila's desk:

"Dear Sheila, I'm so sorry. I accidentally included this in some sensitive materials I was destroying. I tried taping it back together but figured you wouldn't mind doing the rest. All the best, Anne."

Take that, you little apple-polisher. Anne could envision her reddened face as she complained to Mitch about this snafu. *Bring it on, Sheel.*

Sitting in her chair, Anne scooted off her shoes and socks and wiggled her toes as some DJ called PopTart Pete started mispronouncing the news.

Her feet, Anne noticed, were as pale as sand. They'd look a lot better if she painted the toenails.

No time like the present.

In the back of a top drawer she found her next weapon of mess construction—nail polish, left over from a drugstore buy she'd never taken home.

Stretching one foot on her desk, she started painting her toenails Copper Rose, the pungent chemical smell wafting into the office space. Sweet—she looked bad doing this *and* she funked up the air, all at once.

Sheila now returned carrying a cup of coffee from the local Starbucks. When did she get that?—did she leave the meeting? That was odd. When Sheila saw Anne's pedicure position, her upper lip raised in a half sneer and her eyebrows shot up. But she said nothing. Knowing she would discover the shredded galleys shortly, Anne put her nail polishing on hold and stood.

"Sheel," Anne said, her voice melodiously filled with phony regret. "I'm so sorry. I had a little accident with your document there…" She pointed to the taped pages. They looked remarkably similar to a ransom note.

Slowly, Sheila placed her coffee on her desk. She stared at the note and the little pile of destruction. She narrowed her eyes to slits. She breathed fast, clenching and unclenching her hands, doing the same with her jaw. And then…

She turned and smiled at Anne, her eyes as bright as sunlight. "That's all right, Anne. I'll fix it. I wouldn't want you worrying Mr. Burnham about it." And she threw it in the trash, grabbed her coffee, and left again!

Anne's mouth hung open. She was dumbfounded. What the

heck was Sheila up to? *I wouldn't want you worrying Mr. Burnham about it"*?

Anne didn't have time to ponder this conundrum, however, because she heard Mitch's voice roaring around the corner.

"Anne! Sheila! I need to talk to the communications team right now, dammit!"

The CNBC report must have aired.

Chapter 8

From Mitch Burnham's book *All Management Is Crisis Management*:

> *Nothing is free. Everything comes with a price. Stick to*
> *your plan. If offered help, take it only if you can direct it.*

9:48 a.m.

IN THE FEW SECONDS before Mitch rounded the corner to their cubicles, happiness warmed Anne from the top of her short hair to the tips of her newly painted toes. Happy, the same way she'd felt as a kid on Christmas morning, with the absolute certainty that good things were behind the door to the family room and under the tree.

Mitch stormed to their section of the office, Nehru jacket flying open. As he approached, Sheila returned from the supply area carrying a curling iron.

A curling iron? What was she up to? Before Anne had a chance to ask, Sheila had reached her cubicle and plugged in the thing. She glanced at Anne with a smug look on her face that said, "So there," and Anne got it. Anne did her toenails, Sheila did her hair. Anne was beginning to think…

She couldn't think. Mitch was too loud for thoughts to cut through.

"Turn off that radio, dammit," he said to no one in particular. Ken rounded the corner just at that moment and Mitch turned his attention to him.

"Where have you been, Montgomery?"

"I was… running errands…"

Seeing Ken's creased brow, Anne stepped into the breach. "He had to check the rollout of the Burnham Report. It's at the printer today." She improvised. She sometimes went to the printer to see the first newsletters roll off the press, making sure color separations and photo placements were just perfect. Mitch expected that kind of attention to detail and would appreciate Ken's follow-through. Ken nodded his thanks to her and strode to his cubicle.

So there they all stood—the three communications team members—facing Mitch as if ready for execution. No need for a blindfold. Just lock and load.

"The radio," Mitch repeated.

When Anne didn't respond to Mitch's command, Ken reached over the cubicle wall and quietly flicked off PopTart Pete.

"CNBC just aired a report," Mitch began. He stood with his feet apart and his arms crossed. His head was tilted down so that his eyes rolled up at them like some fiendish genie. "They claim to have spoken with someone here about an idea of mine…"

"Yes?" Anne asked, looking and feeling all eager.

"Who would that be?" He looked from one to the other in turn.

"What was it about?" Sheila cut in. "You can't expect us to tell you who gave out the scoop if we don't know the story." She sounded petulant. And she kept curling her hair.

His head whipped toward her. "What the fuck are you doing with that thing? Put it down."

The F-bomb. He was mad. This was good. Very good. Now all Anne needed was for that anger to focus on her. She opened her mouth to speak but darn if Sheila didn't jump in again.

"I'm just following your tenets, Mitch. Look like the job…" She pulled a long tendril out above her ear and meticulously, thoroughly, slowly wrapped the hair around the curling iron, unwinding it away from her head with equal lack of speed. The smell of hot metal and warm hair overlaid the chemical odor of Anne's nail polish. "Anyone have a rat-tail comb? They really come in handy when you're using a curling iron. You put it between the iron and your head and it keeps the iron from burning you."

Sheila was sucking the bad-vibe oxygen out of the room. Anne wouldn't let her steal the show. "Robin might have one," she said brightly. "Maybe you could step over and talk to her."

"Unplug that thing before you short-circuit something," Mitch boomed.

"I can't do it in the ladies' room. There isn't an accessible wall socket." She pointed the curling iron at him. "Not to worry, though. I've called maintenance. They're bringing in an electrician to fix that. I left you a note—didn't you get it? It'll cost extra because of the short notice, but I didn't think you'd mind. I know you like the team to be happy." She smiled at him.

Sheila's performance was so good, it was hard not to step back and stare. But it was diverting attention from Anne's screwup, and Anne had planned it so well, had pinned so many hopes on it.

From around the corner, Anne heard someone cursing. "Who the hell jammed the machine?" a man's voice roared. A veritable geyser of papers shot out from the copy machine tray. Thank God. Couldn't have asked for better timing.

Mitch half turned.

"Oh dear," Anne said in mock concern. "That would be me. I didn't see Sue's note. We need to call the repair service."

Mitch looked at Anne, confusion and irritation wrinkling his brow.

Good. Mitch had come around the corner just a few seconds ago all primed to ream her out and had been distracted first by Ken's late appearance, then by a display from Sheila, the Back-talking Employee of the Month, who was vacuuming all his anger juices dry before they had a chance to explode over Anne. She would top it off by grabbing some of Sheila's negative mojo.

"Sheila's only doing what we've talked about for ages. And you wouldn't want her looking like a hausfrau, now would you?" Anne asked. "She has some meetings today. She'll be representing you." Anne turned to Sheila. "You need some help with that?" Anne pointed to the curling iron.

Sheila did not smile. Her face, in fact, seemed to have ceased moving.

"Let's get back to business," Anne continued. "The CNBC story. Was it about—"

"Cutting my fucking salary!" Mitch bellowed. His foot started tapping. "To—"

"Ten percent above the highest-paid member of your staff," Anne recited, singsong-like. She did feel like singing—and dancing and throwing confetti.

Mitch was nodding, but not in a good way. More in a way that made his head look like the head of a hammer, nailing an unseen stake through the heart of the employee who came up with this idea. Anne liked this nod.

"So that would probably put your salary in the... oh, three hundred-K range, right?" Anne prodded.

"Two hundred eighty two thousand," he shouted then stepped back and straightened as he realized he'd unwittingly revealed what his top officer received. It was probably Lenny's pay. Poor guy should get more than that.

"Let me call the reporter and set him straight then." Anne picked up her phone and began to punch in a number when Mitch stepped forward, grabbed the receiver from her hand, and smashed it down on the switch hook with a plastic-cracking crash.

"What. The. Fuck. Did. You. Think. You. Were. Doing?"

This had to be a record. Although he was not shy about sprinkling expletives in his talks to staff, he used the F-word sparingly, like a gemstone—to accentuate and draw attention to points he wanted to force them to think about. He was not an indiscriminate curser.

Anne put her hands on her hips and met his gaze.

"I. Was. Trying. To. Do. Some. Good. Around. This. Place," she said, imitating his style. Her breath came fast. "It was an idea I wanted to present to you. I'd done up a memo." She grabbed the memo she'd "accidentally" faxed to Darren and waved it in front of Mitch. "And I was faxing out some press releases and somehow this got stuck to the release." Anne shrugged. "He told me he'd hold it, the jerk. He betrayed me."

In a low, simmering tone, Anne continued. "If you weren't so darned inaccessible, I could have talked to you about this long ago. It's just the kind of thing you support. Along the lines of 'fair pay, fair play.'"

His eyes bulged and his jaw muscle worked, and it was as if she was seeing the gears of his brain churning but nothing was coming out at the end of this production line. So she elaborated. She figured yammering on and on was a surefire way to get on his "good" side. Powerful men, after all, were suckers for yammering women. Oh yes.

"Just one more problem caused by your inaccessibility." She pointed her finger at him. "You are rarely available to the staff after eight o'clock in the morning. It's impossible to get a word with you, let alone any direction on what we're supposed to be doing. I mean, letting us use our creativity is one thing. Giving us no sense of our parameters is quite another, don't you think? Is this part of one of your new techniques? Will we see an article appear on this somewhere soon? Are you trying to imitate royalty by being so distant?"

She knew darn well he was. He confided this to her once during pillow talk when she good-naturedly complained of how hard it was to talk to him during the day. "I like it that way," he'd said, "keeps a certain 'royal' distance. Sets up an aura." *Aura, my assa.*

"Anne, let's talk about this later, shall we?" he seethed.

Later? Heck no. There was no time like the present.

"You mean later when I can't get past Robin? That's the problem, Mitch. Your secretary is like a guard dog. Nobody gets past her unless they have the secret decoder ring. It's juvenile. And silly. That's why I didn't get a chance to run this by you."

Something stank.

Not the argument they were having, but something real, something in the air. It smelled like old shoes burning.

From the corner of her eye Anne saw Ken taking a long stride out of his cubicle behind her and around to Sheila's. As he raced into Sheila's area, the crisis became clear—she'd set the curling iron on her desk next to a stack of computer CDs. They'd started to melt, curdling the air with their industrial synthetic foulness. There were now enough bad odors on the floor to qualify it for a Brownfield designation.

Ken ripped the curling iron from its plug while Sheila remained still, kewpie-doll innocent, without batting an eye. Ken whispered to her, "Be a little more careful," but she didn't thank him. Instead, in a phony, distressed voice, she said, "Oh dear, I think those were the backup CDs of the Burnham Special Reports. And the brochures for the camps." She put a finger to her lip. "And maybe a couple of speeches and PowerPoint presentations, too."

Mitch looked at her as if she'd just pulled a practical joke that wasn't funny.

"Surely you have those things somewhere…"

Before he could finish, Sheila was smiling and shaking her head. "No, I was cleaning out my files, doing a swipe of my whole computer, so these backups are all we have." She gestured to them, a Frigidaire saleswoman showing off her wares.

Angry and frustrated, Anne grabbed the rhetorical mic back from Sheila. "There are files on our computers that not even a laser could erase. Don't worry about it, Mitch." Before Sheila could protest,

Anne barged on. "Back to the issue at hand. I didn't interrupt you about the salary story because you are uninterruptable."

"Don't you think that's important enough to interrupt me?" His voice was low and biting.

"You're often inaccessible," Sheila echoed. "Which is why I had to go ahead and order those five thousand camp medals without talking to you. I ordered real gold. I knew you'd want the best."

"What?" Mitch was dumbfounded and so was Anne. She was ordering cinnamon buns and Sheila was ordering five thousand gold camp medals? Man, Anne had to get with the program. Hey, wait a minute—what program was Sheila working here?

Mitch stared first at Sheila, then at Anne, then at Ken. His mouth opened but he said nothing. Ken, too, looked troubled. The worry that had painted his face as he'd arrived on the scene had shifted slightly to confusion.

"Look," Ken said, "everyone's on edge. I'll help find the documents on Sheila's computer."

As Ken spoke, Greg appeared from around the corner.

"Is this a meeting?" he asked, standing next to Mitch and unconsciously aping his stance. When he saw Anne, Greg pointed his finger. "Posted that proclamation, Anne. Sweet." And he bobbed his head.

"What proclamation?" Mitch asked, turning to Greg.

Thank you, Greg.

"About cutting your own salary, man." Contorting his face, he recited from memory: "About how bloated CEO salaries are ticks sucking the lifeblood from their corporations, about how you're setting an example, about how this country is going to hell in a handbasket because of the greed of selfish billionaires who care more about their perks and benefits than they do about their employees, their companies, or even their families." Greg said it all with a childish sense of admiration, and Anne could swear she heard "The Battle Hymn of the Republic" somewhere in the distance.

"Amen, brother," Sheila said.

"So what's up here?" Greg asked, scratching his head.

"Mitch was just telling us how angry he is and that I shouldn't have written that proclamation for him. Right, Mitch?" Was Mitch flinching every time Anne used his name? Good.

"I don't think it's a mistake, Anne," Ken said, trying to smooth things over once again. "Cutting his salary will allow Mitch to look like he's trimming fat. It will boost the stock price. It's brilliant, really." Was that genuine admiration in his voice, or was he merely trying to cover for her? She was torn between feeling flattered and frustrated.

Sheila chimed in as well, echoing Ken's words. "Yes, brilliant idea." She waved the still-warm curling iron at Anne to emphasize her point.

Mitch looked from Sheila to Anne as if they'd just announced they were joining a hair-curling, toenail-painting cult. He was dumbfounded, and he was a man rarely at a loss for words. Anne's mouth puckered into a satisfied smile.

Ken continued his defense, speaking in a quiet yet forceful tone. "We're all under pressure today, Mr. Burnham. It isn't Anne's fault that an unscrupulous reporter took advantage of her goodwill."

"Hey—there you are!" Robin entered the scene, walking toward Mitch while waggling her hand in the air. In it were several phone message papers. "I've got Lou Dobbs holding for you and Neil Cavuto wants to arrange a live interview—something about a salary cut," she said to Mitch. "And the *Today Show* said they'd like you to talk to them about an appearance…"

Mitch turned to her, taking the papers as soon as she neared him. As Mitch scrutinized the messages, Ken continued to try to calm the waters.

"If Anne's misstep signals that productivity is on the rise, the stock will go up. You might not need to cut anyone after all."

Anne felt like slapping him. And hugging him too. And telling him to shut up. And maybe hugging him again. Perhaps hugging him would have that effect, come to think of it.

Mitch's face shot up. "Don't think this is going to take a head off the chopping block," he growled. And he turned abruptly as if he no longer needed to talk to them. As he walked away with Robin, Anne heard him asking her, "Did Lou tell you what the market reaction was?"

9:52 a.m.

Okay, happiness had fizzled out like a bad holiday sparkler. Anne scratched her head, replaying the scene. Had Mitch just come around to thinking what she'd done was a good thing, not a bad thing? How could that be?

She turned to Sheila who had plugged in the iron again and continued to curl her long, shampoo-commercial hair. Her usual sour-lemon look was gone, replaced by self-satisfied mirth. Before Anne could say anything, Ken spoke.

"I don't think he'll hold it against you, Anne. Sounds like it might be a good plan. I'm sure he'll see its wisdom." He returned to his cubicle while Greg headed off to the coffee room.

"How'd you know that stuff about stock prices and productivity?" Anne asked.

"Took some business courses in college." He stood, flicking into a computer program, his strong profile showing as he bent toward the screen. She stared as he pulled up the Annual Report again and ran his fingers through his hair, reminding her again of his boyish charm. He sensed her gaze and turned to her, igniting a blush.

"You okay?" he asked. "I mean, you seem kind of rattled."

"Big day, like you said," she managed to squeak out. "I'll be fine," she added, wishing she could share with him her strategy.

"I'm looking forward to tomorrow." She'd tell him all about it then. His lips lifted in a slight smile and he nodded, before sitting down to work.

Anne turned her attention to Sheila, who also slid back into her chair, taking out a mirror with her free hand. She then sorted out an array of cosmetics and lotions that she obviously planned on queuing up for the next step in her office beauty makeover.

Something smelled here and it wasn't just those melted CDs.

Anne walked over to Sheila's cubicle, entered without permission, and sat on the desk, scooting the makeup out of the way with her fanny.

"We need to talk," Anne said quietly so no one else could hear.

"I'm kind of busy," Sheila replied. Before she could grab her own container of nail polish, Anne whisked it out of reach, holding it up in the air like a hostage.

"I know what you're doing," Anne hissed at her. "And I thought of it first."

"I have no idea what you're talking about," Sheila said.

Greg came back with his coffee and hovered nearby. "That's really something," he said, sipping at his mug. "Mitch taking a salary cut—not many bosses would do that."

Sheila and Anne both looked at him and smiled.

"Nope, not many," Anne said to him. "In fact, go ahead and post on the website that he's cutting it in half. I'll send you a press release in a sec." She turned back to her original target. "Sheila, let's go grab a cup of coffee."

"Somebody just made a new pot," Greg volunteered. "It's great—not as good as this morning's, though."

"Too strong for me. I want a Frappuccino or something like that." Anne grabbed Sheila's arm. "Come on. We won't be long."

Sheila stood but wasn't happy. "I just had some coffee. Besides, don't you need shoes?" She pointed to Anne's naked feet.

"I'll put my shoes on and you'll have coffee with me. End of story."

Sheila hesitated.

"Meet me at the corner coffee shop or I'll march into Mitch's office and tell him how you saved the company a cool half million last week with your suggestion to bundle our printing bids," Anne hissed at her.

Sheila grit her teeth but Anne had done the trick. Sheila's eyes didn't leave Anne's face as she grabbed her purse and headed for the elevators.

After Anne returned to her own cubicle and threw on her pumps, she made a quick phone call to a corporate gift shop they used for holiday gifts for investors and customers. "Hey, Tony," she purred to the account manager. "Anne Wyatt here. Look, Mitch wants to spice things up around here by sending thank-you gifts to the whole staff pronto. What do you have you can send over today—individually gift-wrapped, of course?" Tony had lots of things but Anne settled on leather portfolios and gold-leaf photo albums. "Bill it to Mitch's private expense account. Oh, and fax the invoice today. Make sure you put on it that it's done per my request." Then Anne penned a note.

"Went to Printing Plus to double-check reports. Sheila." Anne slipped this on Sheila's desk before joining her at the elevator bank. On Anne's desk was a completely different note—"Gone fishin' for good coffee and great buns."

Chapter 9

From Mitch Burnham's book *The Mitch Principles*:
> *Join things. The chamber of commerce, the local business club, whatever. Not so much to learn things but to keep an eye on your competition. As the old saying goes: keep your friends close and your enemies closer.*

9:58 a.m.

"I THINK WE SHOULD set some ground rules, that's all," Anne said to Sheila. They sat uncomfortably at a tall, faux-marble table near the window of Cuppa Joe. Anne really didn't get the whole tall-table thing. What did the designers think—that since each generation added a few inches, they might as well plan ahead? Her feet struggled for a foothold on a Mount Everest-high wrought-iron seat.

Sheila sipped a strawberry latteccino through a straw, while Anne wrapped her hands around a mug of chocolate cappuccino with double whipped cream.

"That's silly," Sheila said. "If we're both competing for the same result, let the best woman win. If anything, I think this will make us work smarter to be at the top of our game."

Crap. She sounded like Mitch. She definitely needed to get out of the Burnham Group. Her soul had been snatched.

Anne leaned back and stared outside. It was midmorning but Washington was already bustling. She saw a famous columnist stroll by and she thought she recognized a presidential staffer hurrying toward Pennsylvania Avenue. Even if you weren't involved in the political scene, you could still catch a buzz from all the power wafting around.

"We're both reasonable people," Sheila continued. "It's not like either of us would do anything unethical against the other."

Interesting moral values set there—as long as they were honorable with each other, it didn't faze Sheila that they were burning the flag of ethical behavior with their treatment of Mitch. But it was just like Sheila, everything neatly in its box. That, Anne decided, was what really bugged her about the woman—her thoroughness. Even on a day when Anne was trying to be a slacker, Sheila made her feel like she was… well, slacking on the slacking.

"All right," Anne agreed. "I guess that would work. What do you consider unethical?"

"Nothing from our personal lives comes into play," Sheila said as if she'd done a thesis on this in graduate school and oppo research on Anne in preparation for today's competition. "Nothing that could hurt each other with others in the office. And neither of us reveals what the other is doing."

"Everything else fair game?"

"Within reason."

They drank for a while in silence. Sheila seemed so content, so self-contained, that it was hard not to be envious of her. Anne found herself wanting a little piece of that self-confidence.

"Where'd you get the dress?" Anne asked, pointing at her tangerine disaster. The barista couldn't keep his eyes off it when he served them.

"Mart du Wal." She laughed, pronouncing the "mart" in the French way, with no T. Poor Sheel. She tried to make an everyman joke and ended up sounding like Marie Antoinette. "I bought it for Pizzazz Day, of course," she continued. "Had no idea Mitch would pull this other stunt."

"Why are you quitting?" Anne asked, feeling more comfortable. With Sheila's brains and attention to detail, Anne's guess was she was jumping ship to become CEO at some soon-to-be-successful start-up.

"I'm going to work on Capitol Hill." She mentioned a newly elected congressman who was grabbing headlines with his fresh voice and new ideas. Glamour and influence—not a bad combo. Anne pictured Sheila running up the steps of Capitol Hill in a red power suit, papers at the ready to hand to her boss who would take them with a benevolent smile before he went inside and saved the world.

"As public affairs director?" Anne asked.

"No. Constituent work."

Envy shifted to shock. Constituent work involved handling calls from the folks back home. It was usually reserved for low-level staffers one step up from college interns.

Now Anne's inner picture morphed into something unattractive—Sheila in a cheap summer dress and cotton jacket sitting in a windowless room with a young, scared new hire, answering phones and printing out form letters while a glamorous office manager squawked complaints from the other room.

Going from communications assistant at Burnham to constituent work for a congressman was like trading an executive office suite for a customer service desk. Sheila was taking a step down.

"Why—"

Sheila waved her hand in the air to stop Anne's question. "I've always wanted to work in politics and I don't have any experience in it. Have to start somewhere. I was a poli-sci minor at Tufts."

Start somewhere—Sheila was surely Anne's age and she was starting over, at the bottom of a new career ladder. Anne was envious again, this time of her courage. She saw her in a different light.

"How about you?" Sheila leaned into the table to suck up more of her drink.

Anne gave her the condensed version—how she'd heard of the job opening in San Francisco through Rob, how he'd helped her snag the job with a well-placed word from his boss. Since the hospital was on the cutting edge of research into childhood diseases, Sheila seemed genuinely impressed by Anne's choice. They were both going into service-oriented jobs, Sheila said, patting Anne's arm. But the comparison made Anne uncomfortable. Not because Sheila's was lower on the career ladder than Anne's, but rather because Sheila's was more... altruistic. Sure, Anne was happy to be going to an institution that did life-changing work. But she was moving to a city she loved and she wouldn't even be sacrificing her boyfriend since he wasn't really much of a boyfriend at all.

"So, is that where you're from—California?" Sheila asked, genuine warmth in her voice. In DC, it was natural for people to assume you were from somewhere else. The city was a magnet for transplants.

"No. I'm from around here, kind of. But I've moved a lot..." and Anne told Sheila about her military family background.

Sheila's smile broadened. "My father was Foreign Service," she cried excitedly, "and we lived in Bonn, too, for three years."

They discovered they were there at the same time, as little girls, and had never met each other. And Sheila told Anne of how her own father had passed away a year before Anne's had died.

"My mother still hasn't recovered," Sheila said sadly.

"Neither has mine." Anne looked at her. With her long hair now falling in waves from the curling iron, Sheila looked like a fresh-faced farm girl. Her eyes were big and eager, and her smile was kind. If she'd spent her childhood tramping around the world like Anne had, she probably had lost a sense of home. As if reading Anne's mind, Sheila continued.

"I'm glad I found something close to my mother—she lives in Silver Spring," she said. "My sister Kate is in New York, and my brother Alex works in Tallahassee."

"So you're the designated caretaker," Anne said, thinking of how guilty Jack had made her feel about moving away from their mother. "That hardly seems fair."

"I don't mind it at all. Like I said, I wanted to find a job in politics. I realized it was time for me to stop fooling myself—thinking I'd get around to it 'someday.'"

"But you're good at what you do." Anne couldn't believe she was complimenting Sheila. Maybe she should pinch herself.

"Thanks. But I'm just thorough. I think it will come in handy in my new job." Sheila sipped again at her drink. "How'd you get a recommendation from Mitch—if he doesn't know you're leaving?" she asked.

"Uh… I used an old evaluation he wrote up."

"Same here."

"I was going to tell him today," Anne added.

"Me, too!" She laughed, and slapped the table with her fingers. "Had my letter of resignation typed up and everything. But the severance pay—couldn't pass that up when I'm already facing a salary cut…"

Before they could continue, Anne's cell phone chirped. Apologizing, she took the call.

10:05 a.m.

It was Louise, Anne's best friend.

When she'd moved back to DC, Anne had been able to reconnect with a few old high school pals—Louise and Carla. Both had married right out of college and both had kids. Louise, however, was more like Anne. She'd studied dance at a college in Philadelphia and even did some work with small companies in the DC area before childbearing interfered. While Carla was fun and bubbly, Louise was artsy and reflective. Anne loved Carla, but was more herself with Louise, or at least the old self she had been in college and in

Monterey—a little bohemian, a little free-spirited artiste, and not a regimented Army brat.

Louise's thin voice crackled in Anne's ear.

"Are you busy?" she asked.

"Well, I…"

Louise burst out sobbing. "I just had to talk to someone." Gulping, gasping wails of sorrow cut over the line. An amped-up version of the cries that had lain strangled in Anne's own chest when Mitch used his breakup language in the meeting this morning. Déjà vu jolted through her and she shuddered, looking around to see if anyone had noticed.

Anne covered the mouthpiece and whispered to Sheila that she had to take the call. Sheila nodded and said she needed to use the ladies' room anyway.

"What's happened, Lou?" Anne asked.

"Paul is leaving," Louise stammered.

At the first sound of Louise's anguished cries, Anne had braced herself for some bad news involving Louise's kids, not knowing where she'd find the emotional strength to comfort her. So when Louise blurted out the truth, Anne felt that horrible sense of relief that this bad news wasn't the worst news.

"What?!"

Louise's husband Paul might not have been Anne's favorite person in the world, but she never would have imagined him running out on his wife. Well, maybe—with another guy. A drama teacher at a Virginia high school, he had always impressed Anne as being a little too in touch with his feminine side. For Louise, however, he seemed perfect. They both shared an interest in the arts, but he actually made money at it. Louise was so inspired by him that she'd talked about going back to get a teaching degree when their two kids were older.

"Tell me what happened."

"He… he… he met someone," she sniffled.

"Oh no. I'm so sorry, Lou. Is it Mike?" Anne asked, mentioning the name of a mutual friend who always seemed a bit too pally with Paul.

"What's this have to do with Mike?"

Uh-oh. Wrong conclusion. Anne shifted gears. "When did you find out?"

"He told me! He told me last night!" She said it as if it was worse that he actually told her, instead of coming upon it on her own. Anne understood. If he told her, that meant he was serious, and there was no chance of reconciliation. Telling her was the confession before the inevitable.

"It's another teacher... I know her, Anne. I thought she was nice." She started to cry again, but Anne was having a hard time focusing on her as she knocked out of her head the image of Paul running off with a man. Damned if he wasn't straight. He was so straight he was screwing two chicks. Couldn't get much straighter than that.

Anne brought her attention back to Louise and managed to calm her down by asking her a series of practical questions. Paul had moved out, into an apartment. He'd pay child support. He wanted to see a lawyer. He wanted to marry this woman.

He wanted to marry the woman—it flashed in neon lights in Anne's brain, a marquee broadcasting hopes and dreams, now dead and buried.

Oh man, she had to get past that feeling if she were going to be any good to Louise. But there it was, creeping up on her again, demanding attention... When Louise told Anne that Paul was going to marry his mistress—

Mea culpa mea culpa mea maxima culpa...

—Anne had a flash of post-traumatic envy!

There were so many times—countless times, countless dreams—when Anne would have paid a king's ransom to know Mitch was saying those words to Glynda. *I'm leaving you for a woman I fell in love with at work.*

Anne felt like a monster—her affair with Mitch had turned her into an unfeeling, grasping beast who wished she'd once had what Paul's mistress now had, a lover willing to chuck it all just for her—nice wife, kids, home, everything. *Just gimme gimme gimme what I want.* She recoiled from the person she used to be. Her friend's dismay made clear just how needy and pathetic she'd once been. But she couldn't stop an inner dialogue from rolling through her head like a bad radio play she didn't want to hear:

Old Anne: Well, Louise, maybe it's better this way. After all, if Paul really loves this woman…

New Anne: Oh honey, maybe he'll come to his senses. After all, he has two children with you.

Old Anne: Once love has died, don't you think it's better to just let it go? Let him be free to be with this other woman. I'm sure she didn't plan on this happening.

New Anne: What was the matter with that brazen hussy? She knew he was married. She should have pushed him away!

Old Anne: But don't you think Paul is doing the right thing? He's being honest—with himself and with you.

New Anne: Since when did cheating on your wife become "doing the right thing?"

She shook her head, trying to get those two voices to meld into one soothing song of comfort.

"I'll come over after work," Anne told Louise. "Can you get your mother to watch the kids? I'll take you out."

Louise blew her nose. "Thanks, that's okay. Just stop by. I need to talk." Her voice was congested and she started to cry again. "I… I… I don't know if I can keep the house. I have to find a job. I have to—oh, Anne—I have to start all over."

Start over—there were those words again. Just like Sheila.

Speaking of Sheila—Anne saw her returning just as Louise talked about how she had to go deal with a screaming kid. Anne hung up as Sheila scooted back up onto her chair.

"Everything okay?" Sheila asked brightly.

"No," Anne responded and spilled the beans about Louise. She threw in a bunch of bad stuff about Paul, too, stuff she never shared with anyone, about how he always wanted to be the center of attention at parties, how he split restaurant checks to the half penny, about how he pronounced "chaise longue" *shez lonshje*. Sheila seemed taken aback. Anne suspected she pronounced it the same way.

Nonetheless, Sheila shook her head at the end of the story, showing appropriate sympathy for Anne's friend. In fact, she seemed a bit too sympathetic, a dark cloud blowing over her bright eyes. Through clenched teeth, she pronounced, "She's better off without him."

Anne sensed a Voice of Experience here so she pressed on. "Louise still loves him…"

Sheila shook her head even more vigorously. "He's a cheater. A cheater doesn't break that habit. It's like a disease. Like alcoholism."

"You sound like you know." Anne expected her to confess to betraying a lover herself. For some reason, that would have made Anne like her more—one more imperfection.

"Yes, I do, unfortunately." Sheila sighed and looked at her manicured hands on the table. "You've probably already heard. I was stupid enough to become one of Mitch's conquests."

Chapter 10

From Anne Wyatt's ghostwritten foreword to Mitch Burnham's book *The Action Alternative*:

> *The only surprise in business would be no surprises. When you think you've got all your bases covered, you're probably setting yourself up to lose the game...*

10:30 a.m.

DEEP INTO WORK ON the Annual Report, Ken's mind kept drifting in a thousand different directions but always landing on the same path. He had to keep reeling himself in if he was going to get this draft done before heading out to lunch. Anne owed him the President's Message, too, which would delay it. She'd taken off with Sheila for a coffee break. What had gotten into her?

He'd at first attributed her odd behavior to the insanity of clawing for job preservation during this insane day. But now, he wondered if she was also on edge because...

He thought of her smile as she'd reminded him about tomorrow. No, it couldn't be.

But he couldn't let the thought go. Maybe Anne Wyatt was skittish because she'd decided to ask him out today and had made the date for tomorrow morning. Maybe this Rob person was nothing more than a casual friend and Ken had cheated himself out of the opportunity to get to know Anne because of falsely assuming she was involved. He hoped he'd never given her the cold shoulder as a result.

He leaned back in his chair, smiling, again on the territory that kept tempting him away from the work at hand. Over a relaxed breakfast, he could study her face to his heart's content, memorizing the moment of change from serious reflection to pixie-like delight. Did it happen just as her eyes crinkled into a smile? Maybe that was it—the eyes lit up just a nanosecond before her mouth curved into a grin. No, no, it was something else. It was a subtle relaxation of the face and a slight widening of the eyes—that was the moment when dark turned to light.

Damn! She was hard to capture. Something stirred in him at the prospect of being able to try, at least, to get the essence of her smile.

It wasn't just her smile, though, that intrigued him. There was something deeper there, something searching, something a little afraid of the world and eager to embrace it at the same time, like a child dipping her toe into the water before diving in. Anne's face reflected that inner struggle. That's why she appealed to his artist's sensibilities.

He could have gone on daydreaming for another five minutes or so but the phone interrupted him. Scooting into his desk, he picked up the receiver while announcing his name to the caller. His blood chilled when he heard who it was.

"Felicia!" It had been a mistake to go over to the Arts Consortium. He should have just walked Bethany through the computer problem over the phone.

"Darling, I had quite the time navigating your company's voice mail. Finally, some kind soul in advertising put me through."

"I'm kind of busy right now," he lied. Despite its lyrical quality, her voice was like nails screeching on a blackboard to him now.

"My, my, you're always busy. I hope they pay you enough since they demand so much of your creative energy."

When he didn't reply to this remark, she went on: "But that's why I'm ringing you up. I hope you don't mind but I called Arthur Howard as soon as you left the office and told him about this devastatingly talented young artist struggling to set up his own studio and gallery. I assured him that an investment in this artist would pay off in countless ways in the future—to him and to the community. He wants to meet you, darling! Aren't you thrilled?"

No, he wasn't.

Yes, he was.

Of course his mood brightened at the prospect of having money invested in his plans, money he didn't have to earn himself. But money from Felicia's machinations might hold other strings, ones he'd cut with a quick and decisive blow when he'd quit the Consortium months ago.

"You're speechless," she purred. "Let me set something up. Are you free for cocktails this evening?"

"I... I... don't know..."

She heaved a dramatic sigh and he could envision her smiling and rolling her eyes. She knew she had him in a tight spot.

"Look, Ken," she said in a low, clipped voice. "This has nothing to do with us as a couple. I just can't stand to see a talented artist like you scrambling for an opportunity. Please don't make more of it than that."

Against his better judgment, he penciled in the meeting. After he hung up, he saw Robin flagging him down.

"Just tried to call you," she said. "Mitch has a few moments now. He's interviewing all the staff."

After hearing Sheila's confession about Mitch, Anne had a new mission. She no longer just wanted to get fired. She wanted to ruin Mitch's life.

Anne's first reaction had been to clam up. A plastic smile came over her face as hard and fake as a bad Halloween mask. Sheila was talking. Anne was listening. But she wasn't really here. She was trying to remember the times she saw Mitch and Sheila interact and what, if any, clues might have been in those exchanges. She was trying to evaluate whether he paid her more attention than he did Anne.

In fact, she was reevaluating every interaction he had with all the women in the office, not just those on staff but women who came in for appointments, even wives of board members. What she'd thought of as his harmless, flirtatious charm was, in fact, the high-test toxic brand of the same. And she was realizing that good ol' Mitch used discretion in the office—it seemed like such a virtue during the affair—but loved flaunting his mistresses when they were celebrities he could parade in front of every camera in sight. A double whammy of unworthiness swamped her.

She wanted to get out of that coffee shop and run away. Hell, she wanted to get out of her past life, discarding it like a snake's skin on the harlequin-patterned tile floor.

She did the running away part at least. After Sheila's narrative ended, Anne begged off lingering for some more girl talk—*have to pick up something nearby, errands to run, jobs to do, former lovers to kill, it's been great*—and marched off down K Street as if she were racing to the president with news of peace in our time.

Instead, her mind was a churning war zone. And what did good soldiers do when entering a war zone? They reviewed the terrain.

She flipped back through the relevant time periods. She rewound to April two years ago: Mitch told her about his plans to renew his marriage with Glynda. Anne broke things off with him. He got back together with Glynda.

The reconciliation lasted three months. August of last year, they'd filed for divorce. Anne couldn't remember how long it had taken to be final. All she could remember was that when she'd heard the news of the divorce during the dog days of summer, she'd felt smugly satisfied that she'd moved on. Mitch, meanwhile, had started being seen with a number of women, including Kathie-Rose, the cable news babe.

Anne looked up. She'd walked so far that she was now on the silent closed section of Pennsylvania Avenue in front of the White House. Some tourists gawked. Security guards stared. Behind the wrought-iron gates, camera tripods and primped newsmen stood at the ready for their daily reports. She heard someone asking where the duck was—a nesting duck had set up house in a spindly tree near the Treasury building. The Secret Service had put up a makeshift barricade around it with signs saying "Nesting duck, do not disturb" until the eggs hatched.

That reminded her of Louise and her two kids. It would be hard for her. She and Paul might not have been living the high life, but they had managed to afford a fixer-upper house in Arlington and even a vacation at the beach every few years. Louise liked scrimping, in fact, taking great pleasure in how much she saved using coupons. Anne had always admired her for that—Louise's penny-pinching ways were far better than Anne's when she had been a Bohemian artist. Now, no amount of coupons would help Louise maintain even her modest life. She'd have to find work. She'd have to…

Those words again—*start over.*

Same with Glynda, Mitch's wife. She'd had to start over. Except, of course, with a sizable settlement and monthly checks to boot. And the kid. Louise had her kids, too. Somehow, Anne began to feel they all had more than she did, despite their loss.

Their loss, after all, signified the absence of something substantial. Anne was now not sure she'd had something at all to lose.

Dear Lord, what's the matter with me? I hear devastating news of a friend's loss and all I can think of is my own pathetic need! I learn of a coworker's shame at her affair with the boss and all I can dwell on is my own betrayal by the same lousy cad.

Anne stared into the bright sunlight, triggering her eyes to water.

She walked further, past coffee shops, bus stops, the ornate old Executive Building that shouted out grandeur and forcefulness. She blinked back tears.

Louise had had seven years with Paul. Glynda had had five years with Mitch.

They'd had something real.

She was nearly thirty. Most of her friends and acquaintances were married and settled into career tracks. Those who weren't were like Louise—moving from Plan A to Plan B, starting over. When would Anne get to start *at all?*

Shaking her head like a fighter after a blow, Anne thought of Sheila. She'd had a few months with him. Sheila said she'd broken up with Mitch after Christmas. It had probably taken Sheila a few months to get her résumé together, decide where she wanted to work, and start applications. That meant that Sheila had probably started looking for a job in January, consciously breaking with her past and charting a new direction, not staying in the same office with Mitch, no matter how professionally he treated her after the breakup. Sheila had guts.

Anne bit her lip and turned toward Constitution Avenue and the mall, the long, wide strip of trees and green lined on either side by the museums of the Smithsonian Institute and anchored at each end by monuments and offices of state.

It took Sheila just the week of Christmas vacation to realize she needed to get out of Dodge, leaving the Burnham Group. It had taken Anne nearly two years. And only then because friends and relatives encouraged her. *You should be doing something you enjoy more,* her mother would say when Anne complained about her job. *You're really very talented. Someone would snatch you up in an instant,* Rob had told her after a similar complaint fest.

What had Rob said when he heard she got the job in California? *See—I told you!*

At the mall, Anne sank onto a bench near where a vendor was offering popcorn, cotton candy, and lemonade to hungry and thirsty tourists. She pulled out her cell phone and punched in Rob's direct number. He answered right away.

"Hey," he said in a distracted voice. "What's up?"

His good-natured voice relaxed her. This is what she needed—a comfort zone. Rob was, in many respects, her best friend. She'd met him at a public relations society function and they'd shared a lot of laughs together. He was a high-level staffer so Anne told him about Sheila's new job with a congressman and asked if he knew anything about the staff. He told her a little, all positive reviews.

"Did you hand in your notice yet?" he asked. She heard him whisper directions to someone in his office.

"Not yet." She waited for him to prompt her, but he was obviously involved in something. "We had a staff meeting this morning," she added. "Couldn't talk to him."

"Just leave your resignation on his desk, Annie," he said. *Annie.* No one used that nickname with her besides her father. She'd abandoned it when she gave up Barbie. Hearing Rob use it felt like… a liberty.

"Annie?" she repeated, but he didn't respond.

Irritation and discomfort smoked through her chest. Why should it bother her if Rob used that nickname for her? Maybe because it was an endearment and she didn't really think of Rob in that way. She brushed those thoughts away and went on to describe her reason for dawdling on the resignation.

"You see, he's going to let someone go. Budget cuts."

"That's perfect, then. You can save someone else their job."

There was no point in telling Rob why Mitch wouldn't let go of this plan. Even if the company had a huge influx of cash and stock prices went through the roof, Anne knew Mitch. He had probably already sketched out the article he planned to write about it.

"Wouldn't work," she said. "Trust me."

"What are you going to do?" he asked. Before she could answer, he figured it out. "You're going to try to get fired?" She heard a door squeak open in his office and then he moved his mouth away from the receiver to say, "I'll get back to you on that, Nancy." She tried to remember who Nancy was and an image came back to her—older woman, well-kept and savvy, on the staff from the senator's first campaign.

"I can't believe you're doing this," Rob said.

She told him about the severance pay. "I can go on vacation," she added. "Maybe Hawaii." No, not Hawaii. Not anyplace with a Burnham Group Adventure Team-building Camp located in it.

Rob laughed a little. "That sounds great."

But he seemed far away, uninterested in her plots and machinations. This irritated her as much as his use of "Annie." If there was one thing she'd been able to count on with Rob, it was his sense of humor. What was the matter with him that he wasn't taking this joke seriously?

"Something wrong?" she asked. "You don't think this is funny?"

"Oh yeah, yeah. Great. Can't wait to hear about it." She heard his chair creak as he got up and she could tell he was walking around, then she heard his door close. "Remember I told you that the congressman's being considered for an ambassadorship?"

"Yeah."

"Well… You can't tell anyone, but there's going to be an announcement later this week. He got it!" His words were fast and excited.

"Wow, Rob, that's great. That's… when does he leave?" The posting was in an important eastern European country and she struggled to remember its name. Something -slovenia? Or -ikastan? She came up empty.

"Don't know. But once it's announced, things will probably happen pretty quickly. It's going to mean big changes."

Her heart slowed down. Poor Rob. He'd have to find another job if a replacement was appointed and that person wanted to start fresh. She was just about to offer words of consolation when he broke into her thoughts with more news.

"He wants to take me with him, Anne. Chief of Staff—or whatever title I want. A big pay raise. Incredible opportunities. I can't believe it. He called me his right-hand man. I can hardly wait."

"Oh. Wow." She didn't know what to say as a cascade of conflicting emotions spilled through her heart. She was happy for him, but envious again that here was another person in her life getting the opportunity to start over. Unlike with Louise and Sheila, however, Rob's new start was triggered by good things. Whatever—the result was the same. Anne Wyatt stood still while others moved forward. *Get a grip, Anne! Be happy for him! You're moving, too, to a new job in California. Why doesn't it feel new, though? And Rob—it's not like he was the One for you.*

Eureka moment. He wasn't the one for her. She'd known it. He'd known it. Good grief—even her brother Jack had known it. Where were these Anne Wyatt secrets kept, huh? Would someone give her the key to that treasure chest?

"I'll have to come visit you," she managed to squeeze out, "after I get settled in my job and all."

"Sure, sure. No rush. You need to get yourself in the right track. And I'll be working double time at first. I have so much to learn…" And he proceeded to fill her ear with trade deficit numbers, agricultural negotiation nuances, treaty information, and a hundred different topics she'd be interested in if she weren't waiting for one topic to drop its way into the conversation like a diamond shining through coal dust.

She was waiting for him to say how he'd miss her.

But this was a fool's errand, she realized as she listened to his happy dissertation. Her weak smile faded as truth blasted her with its soul-scouring rays. He felt the same way about her that she felt about him. They were really "just friends." Maybe Rob had wanted more than that, but he'd let her set the pace, and after Mitch, "comfortable" was the pace she'd craved.

She'd found it as fulfilling as a drink of water after a three-month desert trek. *I'll take this,* her subconscious had been screaming. *I'll take this and be content.*

The problem with settling for "comfortable," though, is that it takes up the space that "passionate" and "deeply loved" might otherwise occupy.

At some point, after he was set up in the embassy in Slovikestan or wherever, he'd come to the very same conclusions. It might wash over him the first time she called and he didn't recognize her voice. Or it might occur to him the first time he escorted another woman to an embassy affair and he found himself enjoying her company and wanting to know her better. Or, if he was really busy and a sucker for happy endings, it might take until he came back to the States for a visit and realized what a pain in the ass it would be to fit in a trip to California to see her and his other pals out there.

Some time in the past few months, he'd stopped looking over his shoulder, waiting for her to catch up to where he wanted to be in a relationship. She wanted to shout "Wait up, Rob, I promise I'll hurry," but she knew it was a lie. He wasn't the One.

She managed to say the right things and ask the right questions and they spent a few more minutes on the phone before she told him she had to go. She couldn't stay on. She was thinking of how they were breaking up, when they'd never really been together. He just wasn't the One.

Chapter 11

From Mitch Burnham's article *"Take This Job and Shove It': Human Resources of the Future:"*

If you suspect you have a worker who's a "reluctant contributor," keep an eye on him or her and trim the bad apple as soon as possible before the whole tree starts to rot.

11:13 a.m.

His interview with Mitch lasted exactly twelve minutes, which Ken found ironic since the book on the corner of Mitch's desk at the time was *The Twelve-minute Management Plan.* Had he planned it that way? It wasn't just fast. It was… cursory. Mitch asked only standard-issue interview questions, allowing Ken go to on without interruption. He had the impression he was boring Mitch, in fact, which fed into Ken's notion that the interview was merely pro forma. He was just as glad to get out quickly. He had lots of work to do. He shook Mitch's hand and left, eager to finish tasks before lunch. In a few minutes' time, he was buried in his work again.

He glanced up, however, as Anne returned to her cubicle, lighting a cigarette. Since when had she started smoking? Another sign she was tense.

"Anne," he said in as calm a voice as he could muster. "Do you want anything?" He stood, holding up his mug. Maybe a cup of tea or something would de-stress her. He'd seen a box of chamomile in the coffee nook.

She coughed. Nope, she wasn't used to smoking. In fact, she bent over in a coughing jag and he rushed to her aid, patting her on the back and grabbing an unopened bottled water from his desk for her. When she'd sipped a bit and her cough had subsided, she looked up at him, eyes watery, face red, lips trembling.

Lips trembling? She had it bad. Who knew? Anne Wyatt had a thing for him!

As for him, his hand slipped to the small of her back where it lingered, sending a tremble of a whole different sort coursing through him. He pulled away, feeling his face heat.

"Thanks," she managed to sputter, sipping some more. She wiped her eye and then promptly took another puff from that blasted cigarette!

Sheila stood up.

"Anne, really," she said. "The smoking is a bit much, don't you think?"

"You could set off the sprinklers and ruin the equipment," Ken added, hoping to get her to see reason before Mitch Burnham noticed her transgression.

Anne looked up, as if she were weighing the possibility and liking what she imagined. She blew smoke toward the ceiling.

He had to force her to focus. He grabbed the cigarette and threw it in the Burnham mug on her desk. Then he looked her full in the eyes like a parent trying to reach an intransigent child.

"Anne, why don't you work on the President's Message for the Annual Report now? I could use it to finish my design."

That seemed to do the trick. He could see her attention crystallize.

"I'm sorry. I thought you could just put everything together without it." She touched his arm. "Why don't you go ahead and do that? But I'll go ahead and write that message and get it to Mitch for his approval." She slid back into her seat, took another swig of water, and began typing.

Satisfied that this crisis had been averted, Ken returned to his own work. He had only a few more items to configure on the Annual Report, but he was a perfectionist so he soon lost himself in the little details of moving a header a centimeter here, cropping a photograph there, correcting copy layout to avoid too many orphans, widows, and hyphenations, and catching a misspelling in a headline he'd re-typed when setting it.

He was glad to escape into the steady rhythm of an assignment he could perform well, warmly aware of Anne's presence next door, smiling when he heard her giggle a little as she finished her own task. Good—she was happy with getting something done. He heard the pages of her printer clicking and saw her race off to Burnham's office, papers in hand. Good move, he thought. Burnham, for all his sup-posed business savvy, didn't check his email as frequently as he should. Sticking the actual pages under his nose was the best way to get his attention and approval. Ken was sure whatever Anne had written was perfect. She was a skilled wordsmith, able to take the most banal ideas and turn them into something interesting and even intelligent.

He went back to finishing his task, content in the knowledge that all was right with the world, at least until Anne was rattled once again.

Anne marched to Mitch's office.

When Robin saw Anne, she offered an answer to Anne's un-voiced question.

"Meeting with Lenny. Something I can help you with?" Robin stopped typing and faced Anne.

"Nope. I just need to leave something for him." As evidence, Anne waved the papers in the air, then waltzed into Mitch's office to his desk.

"Leave it on his chair!" Robin called out. "He won't see it on his desk!"

Robin was right. Mitch's desk, so neat and clear at this morning's meeting, was now piled high with magazines, papers, reports, and catalogs. On top of one stack was a sketch of Ken's for an ad layout. Mitch had asked Ken to brainstorm some ideas after growing irritated with the Burnham Group's advertising agency's work on the adventure camps.

She picked it up, admiring its sleek yet compelling design. As usual, he'd hit the mark, and for the first time, she noticed that Ken wasn't just talented. He was sexy. There was a visceral quality to his use of color and shape, the way he forced your eye to move around the page, taking you where he wanted you to go. And there was subtle humor in the layout, too, as if he was saying: This is crazy, but life is too, so there you have it.

She'd have to ask him more about his art when they had breakfast the next morning.

She turned away from the desk and prepared to plop her papers on Mitch's chair. It occurred to her that Mitch's desk, like the man himself, was a phony. Each morning and afternoon, the desk was cleared of papers and clutter, the clean, expansive look of the powerful executive who obviously swept all his work to the "finished" file before day's end.

The desk itself had no drawers—like Lenny's. It was one of those long, table-like things designed to give the appearance of modern forcefulness. The man who sat here, it seemed to say, was so powerful he didn't need filing drawers. Nope, he didn't. Not if he had a woman to clean up after him. Anne had seen Robin stuffing all the material in the credenza drawers at night and fetching it out again in the mornings.

She swiveled Mitch's chair toward her and a small pile of work sat there as well—put in place by other savvy staffers who knew they'd get his attention this way. She remembered once visiting her father in his consulting office when he wasn't back from a meeting. A similar pile had sat in his chair waiting for him. Despite Mitch's progressive new ideas, some things never changed.

Before she placed her document on top, she saw the employee newsletter sitting there. A chipper Post-it note was smacked on its front page: "A rush job but I think it will do. Sheila." Sheila had even drawn a smiley face under her name. Mitch hated smiley faces.

Lifting the note a smidgen to see what Sheila had done with the publication, Anne was shocked and horrified. And mad she hadn't thought of it herself.

Her eye was drawn first to the photo. There Mitch was in all his glory—skydiving from a private jet high above the Arizona desert. His flight suit billowed in the wind, his arms were outstretched in the great blue yonder, and his face lit up with an excited grin. Or maybe that was terror. Hard to tell when his eyes didn't register anything.

But it was the caption that was brilliant, and Anne found herself nodding her head, thinking, "Way to go, Sheel. Well done, my girl, very well done."

The caption was the same one that had run with last week's photo of a clown showing up at an employee party: "Bozo Drops in for Surprise Visit."

The rest of the newsletter was riddled with errors and a shoddy layout. But nothing could top that caption. Knowing Mitch, it would be the first thing he read—after spending a few seconds admiring his image, of course.

Anne looked wistfully at her own attempt at a screwup. It lacked the punch of Sheila's masterpiece.

Hmm… she tapped her finger on the newsletter pages. This should have been her assignment. If Sheila hadn't whisked it out from under Anne's nose, she would have noticed the obvious synergy between last week's caption and this week's photo and done the switcheroo on her own. But perhaps it wasn't too late...

What was it Mitch was always saying—success has a thousand fathers while failure is an orphan? Anne was taking custody of this baby, she thought as she ripped off Sheila's Post-it note, grabbed a fresh one from Mitch's desk, and scribbled her own chirpy message.

"Hope you like it—took me all day! Anne." And she drew three smiley faces all in a happy little row.

She placed it on top of her President's Message and turned to leave the room. As she passed the corner of his desk, however, her hand brushed a stack of his books and they tumbled to the floor. She *was* a clumsy one.

"Everything okay in there?" Robin said from the doorway.

"Fine, fine. No problem," Anne answered, bending to clean up the mess.

Robin harrumphed an acknowledgment and headed down the hallway.

As Anne picked up the books, a copy of a letter fell out of one. "Dear Bernie," it began. Bernie Raisonierre, a major stockholder. Hmm... She read on. It was a glowing description of all the wonderful things happening at the Burnham Group: "The adventure camps are taking hold, slow but sure..." Slow but sure? There was a nice way of saying sales were lower than expected! The letter ended with "thought you'd enjoy a signed copy of my latest book—it won't be on the shelves until July."

Lemons into lemonade. Reassuring jittery investors turned into blatant self-promotion. Only Mitch could be so shameless.

But such a broad gesture cried out for balance, Anne thought. It required some leveling, some tempering, some recalibrating of his cosmic-sized ego. So she grabbed as many books as she could carry and headed for the recycling bin in the supply closet. It took her three trips to chuck them all there and when she was done she penned another fast note to Mitch, this one decorated all around the edges with smileys.

"Took care of book mailing. Not to worry. Anne."

As she placed it on his pile, the smiley faces laughed at her.

Once again she'd chosen a meaningless misdeed. As satisfying as it was to toss Mitch's ego into the dumpster, Mitch wouldn't know she'd dumped the books. Hmmm... unless...

She wrote another note, this one to Robin: "Robin, Thought the book mailing to the board was a waste of time so I canned it. Books are in the recycling—they're advance copies filled with typos. Don't let Mitch know. Thanks. Anne." But she didn't leave this note for Robin. Oh no, oh no. She "bungled" it. This note she left for Mitch, while leaving the one she'd originally written to him on Robin's desk. They'd put the two together soon enough and figure out her skulduggery. Anne smiled. She'd always wanted to be involved in some skulduggery.

With a light heart, she headed back to her cubicle where she was surprised to see that Sheila had left a note on her desk. She must have figured Anne was going to be out for a while. "Delivering proposals to A-list prospects," she'd written in big, loopy permanent marker above Anne's name.

Delivering proposals for camp participation was a crappy task. It was a sales job, really, but Mitch believed everyone in the company should be involved in sales in some way. Whenever he started dropping those hints, they all managed to find other things to do instead of proposal delivery, and usually suffered a sharp lecture about team-work from him as a result. If Mitch saw this note, Anne was surely on his own A-list now. Damn that sly fox Sheila.

No matter. Anne would find other things. The gifts she'd or-dered had started arriving and Robin strolled over with the faxed invoice, shaking her head.

"You did this?" she asked, incredulous.

"Mitch is big on team spirit. I thought this was a good way to promote it."

She stared at Anne over her half-glasses. "How about something like pens or cookies?"

"Hey—that's a great idea." Anne wrote it down.

"Not now, Anne. For crissake—he's going to be furious when he hears about this!"

Ken stood. "Well, don't tell him."

Aw geez, not now, Ken. "She has to tell him," Anne said.

"But not today," Ken insisted. He turned to Robin. "You could hold it until tomorrow. Remember how Anne stayed late a month ago to help you send out board packets?"

Anne's face warmed. Yes, she'd stayed late to help Robin. She'd forgotten about that. Sometimes Robin seemed to be burdened with all the work in the world, and it wasn't like Anne had a full dance card every night.

"I don't usually go over the accounts until Fridays anyway," Robin mumbled.

"That's perfect," Ken said, fixing a problem Anne didn't want fixed.

"But I'll understand if you have to make an exception," Anne pleaded to Robin, who was already folding up the invoice and turning. Her phone was ringing in the distance. Darn.

Ken smiled at her and she couldn't stop herself from murmuring a low "thanks." She was thankful for something—that he'd managed to remind her of a kindness she'd performed, something that didn't have to be fed into the shredder. Before she could say more to him, Ken nodded his head at her and took off from his desk as if the Lottery Commission were waiting with the big check. Rats! Well, there was always tomorrow morning.

❖ ❖ ❖

Another box checked off, Ken thought as he strode toward Mitch's office with the Annual Report layout ready to go. And it wasn't even lunchtime. He could meet Cyndi with a clear head now, not worrying if Mitch was wondering where the hell this project was.

Robin was on the phone when he came up to her but he knew the drill and entered Mitch's inner sanctum to place his work on the growing pile of materials awaiting the boss's attention. How could the man possibly make a decision based on anyone's work today? He'd have to spend another entire day evaluating all they'd done in this productivity free-for-all.

As he plopped the Annual Report on top of the pile on Mitch's chair, he saw the President's Message Anne had been working on. Its Post-it note read: "I thought I'd try a new approach: humor and brutal frankness. Anne."

Ken glanced at her work, sizing up the word count to see if it matched the space he'd left for this piece. He genuinely liked her writing and his curiosity got the best of him. How on earth would she use "humor and brutal frankness" to put lipstick on the pig of the past year's performance?

It didn't take him long to find out.

"Dear Friends," Anne had written on Mitch's behalf…

> *This past year has seen many changes at the Burnham Group, none of them good. Profits are down far lower than we expected. In fact, the last quarter of last year was the worst the company experienced.*
>
> *But, as I've said before (CEO Magazine, June 2004), honesty is not only the best policy, it's the only policy. By facing the truth, we take the first steps toward improvement.*
>
> *Truth is, the Burnham Group is in trouble. Big trouble.*
>
> *Subscription sales of our newsletter are flat. Our quarterly report sales are declining. And my latest*

book—*Don't Kill the Messenger, Promote Him*—*is barely selling through my six-figure advance.*

I've been able to pull us out of the tank in the past by reinventing and repackaging. But this time, reinvention isn't working.

It all started out sweet enough. You'll remember— I rented a plane and coerced a dozen CEOs to skydive with me in a "trust team-building exercise." Everybody covered it—from CNN to CBS, from Newsweek to People. Burnham was back on the map, grabbing stolid business managers by the scruff of the neck and forcing them to look at their teams with fresh eyes.

It was the perfect time for a bold step into the public sector. So I went, tin cup in hand, to Wall Street and Main Street, looking for investors in this latest venture— Burnham Group Team-building Adventure Camps designed for the risk-averse managers to learn the thrill and chill of "riding the creative wave."

Except for that incident involving the software CEO who was bitten by a scorpion, the camps looked like a great idea and investors lined up. (After a year of therapy, the executive in question is doing okay, I'm happy to report. His disability and early retirement are more than adequate to cover the loss of use of his right arm. And leg. And his speech and sexual difficulties.)

A flash in the pan doesn't always start a fire, however. So, too, with the adventure camps. Enrollment rates have been below 50 percent since last spring. And projections show even worse numbers for next year.

I blame this on two things. First, there's that blasted, scorpion-hating CEO's memoir, due out next month. It's gotten more press than my skydiving stunt. And then there's the insurance. We've found that the cost of the special insurance riders participants have to buy is equal to or greater than the cost of the camps themselves. It's only natural that participants would balk.

We're working on that. As I write this, my CFO is negotiating special rates for camp participants. But it isn't the cost, mind you, that's presenting the real problem. It's what the cost represents—the possibility of maiming, disfigurement, or death. Rest assured, however, that we have a crack public relations firm working on this negative subtext, and we're sure we'll work through it with some great ad campaigns in the fall.

In fact, the theme will be one of strength and conviction—if you're too chicken to attend one of these camps, maybe you're not cut out to run a company. We plan to bombard boards of directors at all the Fortune 500 companies with these messages, with the thought of creating a second-tier incentivizing of our first-tier target audience.

In other words, the boards get the message that their CEOs are a bunch of girlie-men if they don't want to attend.

With this strategy, I am sure next year the tide will turn. Burnham Team-building Adventure Camps will take off like rockets. I've even talked to the governor of California himself about taking the state legislature on a camping trip, at his expense. He's interested. I think the Amazon Adventure might be just the ticket as soon as we buy up enough antivenom for the whole crew. To sum up, the Burnham Group will be on the upswing faster than you can say "Who Moved My Defibrillator?"

Mitch R. Burnham, CEO

Ken's fingers gripped the pages so tightly he almost ripped them.

Despite himself, he laughed. Some of it was really good, things he'd wished he could have said to Mitch's face. Things a lot them wished they could say. But she couldn't be serious, could she? Had she thought this ultracreative strategy would show off her imagination and talent? Mitch valued a good sense of humor and had overlooked small mistakes if a staffer made him laugh about them. This stretched the limits, though. Mitch responded to risk-takers, too. But this was more than a risk. This was... diving into a shark pool at feeding time. Maybe—and only maybe—on another day, Mitch Burnham would see the humor in this, laugh it off, and praise Anne for giving him a well-needed chuckle and sense of perspective. Today, however, she was on dangerous territory with this stunt.

But things got worse. Ken saw the employee newsletter mock-up just below this note and it was a hideous piece of mistake-riddled claptrap. Anne's judgment was seriously off-kilter. She never would have left material like this for Mitch in the past. She was clearly three sheets to the wind, throwing herself at assignments with lots of vim but little vigilance. He would just take these projects back to her, tactfully pointing out her errors...

Robin's voice on the phone carried into the room. "Uh-huh, it's all there. Ken's leaving you the Annual Report right now."

No time for Anne to redo things. Robin was at this moment telling Mitch that all the assignments he'd been waiting for were ready for his review. He might be returning to the office any minute, talking on his cell as he walked up to his office. Ken had to take drastic action.

He grabbed a fresh piece of paper and penned a quick note: "President's Message and employee newsletter are on the way. Anne's given them to me. Ken."

He'd have to do the best he could to fix these problems and get them on Mitch's desk by the afternoon.

❖ ❖ ❖

After her latest misdeeds in Mitch's office, Anne was feeling jazzed and pumped, as if she'd really been working on some task that would earn her a promotion and more perks. She didn't see Sheila around so she was thinking of taking those nearly melted CDs with important files on them from her desk and damaging them even further. Maybe take another heat source to them in an attempt to "straighten them out"? Oh yes. Bad smell plus foul-up. Ever since her toenail-painting escapade, Anne was all about the multisensory screwup. Anyway, after ruining the CD files, she could then leave a note for Mitch saying she'd tried to fix them but...

Her phone rang.

"Hey, beautiful," a nasal voice cooed. She slumped into her seat, mentally cringing. It was Vinnie Delgado, a printing salesman who regularly called or stopped by trying to get the Burnham Group to shift accounts to his employer.

"Hey, Vinnie," Anne responded, drumming her fingers on her desk as she tried to think of an excuse to get rid of him.

"How's my Number One Favorite PR Specialist doing?" he asked.

"Fine. But kind of busy so I can't—"

"You have a few minutes this afternoon?" He plunged ahead. That was the thing about Vinnie. He didn't take no for an answer. She'd tried more ways than you could count to get rid of Vinnie when he called or stopped by. She'd hidden in the ladies' room. She'd put him on hold for interminable amounts of time. He was like gum on your shoe. Inescapable and a bear to get rid of. Lucky for Ken, Vinnie hadn't yet discovered that another Burnham employee handled the lion's share of their printing work. Anne and Sheila still got most of Vinnie's sales calls.

"I've got some samples I wanted to drop by. You should see the special laser die cuts we can do now. Unbelievable..."

Placing the call on speakerphone, she straightened her desk while

Vinnie went on and on about new papers and printing techniques and even a "rainbow of new inks that take color to the next level." She was about to make her first attempt to get off the phone by telling him she had an appointment, when he said something that had her reaching for the receiver instead.

"… so I thought if I could get a few minutes with you—or that boss of yours—I'd be able to…"

That boss of hers? Let Vinnie into the Holy of Holies, the Mitch Burnham Sanctuary, give him the Secret Password that provided access to the Man Behind the Curtain?

Yes, she had to do it. It cried out to be done. She would become the patron saint to printing salesmen, doling out goodies to the poor wretches who clamored for crumbs of time.

"Vinnie," Anne said, flipping through her online address book. "You know what? That's a great idea."

"What?" Vinnie didn't sound like he was used to getting positive responses to his pleas.

"I mean, I'm kind of busy this afternoon but Mitch—Mitch would love to hear from you. Just the other day he was talking about laser die cuts and how hard it is to get good ones. Do you have his private number?"

What a shock—no, Vinnie didn't have Mitch's private number. Vinnie didn't have Mitch's cell or his pager or his email address or his home phones—any of them. What a pity! Surely Mitch would enjoy hearing from Vinnie. After all, Vinnie's printing press did great work and they had those new laser die-cut thingies and Mitch was always saying that the best way to get good service was to be available to those who provide it—or she was sure he'd say it if she put it in a speech for him, which she just might do when she was finished with this task.

So she was a good girl and she gave all of Mitch's numbers to Vinnie. She even gave him the number of Mitch's therapist because, as she explained to Vinnie, "Mitch turns off his phone and pager when he's there."

As soon as she got off the phone, she thought how unfair it was that Mitch would be hearing from only one service provider when there were so many more out there he'd adore talking to. She must right that wrong! So she pawed through her files, pulling up every business card she'd ever saved from every salesman who'd darkened the Burnham Group's doors. She created a broadcast email list with all of them and sent them all a perky note. *Mitch Burnham would love to hear from you today. Please feel free to contact him any time, and be sure to mention my name, Anne Wyatt*—and she listed all the information she'd just given to Vinnie.

Five seconds after hitting "send," she heard Mitch's personal line ringing in his office. She made a quick run to the ladies' room in case Mitch came looking for her.

Chapter 12

From Mitch Burnham's book *The Twelve-minute Management Plan*:

If business is a race, then you're the jockey, trainer, and owner rolled into one. The horse either goes your way or no way. So too with recalcitrant employees. You either rein them in or they head to the glue factory.

11:40 a.m.

When Ken returned to his cubicle, both Anne and Sheila were away from their desks. That was just as well. No distractions. He had a little time before heading off to meet Cyndi, maybe just enough time. He'd have to spring for another taxi. It couldn't be helped. He'd save the receipts and keep it for tax time. It was a business investment expenditure, after all.

He sank into his chair and rubbed his hand over his face as he looked at the employee newsletter. He couldn't redo the President's Message for the Annual Report—that was a writing job, and no matter how good his skills were in that area, they were no match for Anne's. Instead, he pulled up a copy of the employee newsletter on the desktop publishing program of his computer. He had the last issue there, complete with Bozo headline (but with the correct photo) because he usually looked it over and tweaked it for Anne before it went to print.

All right. He could delete the stories from the last issue, pop in the right headlines, greek the text just to give an idea of the flow and look, and redo the caption gaffe. That should be enough to be presentable. He deftly moved his mouse around the spread until he had a clean, if content free, version of the publication.

"Will drop in text later," he wrote on a note, before signing his name. He printed out the pages, grabbed his sport coat, and headed for Mitch's desk, leaving the office before the papers hit the chair. As he rounded the corner to the elevators, he heard his phone ringing and ran to his cubicle to pick it up in case it was Cyndi trying him on his office number to change the appointment.

Nope. A printing sales call, forwarded to him by Mitch. How'd the guy get Mitch's number? Ken tried to extricate himself from the call, but it took precious time. After he hung up, he punched in Cyndi's number and left a message on her cell that he'd be a few minutes late, then stuffed his stupid pizzazz tie into a desk drawer before taking off as his office phone started ringing again.

He needn't have worried about being late. For five minutes, he stood in front of a dilapidated storefront on M Street, waiting for Cyndi. During that time, he'd taken three calls from printing salesmen. Mitch and Robin were giving out his cell number in addition to his office phone. As soon as he saw Cyndi's cheerful hello wave from down the block, he threw his cell into silent, letting all calls go to voice mail.

"Ken, sorry I'm late. Traffic was fierce!" She shook his hand, clasping an oversized brown leather satchel under her free arm.

Despite Ken's tense mood, Cyndi's presence cheered him. In a canary yellow suit, she was a ray of sunshine, her dyed blonde hair bleached almost white. She was a short woman and a little pudgy, and she reminded Ken of a tugboat, nudging clients this way or that until they reached the safe harbor of their destination.

"Now, I haven't looked at this myself yet," she said, pulling out a set of keys and trying two until she got the right one to work. "So I have no idea what we're stepping into."

What they were stepping into was a large, empty space, big enough for Ken to see its potential as a gallery at once. It reminded him, in fact, of the large, airy first floor of the Arts Consortium, which was perfect for small shows.

A shoddy drywall partition had been put up near the back with a door cut into it. Behind it was a narrow room with a lone window looking into the alley out back. At a far corner, a tiny bathroom was set up. Dust, paint chips, discarded coffee cups, and lunch wrappers littered the wooden floor throughout the space. And it all reeked of cat urine.

As they walked through the debris, Cyndi read from papers she'd brought with her.

"Previous tenant skipped town without paying the rent and the landlord couldn't lease it again until he'd jumped through all the legal hoops to make sure it was free and clear..."

Ken peered out into the alley. A good-sized parking pad. That was a plus.

"It was some sort of pet store before." She sniffed. "Must not have kept much cat litter around."

Ken walked back to the front room and looked out the soaped-up windows. Northern exposure. Across the street were three art galleries and, as he watched, he saw an embassy-license-plated limo pull up in front of one, and a well-dressed woman alighting from the backseat to go into a gallery. Even without Cyndi saying so, he could tell this block was an art buyer's destination. A quick buzz went through him.

"Didn't fare well in this market. Not a lot of foot traffic right here. Kind of away from the restaurants and shops," Cyndi said, doing her own assessment.

Ken checked out the wall partition, testing its strength. It wobbled easily—it wouldn't be hard to pull down if necessary. "Do you know anything about the places across the street?"

Cyndi went to the window and looked out, making a snap judgment. "Well-established. I recognize one of the names—they have places in New York and Los Angeles, too."

So if Ken set up shop here, he'd be in the same market as already successful galleries. That wasn't a bad thing, he knew from his business background. Better to start up where the business already was, instead of trying to attract it to your doors alone.

He stood, rocking on his heels, looking out at the street. This was it. This was the spot. But he wasn't ready!

"Give me the bad news," he said to Cyndi without looking at her. "What's it going for?"

She gave him the price per square foot, telling him it was a net lease—meaning he'd be responsible for gas, electric, and taxes, too. He sucked in his breath in a low whistle.

"This needs a lot of work."

"I can ask about a tenant allowance," she said. "You know, what he'd pay to get the place to your specifications." She sniffed. "Maybe he'd throw in a case of air freshener."

He looked around at the space and could see it as it would appear once the work was done. He saw it in his artist's mind, a completed painting—floors gleaming, paintings and drawings hanging on removable walls, a small office in the back, and a working bathroom. Again, restrained excitement coursed through his veins. He wanted this place. Bad.

"The electric work could be expensive." A gallery needed special lights for all the displays. He was sure the neighboring galleries hadn't scrimped. That was a disadvantage of being on their turf—he had to look every bit as polished.

"How long do you think this place will be on the market?" he asked.

"Ken, this is prime real estate. He could have someone within a couple of weeks. Could rent it tomorrow."

Ken whirled toward her. "Even in this shape?" He gestured to the mess.

"It's a great area even if the property stinks." She barked out a laugh. "Literally."

"What's the deposit?"

She consulted her papers. "Three months up front, plus first and last months' security—"

"What?!" He exhaled sharply. He did some quick mental math. He had almost that much in the bank, sure. But he wanted to stay at Burnham another year, socking away enough to cover a full year's worth of rent at least. And he had to build his own inventory, too, which was moving way too slowly. Where to get the money he needed? He thought of Felicia's cocktail arrangement for the evening. There was a possibility: Arthur Howard, philanthropist. Why did this prospect make him cringe? Maybe because he couldn't imagine any favor from Felicia coming without strings attached.

Cyndi shrugged. "We can try to negotiate it. Maybe offer a longer-term lease. Lock in for several years, guaranteed payment..." She waved her hand in front of her face. "Whew, this is getting to me. I'm opening the door." She clomped across the wooden floor to the front door, propping it open with a brick. Fresh air drifted in and with it the whiff of Asian cuisine. Georgetown restaurants were around the corner.

Life was around the corner.

"Do you want me to talk to the owner?" Cyndi asked.

Ken thought. If Cyndi let the owner know he was interested, he might play hardball. The property had just come on the market. Then again, he might want to get things settled and make a deal. Business owners liked predictability.

"Okay," he said at last. "Tell him you have somebody who might be interested but that down-payment, security-deposit arrangement is well beyond the bounds of normalcy. I'd pay a month's security and a month's rent up-front, and I'd consider a long-term contract if the rent is locked in for that period—no increases. I'd pay more if it was gross, not net, with him handling all the extras. And... he pays to clean the place and set it up to my specs or he reduces the rent by 10 percent for the first six months."

Cyndi laughed. "I'm glad you're not in my business, Ken. You'd be hell to compete with!"

Even before Ken had left for the gallery space, Anne had been searching out Sheila. She suspected where she was. Anne had seen her watching television earlier in the conference room on their floor. Sure enough, Sheila had the door open and her feet up and was laughing way too loud and long at some Judge Judy patter. That was okay. Anne had been inspired by her television-watching colleague and sent a broadcast email to all staffers inviting them to a *General Hospital* party starting at 2:00 p.m. with preshow discussions. "Since it's Pizzazz Day, I thought this would be a great celebratory break. Before the show, I'll circulate updates on the stories and a ballot for you to vote for your favorite character. Anne W." Robin was included in the distribution, which meant Mitch was sure to hear about it.

As Anne entered the conference room, the aroma of just-microwaved popcorn made her salivate.

Sheila was sitting there in all her lonesome glory, TV blaring, feet on the table, Burnham Special Reports in front of her affixed with personal letters to important clients.

"Hey, Sheel," Anne said, standing in the doorway. "That's a nice touch." She pointed to where Sheila's greasy finger touched the corner of a letter.

Sheila swiveled around and smiled at Anne. "Thanks. I left a copy of one for Mitch to see." She rubbed her hands together. "What's up?"

"We're supposed to have a press conference at noon," Anne said.

"Yeah, I know. I take it you 'forgot' like me?" Sheila winked.

"Not entirely. I wanted to tell you not to worry about it if you have something else more important to do. Like shopping. I changed it."

Sheila chuckled. "Oh. I see." She stood and offered some popcorn. "Does Mitch know?"

Anne took some popcorn and answered after swallowing. "As a matter of fact, that might have slipped my mind—telling him."

"You rescheduled it?"

"Uh-huh." Anne grabbed some more popcorn and snarfed it down. "But I might have forgotten to tell Mitch the new time."

"Oh dear," Sheila said with mock concern. "If he's not there, that'll tick off the media."

"And they already have a short fuse with him," Anne responded in similar tones. Yes, the media had gotten wise to Mitch's publicity stunts. Lately Anne had to cajole and charm more than a few of them to turn up for his regular press conferences. In fact, she'd taken to calling young, new-on-the-job reporters who were more likely to be swayed by strong visuals and gimmicky acts, not realizing the stories that resulted were free advertising for Mitch. He'd worn out his welcome with the regular crew.

"And he'll be mad if he shows up at noon and they're not there." Sheila giggled to herself. "Wish I'd thought of it."

"Well, you're not too shabby with the stuff I've seen you pull. The newsletter was brilliant." Anne didn't tell her how she'd switched cover notes.

"Why, thank you. Giving out Mitch's personal numbers to salesmen was pretty good, too."

"How'd you hear about that?" Anne asked.

"Robin. Saw her a few seconds ago. Mitch must have called her to complain."

"Great!"

Sheila smiled shyly and it occurred to Anne that they were bonding more during this exercise than they'd ever done during any of Mitch's team-building projects over the years they'd worked together. Maybe Anne should have been writing the books on management techniques that inspire.

"You have lunch plans?" Anne asked.

For a moment, Sheila's face lit up with pleasure, then just as quickly shifted into disappointment. "Sorry. I've already called an old friend."

Anne nodded and smiled herself. She saw "long lunch" in Sheila's future.

"You could join us," Sheila offered.

"Nope, that's okay. I have some errands to run anyway."

"Did you try Ken?"

"Yup. He's booked, too."

Sheila raised her eyebrows. "That Ken's a sweetheart." As if thinking Anne would misinterpret that remark, Sheila quickly added, "He was very helpful to me a few times."

In contrast to Anne. Sheila didn't say it, but it hung in the air. Anne had paid little attention to others, especially to "Snooty" Sheila, when she'd first started working at Burnham. Mitch had captured all her focus.

Yet, oddly enough, Anne had thought of herself as a liberated, postmodern feminist kind of woman, too. She'd just figured that she was choosing to be besotted and the choice was the crux of the matter, what separated the traditionalists from the moderns.

"Maybe we can take a rain check, though," Anne said. "I'd love to hear how your new job is once you start."

"Sure." Sheila's mouth twisted into a crooked smile. "Guess we better schedule something soon—before you head off to the Golden Gate city."

"Oh yeah." So many good-byes all of a sudden. "Maybe next week. Maybe later this week! After all, I plan on having lots of free time on my hands."

She laughed. "We'll see, Anne. I still have some tricks up my sleeve."

11:55 a.m.

Ken was still nowhere to be seen. When she returned from her chat with Sheila, Anne had expected to find him in his cubicle working away. Instead, his phone was ringing, but his computer was off and his work area clean—just the way he left it when he left the office. He must have taken off for his lunch appointment.

She sat at her desk and played video games in her cubicle for a few minutes, loudly celebrating her victories and making Robin wait to give her some papers until she'd "hit the thousand-point mark."

After Robin left, Anne restlessly waited. The office had the low-energy noon vibe where half the employees had gone out to lunch and half were sitting at their desks with a sandwich, browsing the Drudge Report or Television Without Pity.

She waited, hoping to see Mitch's enraged face come around the corner after discovering the noon press conference had been canceled. She imagined him standing at the marina by the muddy shores of the Potomac, tapping his foot, looking at his watch, checking his cell, until he finally called in to see what the heck had happened.

While she lingered, she decided that the media invited to the three o'clock press conference would like nothing better than to have their schedules rattled again. So she sent out a quick broadcast email to all the invitees, telling them she was sorry but "Mr. Burnham has to change the conference time to four o'clock… or thereabouts. I'll email you with a precise time after lunch." They'd love that. Not.

She also changed her voice mail message. "Leave a message after the song," she said in a perky voice approaching spontaneous combustion. And then she crooned a few lines of a country song, something about it feeling like today.

As soon as she put the phone down, it rang. Her heart leapt—it was probably Mitch, wondering about the press conference snafu! She picked it up, drawling a lazy hello.

"Anne Wyatt?" a vaguely familiar female voice said over the phone.

"Yes?"

"This is Melanie Simpson from Human Resources at St. Bartholomew's," the voice said, the tone melodic and warm. "I need to schedule you into an orientation seminar. All our new employees go through the orientation. I'm sure they explained it to you in your interview."

As a matter of fact they hadn't, but Anne didn't reveal that info. Melanie sounded so cheerful and efficient, Anne didn't want to burst her bubble.

"I'm looking at that weekend before you begin," Melanie said. "It's a two-day program, nine to six each day with an evening reception."

Ouch—giving up a full weekend before she began the job? Anne was sure that weekend would be crammed with activities related to her move. She had a sublet lined up for the transition period, an efficiency apartment within walking distance of the hospital, but she knew there'd be tons of last-minute items to take care of.

"Is the program there at the hospital—at St. Bart's—or is it off campus?" Anne asked.

Melanie Simpson sniffed. "Uh, I'm sure they'll point this out to you, but we avoid using 'St. Bart's.' The official name of the hospital is St. Bartholomew's Children's Center and Health Care Clinic. When we shorten it, we merely say 'St. Bartholomew's.' And no, the orientation isn't here. We hold them at the conference room of the local Holiday Inn."

The scene unfolded in Anne's imagination in all its ash-gray splendor—windowless room, piped-in music, the ever-pervasive smell of coffee mingling with the scent of industrial-strength cleaner, the room either too cold or too hot, strangers trying to pretend they were happy.

"Okay," Anne said, halfheartedly. "I'll mark it on my calendar."

"Great! I think you'll enjoy it. The first few hours are for new hires and the rest of the weekend is our own version of a management-by-motivation program for veteran employees. I'm sure you're familiar with it."

Oh no, it couldn't be! She felt trapped, surrounded by gobbledy-gookedness. There must be a horror movie about this, an old *Twilight Zone* episode—"Attack of the Business Consultants."

"Yes, of course I am."

"There'll be some role-playing. Everyone is asked to bring a stuffed animal they think most resembles them. And dress for these affairs is casual. So no need to adhere to the dress code."

The dress code? Stuffed animals? Anne gulped.

"You should be getting all that information in the mail this week. The dress code is nothing too restrictive. Nonuniformed employees are expected to wear modest, conservative clothing…"

Anne looked down at her outfit and laughed.

"Is that a problem?" Melanie asked.

"No, no." Anne swallowed. "So what's business casual—the things we can wear to the seminar?"

"Pantsuits. Casual slacks, but no jeans."

"No jeans even at this management-by-motivation thing?"

"Well, no." Melanie Simpson cleared her throat. "And we find these seminars very valuable, Ms. Wyatt. They instill a sense of common goals. And they help our bosses in particular…"

Oh no! Melanie was going to say it. She was going to say…

"… learn to 'use it or lose it.' I'm sure you're familiar with the techniques, coming from the Burnham Group." Her voice changed, to that of breathless fan girl. "I've heard marvelous things about Mr. Burnham. I saw him speak in Orlando last year. He was amazing. It must have been very inspiring to work for such a man…"

As Melanie gushed about Mitch's charisma and spirit, Anne felt like she was going to hyperventilate. She needed air. Warm spring air with no coffee scents, no smell of industrial carpeting or pencils or ink-jet cartridges or die-cut Annual Reports or the musty odor of decaying dreams.

Use it or lose it. When she'd first come to the Burnham Group, Mitch had fired her up with phrases like that. She'd felt for so long that she wasn't using anything, that her energy and talent were withering on the vine. And then Mitch had taught her she could achieve, she could accomplish, she could…

No, dammit. Mitch hadn't done those things for her. She'd done them for herself.

"Uh, I have to go." After a quick good-bye, Anne hung up. She grabbed her purse and ran. She didn't care anymore what Mitch's reaction to the canceled press conference was.

12:05 p.m.

She didn't know precisely where she was headed but found herself in Union Station, just a short walk up from K Street.

When she entered the station, she immediately felt calm in that vast shrine to freedom, where hopping on a train meant unshackling time and distance. Granite and marble, high, vaulted ceilings, the decorative, reverent style of the Beaux Arts period, it was a monument to travel. She breathed in the air, trying to pick up a whiff of that mojo.

The terminal bustled with activity, not just from people catching trains or scurrying to the metro, but shoppers and diners taking advantage of its one-hundred-plus venues.

For one moment, she wished she could just hop on a train somewhere, anywhere, destination unknown, and get away from everything. There was something about motion that made you feel like you really were leaving the past behind, you really were starting over.

Instead, she found a women's wear shop on the street-level concourse, but the selection was limited to what would probably be more than acceptable at St. Bart's—no, make that St. Bartholomew's. Nice suede jackets and matching pants. Monotone silk blouses with discreet stitching along the cuffs. She couldn't stand to look at them.

She rushed instead to a nearly empty shop that specialized in tie-dye and gauzy Bohemian clothes. Her vision zoomed in on a skirt-and-blouse ensemble that took her back. Back to when she'd buy this sort of thing even if it meant going without dinner.

It was an ankle-length tiered skirt of browns and turquoise, decorated with beads, embroidery, and mirror shards. A soft, crushed-velvet tee shirt in deep chocolate complemented it, and the whole thing was tied together with a wide leather belt that ended in strings of rope knotted around jangling bells.

She grabbed it and it felt like she was reaching back through the years and grasping a piece of her past. It felt… girly. Carefree.

A few seconds later, she stared at herself in the dressing-room mirror and liked what she saw. She swirled around, the hem floating out beyond her knees, making her feel like a dance. The bells on the belt jingled! She giggled, her fingers drifting to her mouth.

She stuffed her un-pizzazzy navy blue slacks ensemble under her arm and picked out some hemp espadrilles to go with her new look. While she was paying for the stuff, she spotted some interesting jewelry at the counter and impulsively bought a gold-filigreed medallion on a rope chain for Louise. Maybe it would cheer her up.

Swinging her bag of old clothes by her side, Anne squinted in the sunlight as she left the station. She looked down the street toward the Burnham Group's office. She didn't feel like going back yet. The air was too soft, the sunshine too inviting, and she felt... young.

She impulsively hailed a taxi and directed him to Georgetown. She'd have a three-martini lunch, enjoy the day, return to the office late, and maybe, some time in-between, figure out what was wrong with her life.

And that was how lunch became a dream wrapped in a cloud tied up with a ribbon of candy.

Chapter 13

From Mitch Burnham's book *Use It or Lose It*:

You either grab opportunity, or let it slip away while you dither over risk assessments. You might have a great plan worked out at the end of that process, but that's all you'll have—a plan.

12:38 p.m.

"Anne?" Ken stared. Either it was Anne Wyatt sitting at the small table under a Georgetown bistro's awning or some pixie-like reincarnation of the same. Sipping a martini, her face aglow in the sun, she was a vision of gypsy allure. She smiled when she saw him and gestured to the seat next to her.

"Join me!" As he slid into the chair, she continued, "Your appointment get canceled?"

"No, no. Just took less time than I thought." He'd spent the last couple of minutes walking around the neighborhood, assessing its strengths and weaknesses, and coming to the conclusion this was a great opportunity—just not one he could afford to grab right now. The more he'd walked, the harder reality had hit him. Sure, he had the money for the deposits. But no safety net. He knew what happened to businesses whose owners didn't include contingency funding. If he was going to make this work, make his father realize he could do this, he had to start out the right way, the responsible way. Each step away from that storefront had been a step away from quickly realizing his dream. In this glum mood, he'd decided to pick up a sandwich before heading back to the office.

Now his attitude brightened.

"Well, I'm glad you're here. What serendipity!" Anne told him, and patted him on the knee, making both his knee and face warm. And other parts, come to think of it.

"Nice outfit," he said, after clearing his throat. "Is it new?"

"Yeah. I don't think I'm pizzazzy enough." She pointed to his chest. "Where's your tie? I liked that little Santa!"

He smiled at her friendly exuberance, but inside an alarm went off. She'd been drinking. And he didn't see a crumb of food on the table, so it was probably hitting her on an empty stomach.

"Why don't we order something?" he prodded, grabbing a menu. If he was a little late getting back, so be it. His work was up-to-date.

Besides, it was a beautiful day and he was sitting in a restaurant with an intriguing woman. Maybe if he looked at her enough, he'd be able to capture that Mona Lisa moment on paper.

Spanish music played softly in the background, the floor was polished planking, and the tables were filled with an eclectic mix of power holders and free spirits, leaning in and whispering secrets over small crystal vases of flowers and flickering votives. His painter's eye caught the glow of candles and the glint of sun on crystal, but his artist's soul felt more than sensed the silver of soft laughter, the scent of the hyacinths, the feel of warmth on his shoulder. How did you capture that? He closed his eyes for a split second and let the image fill his mind. The image was of her, though, not the café. He saw Anne, smiling up at him after he'd said her name, her eyes squinting against the sun, her cheeks bleached of color except for tiny freckles across her nose, her lips turned up in that smile—that smile; he'd never be free of it until he caught it.

"You're ready to order?" A waiter hovered nearby and they made quick work of giving him their choices. Anne, Ken was distressed to notice, ordered a glass of wine with her lunch. She seemed a little too caught up in the moment.

"We haven't had a chance to talk much at work," Ken said, looking straight at her, trying to get her to focus. But maybe this was a mistake. He found himself lost in the crystal of her eyes, with his fingers itching to clutch the pencil that would place this elusive image on paper. She had bewitched him. Or maybe it was just the day.

"I know," she concurred. "Especially today."

Ken laughed a little. "Yeah, today is something." He looked down but found his gaze immediately drawn back up to her face, which now peered at him with a creased brow.

"Are you worried—about your job?" she asked.

He shrugged. "Not too much. I have an inside edge. I'm the only graphic designer." He turned more serious. "It's a bad day to make mistakes, though. You have to be careful."

"Yeah, I know. I've made a few slipups." She giggled. "But Mitch is a fair man, don't you think?" She said it with the enthusiasm of someone making a joke to cover nerves.

"You've done excellent work for the company," he said, trying to reassure her. "Your material is always top rate."

She blushed. "I didn't know you took the time to read everything I do."

"Pretty much. You have to read it to get a sense of where to go with the design." Not liking the way that sounded, he added, "I mean, I actually like reading your material."

"I was an art history major in college," she said.

"No kidding!" Something sparked inside him. He should have known. She had a good eye for design, pointing out little elements few others noticed and even crafting her text so that it would fit snugly with images. She was the only one among the team who did that—thinking of a publication as a whole, not just the sum of its parts.

He asked her about her college years and listened as she talked rapturously about studying in California, her first job in a gallery, her dreams, and her disappointments. The alcohol had loosened her inhibitions. He learned more about her in those five minutes than in the six months they'd worked together. His heart went out to her as she told him about her father's death, how much she missed him, and how she still wished she could talk to him. She rambled and he sat back, enjoying the sound of her velvety voice, fixated on her face, those dancing eyes, that elfin smile. She ended by telling him of an art exhibit at the National Gallery she'd been taken with.

"Who was the artist?" he asked.

She mentioned a pre-Raphaelite and his heart raced. He'd gone to see that show! Over a year ago. And it had made an impression on him, too. In fact, he thought of that artist when he thought of drawing Anne. He wanted the same dreamy quality of those paintings married to the reality of her gaze. She'd been there, wandering those cavernous rooms on virtually the same day, having the same reactions to the exhibit.

"You ever been to the Renwick?" he asked.

"Of course!" she answered, leaning into the table. "French Second Empire."

"Modeled after the Louvre."

"I used to daydream about working there," she said.

"Because of the collections?" He racked his memory but couldn't think of anything in the permanent collection that spoke to him. There were fine pieces there, just not his cup of tea. Temporary exhibits were a different matter.

"No, because of the space, the architecture! I used to think how neat it would be to show up to work in a place like that." She laughed. "I went there with my best friends Carla and Louise in high school and the whole time we were there, walking from room to room, floor to floor, I made up a story." She sighed. "I wished I could just stay there after we were done. In that story. In that place."

He saw her in that filly-like stage of girlhood, shy and flirtatious at the same time, giggling with friends. When she smiled or laughed, he saw glimpses of that younger woman shining through the professional veneer, someone more fragile than the stronger person she'd become. "What was the story about?" He leaned into the table, too.

She shook her head, her face turning pink. "I don't remember the details. Something melodramatic and romantic and probably tragic. I think the heroine thought her lover was dead and then he comes back..." She shook her head again, as if chasing away silly thoughts. "It was stupid, I'm sure."

"Doesn't sound stupid. The Renwick inspires imagination. That's why I like it. I can't remember the collections much. Just the space itself."

"Exactly!"

Their meals arrived and she was finished with her martini by now, so she started her glass of wine, lifting it to him in a mock toast.

"You're the designated driver," she joked.

Ken didn't comment but raised his eyebrows. Once she started eating, maybe she'd get rid of the alcohol buzz. He'd suggest a coffee before they headed back.

"I was afraid I couldn't make it as an artist," she said. "I mean, I always drew well. Won a couple of contests in school. But it seemed so impossible to enter that field. It seemed like I'd be sending out engraved invitations to the Gods of Failure."

"It's a tough path." Ken nodded as he ate.

"Do you keep up with it? Or is graphic design your career for good?"

He started to tell her... he wanted to tell her... he wished he could just open up about his dreams and the place he'd just seen.

And how damned hard it was to face the possibility of putting it on hold until he earned more money. Instead he gritted his teeth and looked into the distance.

"It's a good job."

"But you'd rather be painting or drawing," she said, taking another sip of wine and leaning back to study him. "What's your specialty?"

"Oils mostly. But I like watercolor, too—the challenge of it. And drawing, of course." That was dangerous territory. If he said too much more, he'd be spilling his guts. He shifted the attention back to Anne. "So you liked California?" he asked.

"Yup. Monterey, Carmel, especially. It was hard to leave," she told him between swallows. She stopped eating and sucked in her lips. "For a long time, I only thought of wanting to go back." She twisted the napkin in her lap, becoming so transfixed with inner thoughts that for a split second he thought she might cry.

"Is communications work *your* career now?" If he'd hoped to distract her from the gloom that descended with her last answer, he was wrong. Instead of offering a quick yes, her mood darkened even further, shifting from the sunny spring glow to something shadowed and closed. She didn't respond right away, didn't even look at him, but slumped back in her chair, taking another sip of wine.

"Yes, it is." She smiled but after so much study of her face, he could tell it wasn't real. Now it was her turn to change the subject. She asked him about his post-college years and he filled in the blanks, glossing over his business experience at his father's firm and spending even less time on his experiences at the Arts Consortium. This, however, Anne wouldn't let go. Revived, she leaned into the table, gently tapping his arm.

"That sounds like a great job! Why'd you leave it?"

Excellent question, Anne. But he wasn't about to tell her the real reason. He recoiled from it. *I left that job, Anne, because I discovered that my boss, Felicia Lanagan, was a shameless self-promoter more interested in*

what the arts could do for her than what she could do for them, and that
she would use anyone to further this mission, even if it meant bedding the
son of a wealthy man to get to the father's money.

"No room for growth."

She nodded enthusiastically. "Burnham does pay well."

"Yes, it saved me from life as a Document Control Manager."

She laughed, nearly spitting out some wine. "I've seen those ads too!" She put her delicate fingers to her lips. "I remember getting the Sunday paper and sitting at the kitchen table with a marker in my hand, prepared to circle every and all ads. And I saw Document Control Manager. That put everything into perspective."

He looked up, a wide smile on his face. "Exactly."

He remembered as if it were yesterday, the moment he'd realized Felicia's true nature. They'd been at her Chevy Chase–area condo and had enjoyed an intimate dinner and intimate after-dinner. She'd traced his profile with her perfectly manicured finger and started talking about how worried she was about the deficit the Consortium was running when they were in the midst of renovating their building and gallery space. He'd tried to reassure her and suggested that she make some budget cuts instead. Everyone in the office knew that Felicia padded what appeared to be a modest salary on paper with extravagant perks. Her condo, for example, was owned by the Consortium, and she occupied it rent free. Numerous trips and dinners—some of which he'd enjoyed with her—were also billed to the Consortium.

Felicia had not taken kindly to his budget-cutting suggestions. She'd told him that she actually had some new donor prospects she was cultivating. His father was one of them. Two things had become clear in that instant—he was being used, and he could no longer tolerate as eccentricities her profligate ways all in the name of "promoting young artists." He'd handed in his resignation the following day, and hit the pavement looking. What had shaken him most about that experience was wondering how much of her praise of his talent had been sincere. That, as much as anything, had driven him to start planning to open his own place. He had to prove to his father, to Felicia, that he was good, that he could make it as an artist.

"I was glad Mitch took me on," he now said amiably, "when I had no corporate graphics experience."

"Yeah, you can say that about Mitch," she said. "He puts a lot more stock in creativity than credentials."

She peered at him with kind eyes. "I'd love to see your work."

"Are you asking me to take you to see my etchings?" He smiled.

She blushed and a breeze blew a ripple of intimate laughter into the restaurant from a couple walking by and he felt like never leaving this moment.

"This is really nice," she said, wiping her lips with the napkin. "I'm glad we did this. Really glad."

Chapter 14

From Mitch Burnham's book *Fair Play, Fair Pay*:
> *Your employees aren't your family. They're not going
> to stick with you through good times, let alone bad ones.
> Don't think being a good boss means being Gandhi. It
> means becoming a benevolent dictator.*

1:47 p.m.

THEY SHOULD BE BACK at the office. Just because she was on the path to destruction didn't mean she should bring Ken down with her. He'd glanced at his watch twice when he thought Anne wasn't looking. She knew she should suggest leaving but she was feeling... *like paradise.* Like she had felt as a girl wandering the Renwick gallery with her friends. His sandalwood scent, their shared appreciation for that particular gallery, the warmth of his concern for her—she hadn't felt so comfortable in a long time. The only cloud in this sunny hour had been his questions about California. After the call from Melanie at St. Bart's, Anne was feeling less sanguine about her new job.

Well, like feisty Scarlett O'Hara, Anne just couldn't think about that right now. She'd think about it tomorrow. At the moment, she had to make sure Ken got back to the office before he was missed. She'd think of other things to do to draw negative attention to herself. At least her breath was heavily scented with alcohol.

He insisted on treating her, and after they left the restaurant, Ken looked for a cab, telling her it was best if they got back quickly.

She was beginning to think that they were going to be really late and her prank was at the expense of getting Ken in trouble, when she heard a familiar voice.

"Anne?"

It cut through the car engines and jet roar overhead. It zoomed its way straight to Anne's heart as only a mother's voice can, igniting both joy and guilt. She turned, looking through the crowds on the sidewalk.

"Anne, is that you?" Another familiar voice, this one younger and filled with happiness.

Zipping around so fast she nearly twisted an ankle, Anne beheld her friend Carla with a woman who looked an awful lot like Anne's mother.

In fact, it *was* Anne's mother.

"Carla?" asked Anne, peering at her friend as if she hadn't seen her since high school.

"Mom?" Mrs. Wyatt stood behind a stroller holding Carla's five-month-old infant. The baby was sleeping the peace of the innocent, all unblemished skin and chubby cheeks. Anne's mother looked at her daughter apologetically. Ken took a step back, as if giving Anne a wide berth in this narrow sea channel of family currents.

"I was going shopping and I thought Carla would want to get out," Mrs. Wyatt said.

"Your mother is a godsend," Carla gushed. "I don't know what I'd do without her."

Mother and daughter exchanged looks and, as is the way with mothers and daughters, an involved and silent conversation fired back and forth with the unseen atoms between them.

What are you doing here?

Helping Carla, she lives near me, you know.

Carla's my friend.

I like to help her out with her new baby. I'm good at that.
I know.
I know you know.
I know you don't want me to know.
What?

Carla lived just a block away from Anne's mother, and they knew each other from Anne's high school days. It was only natural that her mother, with her motherly instincts, would want to help shepherd this new mother through the tough early days.

Mrs. Wyatt would have shared her Carla-mothering joy with her own daughter if not for the fact that Anne wasn't anywhere near becoming a mother.

Now, as Anne saw her pushing Carla's infant, she knew why her mother had become more vocal about the ticking of Anne's biological clock—she wanted that special relationship with her daughter. Oh geez. Since when had being thirty without kids become something to feed into the shredder? Yet that was how Anne felt, like apologizing.

Anne looked in her mother's eyes where the truth was hidden. Her mother looked down.

Carla's baby twitched and sputtered. As if afraid to telegraph any more of what they both knew to be the truth, Anne's mother stayed at her post while Carla bent to place a pacifier in the child's mouth.

"So what are you doing here, Anne?" Carla asked. "You're such a workaholic I never thought to ask to meet you for lunch. But I guess we better do it soon or—"

"Yeah, I'll give you a call!" Anne interrupted. She couldn't have Carla spilling the beans about her move to California and a new job in front of Ken.

"That would be great!" Carla's voice sparkled, all good cheer and hope.

Carla was a cheerleader. Literally. When Anne had first arrived at high school, Carla had taken her under her wing, had invited her to parties, to her house. It was as if Carla saw herself as the high school welcome wagon. After high school, Carla had gone to the University of Maryland, studied business, and went to work in banking. That's where she'd met her husband. Come to think of it, Anne had caught the bouquet at that wedding. Looking at her mother now, she knew she was remembering that too.

Carla was lucky in the guy department, but not in the baby one. She and her groom wanted to start making them right away—she'd always heard the ticking of the biological clock as if it were pressed up against her ear. But it took years of fertility treatments before they produced little Rose.

Another realization hit Anne. She'd learned of the many sorrowful details of Carla's fertility problems not from Carla herself, but from her mother.

Anne felt oddly betrayed. Anne now wondered how often her mother had treated Carla, taken her out, and by wondering, she felt less than. Less than a good daughter. Less than a loving child. Less than is the threshold to guilt, and guilt is the foyer to resentment. Less than is a ticket to the shredder.

Stop it, her inner voice screamed. She smiled at her mother, who gave her an uneasy grin back. She knew what Anne was thinking. She was a daughter, too, after all. They both looked at Carla, who was fussing over her baby.

Plumper than she'd been in high school, Carla could have been a seductive milkmaid in an earlier time, all curves and softness, with the creamy complexion to boot. Today she wore an apple green, polka-dot top and black pants, as well as green pumps to match her blouse. Seeing Anne eye them, she laughed.

"I never get to dress up anymore. Your mother told me I should do it to pamper myself!"

More looks between Anne and her mother. How much other advice had her mother wanted to dole out to a daughter figure? Did she give any to Marie, Jack's wife? Or had she held back for fear of being an interfering mother-in-law? Had she longed to give this advice to Anne? *Oh, Mom!*

"Have you eaten?" Mrs. Wyatt asked, sounding tentative.

"Uh, yes. In fact…" Anne turned to Ken and gestured limply. "This is Ken Montgomery, a fellow I work with. We had lunch together."

Everybody shook hands. More silent messages zoomed among the womenfolk. In a nutshell, they boiled down to one question—is he a prospect?

"Well, don't let me keep you," said Anne, too cheerfully. "We need to get back."

As if really seeing Anne for the first time, her mother looked at her from head to toe. "Is that new?" She gestured toward Anne's outfit.

"Yup. Just got it," Anne said, not wanting to explain why.

"You look terrific, Anne," her mother said.

"Mm, thanks." Anne nodded. "Really have to get going."

Carla beamed a megawatt smile. "Don't be a stranger. Come by some time real soon. We'd love to see you."

We? Was she referring to herself and her family or to herself and Anne's mother?

As if to answer, Mom chimed in. "I know you're busy, hon, but I'd love to have you and Rob and Jack and Marie over for dinner soon."

Rob and Jack and Marie. Like a wet sheet in the wind, a forgotten promise snapped in her face. Jack was heading out and Anne hadn't mentioned it like she'd promised she would. Damn. *Couldn't do it here, not on this street in the sunshine that screamed happiness and worry-free living, not in front of Carla and her baby, the picture of domestic bliss.*

"Yes, I'll call you. After work today," Anne said. She was about to offer to stop by when she remembered her similar promise to Louise. Okay, if she did stop by, it would be a surprise, which would initially please her mother until she shared the worrying news of Jack's deployment. Anne was doomed to disappoint today.

They repeated their good-byes and Anne watched them for a few moments trudging in the opposite direction, her mother leaning toward Carla, telling her something, something Anne suddenly wished she could hear too.

Ken soon flagged a taxi and they piled in. It was a quiet drive, both of them lost in thought. When the cab pulled up in front of the Burnham building, Anne offered to pay the driver but Ken insisted.

"It was my treat," he said. The brightness was gone from his voice, and Anne wondered if it was because they were back at work.

As he helped her out of the car, he asked, almost too casually, "Who's Rob?"

2:19 p.m.

Uhm… that's a good question, Ken.

Who was Rob and what precisely did he mean to her? It sounded like a question that should be written on the blackboard during philosophy class. *And so, students, ziss is vhat ve must consider today—who is diss Rob person and vhat exactly does he mean?—here is the central question of existence, ja?*

And it was a key question, the answer to which would unlock the secrets of her universe. Why had she wasted Rob's time, let alone hers, if she wasn't prepared to get serious at some point? Well, maybe because she'd given herself a great talking-to after the Mitch affair ended. Annie, she'd said (she used her nickname with herself because she was usually so close, her ego and her), you need to stop futzing around. No more jumping into bed with Mr. Wrong. Easy to spot him. He's the one with the wedding band on his left hand—or the tan mark where it should be.

She'd followed her advice with the zeal of… well, a zealot, and that's why she'd ended up with a boy *friend* as opposed to a *boyfriend.* But more importantly, she'd used the boy *friend* to keep her from even thinking about getting anywhere close to a *boyfriend*. He was a shield against possible heartache.

Somehow, she didn't think Ken wanted to hear all that. She didn't want to hear it herself.

As they walked a short block from the cab drop-off to the office, a distraction presented itself that kept her from boring them both with the answer.

Up ahead in the window of a very swanky restaurant, the kind decorated in black and white with arrogant waiters and menus without prices, she saw Mitch. He sat across the table from a perfectly coiffed and made-up woman, a model-perfect gal with not a hair astray nor a wrinkle on her clothes. Kathie-Rose. The news babe. He held her right hand in his on the table and stared at her with an intensity that Anne thought she'd once enjoyed, and it felt like she was watching a rerun except the woman they'd hired to play her looked way better than she ever had.

"Mitch," Anne mumbled. "I thought he was supposed to be—" Supposed to be at her aborted press conference, or at least looking like he was mad as all get out about it being canceled. He must have found out! Probably from Kathie-Rose herself.

What was he saying? Maybe if she stared long enough she could read his lips…

"Anne, did you need to tell Mr. Burnham something?" Ken gently touched her on the elbow.

"I—no, I was just thinking… he was supposed to be somewhere else. It confused me. That's all." She walked away from the window, still trying to peer at Mitch from her peripheral vision.

"At an interview? I had mine this morning."

"What?"

"He's talking to all of us. Individually. Sort of an interview for the job—why he should keep us."

"You're kidding."

"No. Remember? He mentioned it at the staff meeting this morning. I thought you'd had yours already. You were out of the office a lot this morning."

If Ken only knew...

They reached the front doors to the Burnham Group and Ken held open the door.

"What was it like?" she asked.

Ken shrugged. "The usual questions about goals and assets and faults."

"Did he ask you what your worst trait is?"

"Of course!"

She groaned. That was so old school. Yet Mitch believed in it. When she'd told him once that everybody lies—telling prospective employers things like "I'm too much of a perfectionist"—he had just smiled and said, "I know. I judge them on how original their lie is."

"What did you tell him?" Anne asked Ken.

"I told him that I was afraid to take risks."

"You told him the truth?"

"Yeah. I figure I have nothing to lose."

"That's a risk."

He paused. "I guess it is."

They stood in front of the elevator bank. She wondered if Mitch would want to interview her and when he'd fit it in his afternoon schedule. Or maybe he'd be too besotted by his lunch with Kathie-Rose, Mistress.01 version. An interview would certainly present Anne with the opportunity to do more damage.

But every time she thought of being called into his office, she imagined herself being the one asking the questions. *How long have you known this Kathie-Rose person? What were you saying to her at lunch? And why the hell didn't you ever look that way at me, you rat bastard?*

"You never answered my question before," Ken said as the elevator arrived and the door opened. His voice was more serious. "Who is Rob?" He looked straight ahead, not at Anne, and his jaw worked. He wanted to know if she was available or if he'd be wasting his time. Good planning, Ken. She had to get a hang of this not-wasting-time business. She'd missed the course on that.

Sometimes when she was stressed, Anne saw herself—an alter ego, if you will—as a character in a French movie. In that movie, she was cool and unflappable. Confusion might surround her, but when she opened her mouth, she was speaking a romance language, which seemed to make everything all right.

Ma vie est une catastrophe. Mais oui, bien sur, certainement. Je ne pense pas. Je vais chercher du bon vin à la cave.

So when Ken repeated his simple question about Rob, a question that on its surface seemed quite reasonable but that was fraught with peril below, she wished she could throw a torrent of sophisticated-sounding French his way that said a lot without answering anything.

She just didn't want to blow this mood, this sense that she was on the verge of… something.

Instead, she shrugged. "Just a friend." They stepped onto the empty elevator.

Wait a minute—if he wanted to know about her availability, shouldn't she also know his?

"You know," she said in what she hoped was a lighthearted tone. "I've overheard you on the phone sometimes with a… Cindy? Is she your sister?"

She felt him stiffen.

"No," he said. "She's…" He stopped, gritted his teeth. "Just a friend."

So he had one too, a "placeholder" for the Real Deal.

She glanced at him. He was staring straight ahead, as if memorizing the look of the elevator doors.

She didn't know whether to be angry or sympathetic. Why had he gone and spoiled the glow of the day just because she'd revealed her "just a friend" when he seemed to have the same game going on in his corner of the world?

"Look, Ken," she said, pulling his sleeve so that he turned to face her. "I think that's great that you have a friend too. I mean, we all need friends, right? I mean, I'd love it if you were my friend, too…"

Dear Lord, what was she saying? That darned wine/martini buzz was making her sound like a moron. She was blabbering on about friends and their importance so much she might as well have started warbling through the Carole King songbook.

"I mean…" She looked up at his face, now more worried than irritated, those brown eyes searching her own, that tan skin, that sandalwood scent… It was as if she'd had another glass of strong, sweet wine in one quick gulp that immediately went to her mind and heart.

She sighed. Her hand remained on his arm, so warm and inviting. And then…

Time stopped. Wordlessly, he traced the line of her chin with his finger, his gaze so intense that she almost couldn't bear it. His finger lingered around her mouth while his own mouth opened a millimeter as if in wonder, his eyes voicing a question, and she couldn't help it. On tiptoe, she leaned forward and brushed his lips with her own, unlocking that penetrating stare, breathing deep the odor of warm sun lingering on his jacket.

He didn't pull away but enveloped her in an embrace, one hand on her waist, the other behind her head, those long, graceful fingers in her short hair.

His kiss was searching and needy. She felt his body stiffen against her, his breath become ragged, his grasp search and tighten and search again.

And then the elevator dinged and they were at their floor.

Chapter 15

From "Confusion Keeps Them Guessing," an article in *Tomorrow's Leader* by Mitch Burnham:

At your next departmental retreat, try this to liven things up—insert a "surprise" page in your PowerPoint presentation: something that will amuse, startle, or even better, offend. No reaction? Guess what—your employees have only been humoring you, paying lip service to your leadership.

2:22 p.m.

Sweet Jesus, how he wanted her!

As the elevator opened, they quickly disengaged. He mumbled something about getting together again. She mumbled an okay and they scurried to their cubicles like guilty sinners.

Ken stood in his a moment, disoriented. What had just happened there? He'd been disappointed she had a friend, someone her mother obviously thought of as part of a couple, and then she'd started explaining it and looked at him and—

And he'd seen it. That moment when her smile lit up her face. It had happened as if in slow motion and he could recount every muscle movement, every eye crinkle, every angle, every stroke. He hadn't been able to stop himself from touching her face, from searing into his artist's hand the feel of the image he wanted to capture on paper.

But she'd followed through with the kiss. She'd initiated that. Not him.

Couldn't stay here. Too distracting, too hard—

His phone rang and he picked it up. Another printing salesman forwarded by Mitch or Robin! As soon as he got off and hung up, it rang again. Same thing. He checked his silent cell—five missed calls, all printing reps. What the—

As his desk phone started ringing yet again, he murmured, "Can't work here." He grabbed his flash drive, some CDs, a few files, and… and his leather portfolio. He'd find a quiet place to work until things settled down. Until his phone stopped ringing.

Until his heart stopped throbbing.

Anne sat at her desk staring at her computer screen. Her whole body tingled with an electric buzz. She felt like she'd just gotten out of the pool after swimming thirty laps—blood pumping, all cells firing, breath fast, ready for more. That kiss—what a stupid thing to do. No, not stupid. Comfortable. Fun. Exciting. But she was moving away and Ken was staying here and maybe one shouldn't try to begin a relationship with a boozy lunch and an impetuous snog in the elevator on the way back to work.

Maybe Ken would move to California? Maybe if she mentioned it…

Anne looked around for Sheila who, for some reason, she was beginning to think of as her anchor in this wild sea of a day. As Ken strode by mumbling something about needing a "quiet space to work," Sheila appeared like a hangover vision coming around the corner from the hallway by the elevator bank.

And what a vision she was. She had traded in her tangerine halter dress for a crop top and short shorts—in a shade of fuchsia Anne was sure had never shown up on a printer's PMS color chart.

It looked like someone had mixed children's aspirin orange with hot pink and had thrown in a soupçon of iridescent green undertones. It was vomitous. Across the butt of the shorts was written: "Bite Me." She'd paired this ensemble with gold platform shoes that looked like they came from an Austin Powers movie, and her hair was teased and vamped into a style that brought to mind the Bride of Frankenstein meets Mary Tyler Moore. Not quite wild enough for one, but rather an unsettling version of the other. Anne was impressed.

"Sheila," Anne called out over her cubicle edge. "Got a moment?"

"Sure, sugar." Sheila's voice was a little slurred. Damn. She'd thought of the three-martini lunch too.

"Ladies' room," Anne said, looking around. She wasn't sure when Ken would come back. Sheila nodded with a serious expression on her face, the face of a spy about to take on a dangerous mission, and they both headed around the corner into the sanctuary of the bathroom.

Anne brushed her short hair while Sheila leaned against a sink and talked.

"Nice skirt," she drawled at Anne.

"Sounds like you had a wet lunch."

"Hey, I'm not driving." Sheila hiccupped.

"Neither am I—for a few hours." Even now Anne's alcoholic buzz was starting to fade, a mere ship drifting from its moorings toward a vanishing horizon. A different kind of euphoria remained.

Trying to look casual, she touched up her makeup while she talked.

"Do you know much about Ken?"

"He's nice, like I said earlier." Sheila leaned into the countertop, staring at Anne's reflection. "What happened?"

"Nothing. We just ran into each other and had lunch together after all."

Sheila smiled broadly. "And a spark was lit."

"It's too early for that!" Yeah, sure. But not too early to plant a big wet one on him in the elevator. Just the thought of it zinged something from her espadrille-clad feet to her brain.

Sheila turned to face her. "But you're moving…"

"Exactly. I can't get involved with someone right now." Anne had meant for it to sound responsible and mature, but instead it sounded like something from a really bad drawing-room comedy… or a really good Russian drama.

Sheila studied her. Anne couldn't look her in the eyes, though, because she was afraid she'd reveal too much with her own puppy-dog look of confusion. So she continued powdering her nose until it was almost white.

"Anne," Sheila said, "if you like Ken, there's no reason you can't still pursue a relationship. He could visit you in California."

Sure, just like she was going to visit Rob in Berserkistan.

"Long-distance relationships don't work well," Anne said, again trying to sound worldly wise. This time she just sounded fake. Inside she was screaming: *But I'd like to try!*

"I guess they're hard. But not impossible." Sheila crossed her arms over her chest. "If you want my advice—and I assume you do or you wouldn't have asked me in here—I'd just tell Ken you're interested in getting to know him and invite him to San Francisco as soon as you get out there. Who knows? Maybe he'd like the place so much he'd jump at the chance to move there."

"He just started at Burnham six months ago!"

"I'm just saying you never know." Sheila wagged her hand at Anne. "Don't rule it out. He's a sweet guy."

Anne tried to envision Ken coming out to visit her. Oh, it was a nice picture, but really, Sheila must be in the throes of alcohol optimism to think a fellow Anne had just… gotten to know… would want to follow her somewhere. To keep that painful reality from stinging too long, she changed the subject.

"What's up with Mitch and News Babe?" Anne asked.

"Huh?"

"Kathie-Rose."

"Oh, he's been seeing her for a few months. They're an item."

"I thought he was playing the field." Anne stopped with the powder and applied fresh lipstick. But that only made her think of the kiss again so she hurried through the application.

Sheila laughed. "He plays and then he stays. Who knows what's up with this one? Although—"

She leaned to one side and nearly fell.

"Damn shoes. Bought them from some fellow on the street," she said

"Whoa, big girl," Anne said, catching her. "You need some coffee."

"I need some water." Sheila looked at herself in the mirror and fluffed out more of her hair. "Of course, if I drink water all afternoon, I'll pee like a horse."

"But bathroom breaks in increasing frequency should look well on the tote board, don't you think?"

Sheila giggled and nodded her head.

"Sheel, do you ever wish you had a shredder?" They headed for the door together.

Ken found an empty office around the other side of the elevator bank. He switched on its computer after closing the door and darkening the blinds at the glass window fronting the hallway. With a grateful sigh, he sank into the chair and ran his fingers through his hair.

What was he going to do about this?

About what, man? It was just a kiss. She'd had too much to drink at lunch. When she wakes up completely, she'll be embarrassed, offer apologies, and everything will be back to normal.

Normal. Who wanted that? Dammit. No phone calls interrupting him here, just his confused thoughts. He plugged in the flash drive and pulled up a brochure. After ten minutes of trying to focus, he gave up and brought his portfolio onto the desk, slipping out the drawing of Anne.

Oh hell, he'd finish this and get it out of his system. He could do it now. He knew exactly how to draw her. He grabbed a pencil and turned the page on his drawing pad. He'd start afresh.

With swift, sure strokes, he worked with an intensity and excitement he'd not felt in a long time. That was it, that was the way her lips looked at the beginning of the smile, the tiniest wrinkle around her nose, the slightest narrowing of the eyes, the nuanced uplift of the entire face from gray to sunshine, from dark to light. It would be finished in no time now. Another piece for his collection.

He was so intent on his drawing that he almost missed his cell phone vibrating. He was about to let it go to voice mail, figuring it was another print salesman calling, when he glanced at it and saw Cyndi's number. Maybe she had an answer from the landlord. Sometimes these negotiations could drag out for quite some time. If he could get this one to move slowly, that was to his advantage.

"Ken, good news," Cyndi said as soon as she heard his hello. "He'll meet your demands. Every single one. He's eager to get the place rented and he thinks a gallery has a good shot there and will be a good risk…"

She went on for a few minutes with details but all Ken could do was sit still and quiet, his mind a blur. Instead of elation, he felt confusion. He'd assumed the landlord would turn down his offer outright. That's why he'd made it so damned unreasonable. But the man wanted to settle and get the place rented. Ken hadn't planned for that at all. He'd counted on an obstacle, a rationalization for not moving forward.

He felt as if the rug had been pulled out from under him.

2:31 p.m.

Back at the cubicle, Anne remembered one of the things she'd wanted to ask about Kathie-Rose, and it was a legitimate question. So she went into Sheila's territory and whispered to her.

"Mitch met Kathie-Rose for lunch. So he probably knew the news conference was rescheduled."

Sheila, to her credit, looked genuinely crestfallen for Anne. "Damn. That was such a good plan, too." Movement caught both their gazes and Sheila pointed to the elevator hallway where Robin was coming around the corner. "Talk to her," she said, holding a pencil like a laser targeted at the secretary.

"Ask her if Mitch knows, you mean?"

"No, you don't want to tip her off. Just find out if his schedule's changed this afternoon." She hiccupped again.

"I rescheduled it again, you know. Now it's at four."

"Brilliant." She beamed at Anne. "Go check with Robin. Shoo, shoo!" She waved her hand at Anne. "Robin will know if he shifted anything around. Robin sees all, knows all."

"Aye aye, cap'n." Anne saluted her and marched toward Robin's desk.

Robin heard Anne jingling and bangling, so by the time Anne was in the secretary's sight lines, Robin had already raised her eyebrows and frozen midtask.

"You know, I think this is the last Pizzazz Day this company is going to see," she said. This hurt. Anne actually liked her new outfit. Robin resumed stapling some reports together as Anne stopped in front of her.

"Mitch's schedule—what is it this afternoon?" Anne asked.

Robin put down her work and moused her way to a calendar on the computer, with color-coded appointments lighting up the page like a multiseasonal holiday exhibit.

"After lunch he meets with Sheila. Then he sees Greg. Then I have an investor meeting lined up."

"That's all?" Good, no press conference. Robin would have had to reschedule the investor meeting to make way for the new press conference time. Still, something wasn't right…

"Sheila and Greg?" Anne remembered Ken saying he'd met with Mitch, too. "Are those the interview-type things he's doing with everybody before he cans one of us?"

Robin gave a noncommittal shrug. "I just schedule them. I don't ask questions."

"When is he going to do mine?"

"He hasn't told me to schedule one with you."

Her ears burned. He didn't think she was worth scheduling an interview with? Why, the tyrant—she'd show him.

She stabbed a finger at the schedule. "Well, I want one. Put me down after Sheila or Greg."

Robin peered at her over half-glasses. "That won't work. Investor meeting is then."

"Then squeeze me in after that." She would not be denied.

Robin shrugged again and grabbed a pencil, writing the appointment information on a Post-it note. Anne didn't even rate an entry on the computer calendar. "I'll ask him about it when he gets back, okay? I'll let you know the exact time." Robin was acting like she was afraid of Anne. Perhaps Anne's voice *was* a tad loud.

"Anne, nothing personal, but have you been drinking?"

Anne stiffened. "Maybe." Then, realizing that Robin was her conduit to Mitch's bad graces, Anne proudly proclaimed the truth. "Yes. Had a few martinis with Ken at lunch. Got a problem with that?"

"Ken and you boozed it up?"

"No, no. Not Ken! Just me. I decided I'm a little too rigid. Need to unwind." Anne gestured to the wider world. "Need pizzazz."

"Wouldn't have thought he was your type." Robin said this with what Anne thought was a bit of sarcasm. But she couldn't tell for sure because she had this big, invisible emotion-muffler surrounding her right now. She must have picked it up this morning when she'd killed that bluebird and had added to it throughout the day by numerous angst- and guilt-laden encounters with family and friends. Nonetheless, she was offended.

"Why not?" Anne demanded.

Robin shot up one eyebrow. "Ken is…" Robin stopped, twisted up her mouth as she obviously evaluated how to say something without being offensive, and then finished, "… more realistic…"

"More realistic?" Was steam coming from Anne's ears? It felt that way.

Robin dodged. "I mean more… down-to-earth, maybe."

"You think I'm elitist?" Anne's face flamed so hot one could roast chestnuts on her skull.

"No, no, I mean… more grounded, maybe…"

"You think I'm unstable?"

Robin threw up her hands. "You're the word girl. I don't know what I mean. Maybe Ken *is* your type. You're both artsy. You're both good at your jobs. For all I know, the stars have determined you're meant for each other, okay?" She let out an exasperated sigh. "Look, I'll tell Mitch you want to meet with him."

Anne wasn't quite satisfied but she didn't know what else to say. She was rattled on two levels—that Robin wouldn't consider her Ken-worthy and that she wanted to be Ken-worthy in the first place. This was ridiculous. One impulsive kiss and she was as giddy as a schoolgirl, trying to get the scoop on her crush. *Get me out of here!* She couldn't think about this any longer! She turned to go, but Robin called after her.

"Hey," Robin said. "Some folks were wondering where you were at two. Something about a *General Hospital* party in the conference room?"

Darn. Forgot about the soap opera event she'd scheduled. "Oops," was all she managed to say.

"Lenny was mighty disappointed when you didn't show," Robin said. "I think he left it early."

"Thanks." Anne stopped. "Did, uh, Mitch know about the get-together?"

Robin peered at her over her glasses again. "You included him on the invite list."

At least that had gone right. She strode back to her desk, focused on why Mitch hadn't scheduled an interview with her. Maybe it meant she was winning. That is, losing.

"What'd you find out?" Sheila asked when Anne returned. Anne noticed she had a large bottle of water on her desk. She was already swigging the hangover antidote.

"No press conference listed," Anne muttered. "But he's seeing you and Greg, and not me!" She crossed her arms and leaned on her desk.

"Wow." Sheila swigged some more water and wiped her lips with the back of her hand like some cowpoke. "That's great."

"I don't know…"

"Hey—if he's not meeting with you, that means he might be thinking of you as the One. He might have made up his mind already."

Why did even this victory scenario make her feel all itchy and uncomfortable? She really was nuts. *Must make a note to schedule an appointment with a shrink when I get to my new job. At least there would be plenty within reach, working at a hospital.*

Sheila twisted her mouth to one side. "Maybe I shouldn't go to my interview. I mean, I thought I had it all planned out. Have a few drinks, change my outfit, come in late to see him… but if he's already leaning toward striking you, I better ratchet things up."

Anne wasn't sure how Sheila could ratchet things up any further short of parading naked through a board meeting, but she was willing to place bets on her abilities.

Before Sheila could decide what to pull out of her hat, they both looked up as Mitch rounded the corner. He held his cell phone out before him as if reading a text message and he was scowling. He was barely two steps into their area when he started barking orders to Robin.

"Is Calvin here this afternoon?" he asked, referring to one of the investors. "I need to talk to him." From the corner of his eye, he caught sight of Sheila and Anne. Anne managed to race around outside the cubicle, swinging her skirt so that it jingled like wind chimes in a hurricane. She was hoping her alcohol-laden breath carried the few feet to his face. She couldn't tell. But he did wrinkle his nose as he stopped to look at her, then Sheila, who chose that moment to appear by Anne's side.

"My God," he said, scratching his head with one hand and closing his phone with the other. "Have you joined some sort of theater group, Anne?" To Sheila, he just nodded. "See you in a few." And then he was off to his office where no employee could enter unbidden.

2:36 p.m.

Sheila considered not going to her meeting but ended up deciding she'd do more damage to herself in front of Mitch than by just not showing up at all. She told Anne she was seriously considering singing all her answers. It was Pizzazz Day after all.

When Sheila left a few minutes later for his office, Anne slid into her seat, feeling as if she were a character in her life, but not really living it. Maybe it was the new clothes.

No, it was the spring air, that was it. There had been hyacinths in the restaurant at lunch and they always smelled like spring to her. Like Ken's sandalwood aftershave, they whispered something. Something was going to happen. She didn't quite understand and wanted to know, but was afraid to know.

Something did happen. A man from IT showed up, Greg by his side, to look at her computer.

"Dude, you're not getting a Dell," Greg said, pointing his finger at Anne as if it were a pistol. "Something's wrong with the system, man. Infected every which way to Sunday. Viruses, worms, Trojan horses." He went on to list a witch's brew of software diseases, becoming more animated as his recitation proceeded. Anne swore he was going to jump up and down and clap his hands before he was finished.

The IT fellow—Gordon was his name—took Anne's seat and started whizzing through programs. He inserted one CD and then another and the clicking and clacking her computer had been making was fast disappearing. Damn.

Greg, meanwhile, fingered the fabric of her skirt. "Nice. Did you get this at Babamama's?" he asked. "I shop there."

"Uh… yeah." She didn't remember the store carrying any men's clothing, though. She looked at Greg with new eyes.

"Looks like something…" He stopped and thought. It took a while. "… like something those people in that movie, the one with the airplane and the guy who has to land it. Anyway, the people in the airport with the orange outfits."

She actually followed this, which mildly disturbed her. He was talking about *Airplane* and the scene with the Hare Krishna. It was just on television the other night, which Greg proceeded to remind her of in the next sentence. Yet her outfit was not orange. Nor was it anything like a Hare Krishna getup. But she figured the orange in Sheila's morning dress had combined with the gauzy fabric in her own skirt into one big blur in Greg's addled mind.

But this little trip down the byways of Greg's brain was making Anne think of her next step, especially given how vulnerable Greg himself would be to the job guillotine. She'd really have to pull out all the stops to race past him. Hmmm… he thought her outfit looked rather cultlike. So why not live the dream, huh?

As soon as Gordon was finished with her computer, Anne was going to find herself a cult and get some new members. She thought the staff of the Burnham Group was fertile ground for recruitment.

Perfect—religious proselytizing on the job. That should earn her a few more black marks. She was ready.

Chapter 16

From the article "Never Too Late," by Mitch Burnham (from *Entrepreneur International* magazine):

You need to bolster the bottom line? That means cutting staff. You need to sell more product? That means undercutting competitors. You need to draw attention to your company? That means doing whatever it takes—including dancing in the street naked with a sandwich board around your shoulders.

2:57 p.m.

KEN STARED AT THE paper in front of him, rows of scratched-out sums, figures, notes, and even a sketch of how he would like the gallery storefront to be renovated. As far as he was concerned, that was the only good thing on the paper. The rest of his notes were filled with crossovers, strike-throughs, and circled figures with exclamation points beside them.

In a growl of frustration, he tore the page from the pad, crumpling it into a ball ready for basketball discard. His hand wavered. He couldn't do it, dammit. That drawing of the gallery stopped him. He unfolded the paper, picked up the pencil, and adjusted the opening in the wall, the configuration of the office in the back. Oh man. He couldn't do this. He was caught in a hell between not being able to let go and not being able to grab what he wanted with both hands.

It was too much money. Even with the deposit cut back, the tenant allowance, and the discount on the rent for a long-term lease, he'd still eat up his savings in the first six months—and that was if nothing went wrong and he stayed within budget. And that budget was for day-to-day operating expenses. He hadn't even done up a budget for the gallery opening, which would have to be a classy and costly venture in that neighborhood.

Working in his father's finance firm, as well as the business courses he'd taken at his father's request, had taught him that without a safety net, business owners could easily and quickly fall into making bad decisions that ultimately led to their downfall. Desperation wasn't a good place to be when you needed to figure out if more investment, advertisement, inventory, or staff would tip you over the edge into success.

He threw the pencil on the desk. Crap. Why'd he go look at that place anyway? He should have waited until he had more money. He'd gotten started too soon because he was so damn eager to make a break, to prove to everyone he could do this. He should have gone about this coolly, rationally, patiently.

At least he'd had a nice lunch with Anne.

Anne—again he thought of her erratic behavior today. In some respects, she'd seemed like a giddy teen. Maybe it wasn't just the alcohol. Maybe she did have a thing for him, had had it for a while and now it was all bubbling to the surface as her controls were knocked out of alignment because of Mitch's crazy scheme. Every time he thought of this possibility, he pushed it aside, then immediately embraced it again. Now he embraced it with pleasure. At lunch, they'd discovered they had a lot in common, so it was only natural that they—that she—be attracted.

Stop it! Replacing one daydream with another isn't the way to get a grip on reality.

He shook his head and looked back down at the gloomy scenario the figures painted, not the happy future the drawing showed. His hand reached for the phone on the desk. One call. He could call his father, explain he needed money for the investment…

He pulled his hand back, remembering with pain their heated argument after he'd left the firm, as well as subsequent remarks his father had made about what he was up to. Oh, he'd always sounded interested, but there was an undercurrent, a sense he was disappointed. When Ken had landed the Arts Consortium position, his father had said: "Don't undervalue yourself, Kenneth. Even a nonprofit should pay you what you're worth." And when he'd left there suddenly, his father had actually approved, especially of the move to Burnham: "Give yourself a year and you could be running that place."

He couldn't ask him for the money. He couldn't face the humiliation of a turndown. He sighed heavily. At least he had that cocktail appointment with Arthur Howard. He'd seen Felicia go after prospects enough to know the drill. Of course, Felicia's donor cultivation was mostly about creating a perception, a dazzle that made prospective contributors feel they were the ones who were being given a gift, not the other way around.

Well, he wasn't going to approach this as if it were charity. He'd present his ideas in a way a businessman would understand them, as an investment with a return.

That reminded him—Felicia hadn't designated a place for this meet. He picked up the phone to call Bethany. She'd know.

Anne cruised through dozens of Internet sites for religious groups she never knew existed. In fact, she was glad she never knew. Some of them engaged in animal sacrifice, for crying out loud.

None of them quite suited her, though, so she decided to make up her own. Temple of the Divine Crusade. The Crusade would be aimed at one overarching goal—to make the world a better place through the regular use of tobacco products. Oh, and weekly dance festivals to allow one's spirit to roam beyond the confines of mortal and preconceptual boundaries, elevating it instead to the higher realm of ego-loosed reality, a semicomatose, semihypnotic state akin in many ways to hallucinogenic drug use except, of course, the Crusade didn't advocate the use of drugs. Nicotine didn't count.

She wondered how long it would take before Mitch used some of this lingo in an article.

She printed out a bunch of hastily composed flyers on her new religion, grabbed her cigarettes, and decided to start her personal crusade through the halls of Burnham. What better place to begin than with Robin? As Anne came up to her desk, she heard someone singing. Holy moly! Sheila was true to her word. She was in with Mitch right now. Sounded like something to the tune of "The hills are alive with the sound of music…"

Anne handed Robin one of the flyers. "This is really important to me. Could you make sure Mitch sees it?" she asked. "I'll be holding a meditation meeting later today."

Robin glanced at the paper. Anne left before the secretary had a chance to say anything.

For the next quarter hour, Anne skipped and ran through the kingdom of Burnham, delivering her religious messages, urging followers to come to her afternoon revival. She smoked, of course, when she talked to many of them, telling them of the "government conspiracy" to blame tobacco companies for the world's ills because it focused the public's attention on a "big, bad corporation" and away from the corruption at the heart of the republic. Most waved the noxious fumes away but damned if Lenny didn't inhale deeply and then, with more than a little regret, told her he rued the day he had to give up the weed. He also said he was looking forward to her "meeting" and marked it on his schedule. "So this Temple says smoking is good for you, huh? And it took me twelve years to really get off it."

Crap.

After telling Lenny that there were different "levels" to her group and perhaps he should stay at the "nonsmoking level," she headed back upstairs just in time to see some secretaries being shooed out of the conference room by Delaney Margrave, a she-witch from human resources who apparently didn't approve of *General Hospital* parties.

"Anne, I thought you said this was approved by Mitch," one of the secretaries said, waving the soap opera–party flyer as she walked by.

That *General Hospital* thing was so yesterday. Or rather, so last hour. Anne was all about the Temple of the Divine Crusade now. She sat at her desk and wished she could light a candle. She did the next best thing. She stuck a cigarette in a wad of poster putty, put it on the floor, sat cross-legged in front of it, and waved her hands over the smoke while chanting loudly, "ooooohhhhhhhmmmmm."

Thank God Ken was out of his cubicle right now. Away from her lunacy was the safest place for a kind soul like his.

Sheila stepped into Anne's cubicle entrance and clapped. "Very, very nice."

Anne stopped meditating to look up at her. "How'd your meeting go?"

"Call me irresponsible…," she crooned.

"I heard you singing. Didn't think you'd really do that."

"He wasn't paying much attention to anything else I said so…"

"What'd you say when he asked you your worst attribute?"

"I told him I was a compulsive liar but with the help of my shrink I was getting past those issues."

Anne smiled. Sheila was one creative whiz.

"How long you doing this?" She pointed to Anne's meditation getup.

"Dunno. I was hoping Robin or Mitch would come by."

"He's in with Greg now."

Anne stood. "Perfect!"

3:15 p.m.

Anne had a plan and the means to implement it, but she was delayed because of the fresh-from-the-runway appearance of the woman of the hour herself, Kathie-Rose Kimball.

From the corner of her eye, Anne saw her get off the elevator, followed by her heavily laden cameraman, both heading for the conference room. Snicker—she hadn't gotten the news of the latest change.

Hmm... Anne could wait and let her slowly simmer as she realized her time was being wasted. But no, Kathie-Rose might tramp on down to Mitch's office and let him know about the postponement again. Better cut that off at the pass because Anne had the press conference scene already staged in her head and didn't want it ruined.

Anne hurried to the conference room, her outfit creating a breeze of sound.

In the conference room, Kathie-Rose was talking to her cameraman. When she saw Anne, she looked up and laughed. Now Anne was really irritated. So she wasn't wearing a corporate pencil skirt and three-inch heels. That didn't make her worthy of scorn.

Immediately realizing the inappropriateness of her chuckle, Kathie-Rose covered her mouth and coughed.

"Am I too late?" She gestured to the empty room.

"Mitch didn't tell you?" Anne simpered. "He had to reschedule. Again." She rolled her eyes in a "what a jerk" sort of way.

"What time should I be here?" Kathie-Rose asked dryly. Her cameraman picked up his equipment and let out a curse.

"Oh. Four should do it. I'll send you an email if it changes again."

Kathie-Rose reached in her pocket and pulled out a card. "Here," she said, handing it to Anne. "My cell is on this. Call me if the time changes."

Sensing her irritation, Anne decided to feed it.

"Look, if you're not happy about it, go ahead and complain to Mitch."

Kathie-Rose said nothing and brushed past Anne, the cameraman following her like a drone coming after the queen bee.

Anne took the card and headed back to her desk where she tossed it into the trash can. Chances were Kathie-Rose wouldn't be showing up at four if she had something better to do. And she surely had something better to do than come to a Mitch Burnham "Look at me" press conference.

That accomplished, Anne returned to her original task. A gathering of her disciples was in order, complete with music and dance, a part of her religion's rituals, after all.

First, she found a Latin-beat collection on the computer and started it up, playing as loudly as her computer speakers would go. The thwump-thwump-thwumpa of a fast number immediately set the air on edge. Then, she sent a broadcast email to the entire staff about an "important meeting" on her floor. Then she turned the overhead lights off so the office was lit only by the ambient glow from computer screens and desk lamps. And then she started doing some combination salsa thing, two-stepping her way around the cubicles and offices, calling her followers to her side, clapping her hands above her head and swinging her hips left and right, sending her beads a-jangling.

She thought she'd feel freakish. But as she let herself be moved by the music, the concerns of the day lifted off her shoulders. Everything flew into the air—guilt, worry, shame, fear, longing. It was as good as a shredder. Which was kind of creepy, she realized. It was turning into what she'd said it would—a liberating experience that unleashed inner creativity.

"Come on, it will be good for you! You won't be sorry!" And she threw in some mumbo jumbo about life forces and undiscovered passions, and even said something about the force being with them and Landrieu beckoning them to dance, dance.

The elevator opened and who would show up first but good ol' Lenny? Anne shanghaied him as soon as he stepped off and he got behind her. Sheila shrugged and said "might as well," joining behind him. They had the beginning of a conga line.

"It's Pizzazz Day," Sheila said, getting into the spirit. "Mr. Burnham expects this! Come on, stand up and dance or face the consequences!"

Sheila didn't say what the consequences were but her voice and demeanor implied they were worse than making a fool of yourself in an office-led conga line. Sheila really got into this. If anything, she was better at browbeating people to join the conga line than Anne was. Sheila was practically a Conga Nazi.

It didn't seem to matter, though, because the *General Hospital*–party secretaries were ready to do something out of the ordinary now that their soap discussion was ruined. And others on the floor just seemed eager to take a break in the middle of midafternoon doldrums on this day when pink slips were floating into unfortunate staffers' boxes. Somebody tripped and knocked over a tray of papers. Anne picked them up and threw them into the air like giant confetti. Inspired, she also grabbed a bunch of shredded documents from the waste bin and tossed those as well. Some of her followers liked this and did the same when they passed by.

By the time they wound their way to Mitch's office, they had at least two dozen people in tow. Sheila was doing some weird "brrrrrr" thing with her voice and Lenny was asking Anne if he could have a cigarette when they were finished, and exactly how many this Temple said they should smoke a day for good health anyway. "I always thought that Surgeon General's warning was a snow job," he whispered knowingly.

At Mitch's office, it took all of ten seconds for the door to fly open and there was Mitch standing in the doorway looking at them and not knowing what to say.

Anne was about to shout out her religious spiel when Sheila beat her to the punch. "Pizzazz Day activity," she cried. Dammit, Sheila was stealing the show again. Anne no longer felt guilty for taking credit for the employee newsletter foul-up.

Good old Greg couldn't pass up this opportunity. He pushed past Mitch—which brought a quick grimace from the boss—and joined in the line, like a big puppy following a man dropping bacon bits.

"C'mon!" Sheila yelled to Mitch, but he stood and stared, mute. Anne didn't know what he was thinking but her guess was it was along the lines of ##@%&@!!!!.

"Religious observance," she managed to sputter, but she didn't think he heard her. Sheila grabbed his hand and put him in line right behind Anne and in front of Lenny. So Mitch's warm paws were grabbing Anne's midriff. Now there was a trip down memory lane she hadn't counted on.

The music was chu-chumpin and rattling, mariachis shaking in the background of some Gloria Estefan tune directing them to get on their feet. Anne heard some laughter and good-natured shouting behind her and she knew Mitch was probably steaming because his Pizzazz Day concept had been taken in directions he'd never intended. And he wouldn't be able to wring an article out of this exercise.

Anne should have felt another rush of victory, another claim to bad-employee fame. Instead—well, instead, she felt Mitch's hands on her waist and his breath on her neck and all she could think was how uncomfortable it felt, how her skin now crawled at his touch.

Get me out of here. Whose idea was this anyway?

Robin, she noticed, was chugging some aspirin. Her phone must have been ringing because she picked it up, tried to hear, then put it on hold and went into Mitch's office where she closed the door.

For another few minutes, they all congaed around the office, but what began as a great way to push Mitch beyond the limits of his patience ended as a test of Anne's ability to concentrate. She'd had this entire speech prepared, you see, filled with grand narratives about her newfound faith and wild claims of what it could mean to those who took up the Crusade with her, and a long-winded rant about multinational forces stealing individual freedoms away. She'd planned on buttonholing Mitch in front of everyone, embarrassing him before his team.

But now she kept thinking of the last time he'd had his hands on her waist and it brought back all the shame and anger and regret that had so magically rocketed out of her at the beginning of this dance. It wasn't fair!

It had been on a fall trip to West Virginia. He'd gone to scout a location for one of his camps when they were flickering from idea into action. And he'd taken Anne along to "help with communications opportunities." The foliage was magnificent—it had rivaled New England's that year—a bright canvas of reds and yellows so vibrant that the leaves looked backlit. It was damp, too, from a recent rain, so when they went walking up a steep mountainside trail, she'd nearly tripped and Mitch had grabbed her around her waist. One hand on either side, firm and steady. He'd said, "Be careful. You scared me there."

She'd felt so cared for, so happy, so sure of her future even though it was built on slippery inclines as treacherous as the ones that had made her slip.

The music stopped. He dropped his hands. Immediate relief.

"Okay, let's get back to it, shall we?" he said, neither angry nor exhilarated. The music shifted to a slow ballad and the crowd began to disperse.

"Mitch!" Anne followed him, feeling like a child running after Papa. He turned at his office door.

"You can't shut this down. It's important to me. I've joined a new church and this is a religious observance." It sounded pathetic instead of crazy so she made her voice more forceful. "The Supreme Court ruled that employees have the right—"

He held up his hand. "Just keep the noise level down." He turned to go back to his office.

What? He can't go back to his office! What's the matter with him? Why will nothing penetrate? She followed him, practically stepping on his heels.

"You haven't met with me," she said to his back. "You've met with everybody else."

He stopped and turned. Half his mouth smiled. His eyes stayed the same.

"You know," she continued, "about the job. About who you're going to let go." She was insistent. And pathetic again.

"I don't really think we need to meet. But if you insist, talk to Robin."

He walked into his office.

"I've already talked to Robin," Anne said. It sounded like a whimper. His door was now closed.

Ken's desk was shaking. Someone had a radio turned up so high in the other part of the office that the beat was making everything in the room tremble. Good grief—maybe Mitch should write an article on office etiquette.

Flipping his cell open, he clicked through incoming calls until he got to the Consortium number and dialed it. Bethany answered with a perky greeting on the second ring.

"Hi, Beth, I was wondering if Felicia was around."

"Nope. She's downtown at a meeting. Can I help you with anything?"

"No... well, maybe..." Bethany kept Felicia's calendar. "I'm supposed to meet her and Arthur Howard for cocktails after work but we didn't set a spot. Did she mention it to you?"

"No, but actually, no need to worry. Arthur Howard can't make that meeting."

"Oh…" Disappointment pushed out a sigh. Despite his misgivings, he'd now begun to count on this get-together. He looked down at the scrawled figures on the notepad, which was dancing across his desk because of the strong backbeat from the distant music.

"I was going to call you but Felicia said she'd take care of it," Bethany explained.

"I've been away from my desk," Ken said. Now what? He paused.

"Hey, thanks again for coming by earlier to help me out. I was able to whip up the piece for Felicia in a few minutes."

That kind of project was what he'd handled when he was there. Now Bethany was doing it with far less expertise and Felicia would probably find it acceptable. How could she appreciate his artistry if his work was interchangeable with Bethany's? Bethany was a good worker, but she didn't have his eye.

"No problem. You take care, Beth."

When he got off the phone, he sucked in his breath and finally crumpled the paper into a ball, tossing it into a nearby wastebasket. He put aside thoughts of his plans, of anything but his work at hand, and finished a brochure and an ad layout for Mitch. By the time he was done, the music in the other area had stopped. So, too, had the calls from printing sales reps. His cell phone hadn't recorded one in nearly an hour.

He put a call into Cyndi, getting her voice mail. "It's Ken. I've made a decision about that property. I just can't afford to take it right now. I'm sorry."

3:32 p.m.

The dance party drifted to a close the way most parties do. Laughter petered out, lights went back on, someone turned Anne's speakers down when an important phone call came in at a desk across the room.

Ken came back to his cubicle and looked around, assessing what he'd missed. If only he knew.

Sheila hummed to herself, which was a bad sign—she obviously had a corker up her sleeve that she wasn't sharing with Anne. When Anne looked over at her, however, all she saw was a happy employee blithely collating and stapling materials for the next board meeting. Unfortunately, her idea of collating today was stapling all the page 1's in one pile, the page 2's in another, and so on.

When Sheila left her desk for a break a few moments later, Anne scurried on over and pawed through her papers. Sheila was good. The papers were not only stapled together wrong. They looked like they'd come out of a computer printer gone haywire, with half of some pages blank and type bleeding to the top edge on others. How had she done that?

Underneath the stack Anne found a business card: Window Cleaning on the Spot. Why would Sheila be calling for a window cleaner, Anne wondered? She wrote the number on her palm and headed back to her desk as Sheila returned from the coffee room carrying a garlicky-smelling plate of hors d'oeuvres.

She smiled at Anne. "Go get some, Anne. They're great." She held her plate in the air. It was piled with meatballs, stuffed grape leaves, phyllo-encrusted bites—all exuding a strongly herbed odor. She looked over at Ken as well. "You, too, Ken. Help yourself!"

"I take it you ordered those?" Anne asked. Ken just shook his head while checking his voice mail.

Sheila nodded between mouthfuls. "They came during the dance. I slipped out and signed for them."

"Mitch hates it when the office smells like food."

Sheila said nothing and slipped into her chair, dripping oil onto her papers. She really had that grease-stained paper routine covered.

Anne headed for the conference room where she grabbed the phone and dialed the window cleaning service.

"Hi there, I'm calling from the Burnham Group," she said, all chipper and friendly. "Just checking on an order we placed. Can you go over that with me?"

Oh yes, he'd go over it with her. It was a special order. They'd never done something like this before. A crew was on their way to the Burnham office right now—rush order, triple the usual price plus a 30 percent bonus for the extra work involved—loaded with extra soap because Sheila had asked them to soap a special message on the windows. *Happy 57th birthday, Cal,* it would read when it was finished. Anne's first inclination was to cancel it. But the man on the phone did a quick check on the crew's progress and told her they were already on the job, setting up.

Anne hung up the phone, smiling to herself despite her envy. Sheila was good. "Cal" was Calvin Theopoulus, the board member and big investor Mitch was slated to meet with at four. He was devoutly religious and devoted to his family. And, a little on the vain side. His hair was more Grecian Formula than Greek and he was sensitive about looking his age, which was fifty-four, not fifty-seven.

Sheila was really, really good. She must have looked up his file, found out today was his birthday—hey, Anne was going to get in on this action. Two could play this game. She grabbed a phone book from a bookshelf in the corner and turned the pages until she found what she was looking for. Then she punched in the number and heard it ring twice before a gravel-voiced woman answered the phone.

"Party Hearty?" Anne asked, leaning back. "I'd like to order a stripper for this afternoon. Pronto, in fact. Do you have any available for the next hour?" As the woman gave Anne their rates and explained the various dances that were available, another inspiration hit.

"Do you have male strippers?" Anne inquired. "Because I think our birthday boy would enjoy that the most."

Chapter 17

From the article "Cut Your Losses" by Mitch Burnham
(from *Entrepreneur International* magazine):

*Once failure is staring you in the face, there's only one
solution—get the hell out. You can proudly point to your
prescience at knowing disaster was but a breath away.*

3:53 p.m.

WHEN KEN DROPPED OFF his latest bit of work to Robin—Mitch
was incommunicado in his office—she made a comment to him
about "missing the party." He didn't ask.

He wasn't in a partying mood. Wasn't sure he would be any
time soon.

When he'd come back to his cubicle, he'd checked his voice
mail. Three more printing rep messages and one message from
Felicia telling him what restaurant to meet her at for cocktails. Yet
Bethany had told him Arthur Howard had canceled and Felicia
knew it. Felicia had told Bethany, in fact, that she'd handle notify-
ing Ken.

Like a detective, he worked through the timeline of his conversation with Bethany and the message from Felicia. There was
no getting around it—Felicia knew when she left her message that
Arthur Howard couldn't make the meeting, but she still wanted to
get together with Ken.

What had she planned on saying when he showed up? he wondered. *Ken, darling, poor Arthur called at the last minute to postpone, but I thought we could discuss your plans anyway?*

And then would she lead him on with promises of a future meeting? Felicia was so predictable. It was his mistake for deluding himself into believing she really did have his best interests at heart. She wanted to get back into his good graces and it didn't really matter why. Even if she wasn't after his father's money now, she would be eventually. She couldn't stop herself.

Back at his desk, he looked over at Anne who was busily preparing for a press conference. Sheila was at her desk as well, on what sounded like a personal call. Was she wearing something different? That reminded Ken—he'd yet to put back on his pizzazzy Santa tie. To hell with that. He'd shown his team spirit. He was sure Mitch Burnham rued the day he came up with this crazy idea anyway.

With a sigh of resignation, he thought of Felicia again. Then he thought of Anne. No way was he going to start another office romance. He couldn't afford to leave the Burnham Group if it went bad. Maybe he could ask Mitch if that office he'd been working in earlier was free. If he was away from her, he wouldn't be distracted by her so much.

Anne smiled at Ken and stood to head to the conference room for the press conference. Poor guy looked kind of glum. She made a mental note to find out why as she thought through her plans for the rest of the afternoon.

The male stripper couldn't get there until four thirty, but Anne wasn't sweating it. She knew that Mitch would keep Calvin in his meeting for a long time. He never rushed big money and Calvin was big all right, with a tidy pile of assets and holdings in companies too numerous to mention. In fact, Calvin was big in other ways—he struggled with his weight and Mitch was careful to order low-fat snacks whenever Cal was attending a meeting.

Anne had ordered a double buttercream cake with the message "With appreciation from Mitch. Happy 57th!" It should arrive around the same time the stripper came.

She was feeling confident as she waited in the conference room for the media to show up. Not only did she know Mitch was clueless about this postponement—otherwise Calvin wouldn't be on the books at four—she was also giddy with anticipation for the moment her little treats arrived. She'd apologize, of course. Loudly and profusely. Wouldn't want Sheila getting the credit this time.

Speaking of Sheila, she popped her head in the room as the elevator door opened and Darren, the CNBC reporter, headed their way. His eyes became saucers as he took in Sheila's ensemble.

"Looks like this should be a success," Sheila commented, pointing to the room where Anne had arranged the podium with its Burnham Group logo slightly askew and the chairs bunched up in one corner.

"Hope so," Anne said.

Darren brushed past, slim reporter's notebook in hand. "Any press releases?" he asked.

"Darn. I forgot," Anne said. Sheila laughed and left the room. Anne wished she'd stay. Not for the moral support, but so Anne could be sure Sheila wasn't engaged in any bigger and better screwups during the half hour or so this task would take.

As Sheila turned the corner, Anne saw the elevators open again. More reporters straggled out but so did Mitch's four o'clock, Calvin Theopoulus. Could this possibly be going any better?

Another elevator opened and a few more news folks came in, including Kathie-Rose. *Must be a slow news day.* Last to step off was the bakery deliveryman—*wow, were they fast.* Guess that's what happened when you were willing to pay four times the usual price. And Mitch was willing to pay. Or at least his expense account was.

"Calvin," Anne said, holding out her hand. "Let me give you a great, big birthday hug!" She rushed over and embraced the startled man. A startled man who wasn't big on physical contact. He put his hands on Anne's arms as if he wanted to keep her a yard away. His doughy face looked both appalled and disgusted.

"Oh look," she said, gesturing to the birthday cake delivery. "This is for you. Mitch wanted your day to be special!" She grabbed the deliveryman's sleeve, forcing him to stop, and she opened the cake box to let Calvin view the offensive sweet.

And here again, the Workplace Gods were smiling on her because the bakery, in its haste to decorate this cake, had misspelled Calvin's name! Happy 57th, Calvin *Theopolas,* it read. He was a stickler for getting his name right. Really touchy about it. She hadn't even thought of adding that flourish!

He sputtered and his mouth moved but before he had a chance to say anything, Sheila was hurrying over, her arms outstretched as if she was going to grasp him to her bosom. She was doing the birthday-greeting thing, too, but in her skimpy shorts and low-cut top, it was far more fearsome for a man like Calvin. He avoided her entirely and took off for Mitch's office like he'd seen a ghost with no clothes on. Sheila raised her eyebrows and turned on a dime, following him. Damn. She probably had more planned, but Anne was stuck with this press conference. No matter. It would be over soon and she could return to the battlefield.

4:05 p.m.

Several reporters commented on Anne's outfit—one even complimented her—and she gave them the Pizzazz Day explanation, making it sound even sillier than it really was. She threw in something about it being Mitch's latest "scheme," a word she knew would make him cringe if he were there.

While the reporters focused on her ensemble, she was able to take in the neatly outfitted Kathie-Rose Kimball. It was obvious why she'd look down her nose at peasant chic. She was all upscale mannequin, not a thread or hair out of place.

She stood in the back of the conference room primping, looking at herself in a large pocket mirror while she fluffed up her already perfectly tousled hair. She patted a little powder on her perfectly made-up face and smacked her perfect lips together to make sure her shiny gloss was evenly distributed. She wore a geranium-colored suit with matching silk blouse. Her earrings were glistening gold disks peeking out from behind her shiny tendrils. She blinked her eyes and then smoothed up her long, dark eyelashes.

Although her legs wouldn't show on camera, they were long and curvy and her shoes were stiletto pumps. Her French-manicured hands wrapped around the microphone in an almost-erotic gesture as she cleared her throat and practiced her lead. "Entrepreneur and business consultant Mitch Burnham announced today…"

So this was Mitch's latest. Of course. Kathie-Rose not only had beauty and the power of the media, she had the acquirable factor times ten. From reading the gossip columns, Anne knew her one very brief marriage had been to a man flashier, richer, and more entrepreneurial than Mitch—a New York real estate and media tycoon, a fellow who once paid nearly a million dollars to hold a party in Central Park to celebrate the opening of an art exhibit his real estate company was cosponsoring. Of course, his real estate company had also been trying to sway city fathers at the time to shift some zoning laws on his behalf. And darned if he didn't get what he wanted. It was a maneuver worthy of Mitch.

Kathie-Rose's extra appeal was that she had left this fellow. She'd not only left him, she'd devastated him, if the media reports were to be believed. He checked himself into a spa for depression after the separation and probably took Prozac to this day. She'd issued a terse statement after the breakup that merely said she was "sorry for not adequately knowing my own mind and heart." In short, she hadn't really loved the guy. And because she herself was the daughter of tycoons, it wasn't money that had lured her to the altar. She refused to pursue a financial settlement.

What a catch—independently wealthy, sexy, desirable, and powerful. Perfect Mitch bait. Anne wondered how long this one would last.

Just as Anne thought this, a scruffy newspaper reporter came up to her and asked her the very same thing: "How long you think it'll last?" She was about to say, "With Mitch, you never know—he stayed with one lover for a year," when she realized the guy only wanted to know how long the press conference would go on.

"Uh, not long," Anne said.

The small room was crowded. The earlier news of cutting Mitch's salary had drawn out more people than expected. This was good. Several print journalists sat around the table, their jackets and blazers open and shirt collars loose. A few more television reporters were in the back, as neatly combed and pressed as Kathie-Rose but not nearly as charismatic. Darren smiled at Anne. There was even a reporter from a radio syndicate in the room. This was a good turnout, Anne thought, proud of herself. Too bad it would be for nothing.

It wasn't unusual for press conferences to start late, but Mitch was famous for his punctuality. It was now ten minutes after the hour so she thought it was safe to do her little bit of acting.

Her plan was to step out of the room to check with Robin, only to "discover" what she already knew, that Mitch was in an important meeting and didn't know about the press conference. She already had her reaction to that choreographed. First, indignation that he'd double booked. Then—hand to head, slapping her brow, muttering curses that she'd immediately apologize for, and finally, the admission of guilt. "Oh geez, Robin, I must have forgotten to tell him. All those reporters—they'll be so mad! Can you just interrupt him a second?"

That was the key—getting Robin to interrupt his meeting for this bit of business. He hated interruptions in meetings. Hmm… maybe she should offer to interrupt the meeting herself. When he was informed of the reason for the interruption, she predicted a blast of profanity. Being a media hound, he'd probably opt to fly around the corner and come to the press conference, but by then, the reporters would be in a stew of irritation and Anne would advise Mitch to bow out. "I'll handle it," she'd tell him.

Straightening her shoulders, Anne headed for the door.

"Be right back," she said to the group in the room, "I'll just see what's holding him up."

She walked slowly into the hallway. There was no rush, after all, and she wanted to savor this wonderfully well-executed plan. It occurred to her that it was, in many ways, the very kind of plan Mitch encouraged business leaders to make—a bold step that required courage and ingenuity and, if successful, would yield a tremendous payoff.

As she rounded the corner to Mitch's office, Anne heard his voice.

His voice? He was supposed to be in a meeting, hunkered down with Calvin. Maybe he'd just stepped out to give Robin some instructions.

Yes, that was it, Anne thought as she saw him standing in front of Robin's desk. Calvin was in the doorway, waiting for him.

"Tell Brenton I can talk to him at one tomorrow. And here—I got another sales call on my cell at lunch. Give it to Ken." Anne grimaced. Maybe that's why Ken had been so grim. He was getting all the sales calls to return. Ouch.

Robin nodded and looked up at Anne as she came into the secretary's line of vision. Mitch followed Robin's gaze as he continued speaking: "Cal and I…"

Okay, here goes. Taking a deep breath, Anne plastered a smile on her face and walked toward him.

"Mitch, I've got everybody ready in the conference room," she said.

He stared, wide-eyed. *Good, good.* He was confused. He patted his jacket pocket. Was he looking for his BlackBerry? He could just ask Robin to look at his calendar. His brows furrowed. *Very good. He was going to ask soon what this was all about because he has an investor waiting for him and he has nothing on his calendar to indicate—*

"Okay, Anne. Sorry I'm a few minutes late." He turned back toward Calvin. "Come on with me, Cal. You should enjoy this." He walked toward Anne, talking to Calvin. "I'm a bit nervous."

Nervous? And how had he known—

"Thanks for rescheduling this so Kathie-Rose could make it," he said, touching Anne lightly on the elbow as they headed toward the conference room. "It would have been a disaster without her here. You always were good at figuring this stuff out."

Kathie-Rose. She must have told him after all. Even after the second postponement this afternoon—she probably called him, the vixen. Did that mean he didn't even go to the river at noon? That he'd headed straight to lunch with Kathie-Rose?

Answering her thoughts, he said, "Robin says the marina called. You must have forgotten to let them know we were canceling. Give them a ring and make nice with them, will you? I might want to use that idea in the future. I talked with the MicroBeers fellow—we'll reschedule something with him."

Anne was speechless. She mumbled something and tried to keep pace with his long strides. Something was wrong here. Not only had he managed to "fix" her screwup, he was complimenting Anne on how good she was at figuring things out.

She was awash in frustration and… something. Something regretful, something angry. Something that said, "Yeah, I was good at figuring out what you wanted, too bad I never did it for myself."

She said nothing. They arrived at the room and now she felt silly in her outfit, like a child at a grown-up's party.

Once in the room, she went through the motions and played her part. She introduced Mitch after apologizing for his delay. She tried to throw in something about how he shouldn't have spent so much time talking to his pretty secretary but it sounded petulant. And it didn't score her any black marks because Mitch was oddly distracted. And yes, he *was* nervous. He was looking up at the ceiling as if trying to remember what he was supposed to say and he kept fidgeting, rolling his shoulders as if they were stiff and out of whack. When he stepped to the podium, he didn't give the usual Charming Mitch smile but quickly thanked people for coming before launching into his talk.

Anne stood to the side, hands in front of her, listening as he began his spiel about the latest camp. He spoke confidently and quickly, but his body language told a different story. He moved around a lot and kept patting his pocket. She wondered if he'd left his cell phone in there and was afraid it would start ringing. She hoped it would. She began sending it telepathic messages to ring. Perhaps she could slip out and dial that number herself.

He also kept avoiding Kathie-Rose's gaze. Maybe that was it. Maybe he was going to break it off and he was feeling uncomfortable. But then why would he have been so glad Anne rescheduled so Kathie-Rose could be here?

Mitch rushed through the press conference. After a few minutes of monologue, he threw the floor open to questions and got a few tepid inquiries about how the new camp would work and who would be its first participants. He shrugged them off with a quick reference to the fact sheets in their press packets. Here at least Anne could score. She'd provided no press packets. She was about to step up and confess to this gaffe when Mitch turned the tables on everyone—the reporters, Kathie-Rose, and most of all, Anne.

It started when the CNBC reporter asked about the salary cut and how it related to the stock slump.

Mitch held up his hand as if to fend the fellow off and shook his head.

"I have another announcement to make," he said, and Anne saw that smug smile start to lift his lips, that smile that said he had a secret that would make this boring event worthwhile, that he'd looked out for them after all, that he was about to pull a rabbit—or even an elephant—out of his hat.

"There are bigger adventures than the ones we take in my team-building camps," he said, his pace now slower, his hand sliding into that pocket again, and his sure-footed stance back. "In fact, I'd say the biggest adventure a man can take is when he decides to commit himself to one woman…"

Anne's body stiffened. *Oh no oh no oh no.* She knew what was coming next. She "figured it out" because, after all, she was so good at figuring out what he wanted. Dammit to hell.

His eyes gazed straight at Kathie-Rose. Yes, Anne knew what he wanted. He wanted Kathie-Rose.

"… so I thought I would use this occasion to announce an adventure with relevance only to me and one other person in this room. Kathie-Rose, would you step up here?"

"Mitch!" Kathie-Rose was blushing and rattled, but had that giddy schoolgirl look that telegraphed what her answer would be. In a second, she had stepped to the front of the room, her microphone still in her hand, limp at her side.

Mitch pulled his hand out of his pocket and he was holding a small velvet box that he opened with one deft movement. It was the kind of velvet box that contains only one kind of jewelry.

After removing the ring—an emerald-cut diamond surrounded by emeralds on either side—he pulled up her left hand and looked into her eyes.

"Kathie-Rose Kimball, will you join me in the greatest adventure of a lifetime and do me the honor of becoming my wife?"

Tears were streaming down her face and she was nodding and mumbling "yes, yes," and as cameras flashed and even the toughest reporter in the room was cooing out a soft "ah," she threw her arms around him and gave him a huge hug.

As for Anne, she murmured no "ah's." She did not clap with the others. She did not coo or cheer. She couldn't even feel her usual sense of admiration for the guy's spot-on sense of publicity. She felt sick.

The jerk. The arrogant manipulative rat bastard scumball dirtbag. Anne wished she had her brother's gift for profanity. She couldn't think of enough blue words to mentally hurl at Mitch.

She wondered how he'd planned on pulling this stunt in a canoe if they'd gone ahead with the originally scheduled noon event. Maybe have her get in the boat with him to demonstrate how safe it was? That made sense, come to think of it. Kathie-Rose liked the thrill of joining in the story. She once did a remote from inside the lion habitat at the National Zoo.

The daggers in her eyes must have been misfiring because Mitch was impervious to her stare. He and Kathie-Rose kissed, and Anne could already visualize that night's television coverage and tomorrow's front-page photos. *Mitch Burnham Starts Two New Adventures.*

Anne imagined too, Glynda, the former Mrs. Mitch Burnham, reading the news in the *Washington Post* over her café au lait and croissant, served by a silent maid. And this, for some reason, made Anne's eyes well and blur and she had to blink fast or risk looking like a sentimental sap. Poor Glynda.

Mitch, in all his bastardly-ness, had actually made Anne feel sorry for the woman she once wished would have disappeared from his life to make room for her.

Mitch Burnham had never made room in his life for Anne. She had been a diversion, not a relationship. She had been the in-between girl, the "Next One," who'd hung around while he tried to decide if he should stay married or not. By tolerating Mitch's treatment, Anne had allowed herself to be used. He'd brought out the worst in her.

Kathie-Rose answered a question about whether she'd change her name. She hadn't changed it for Mr. Billionaire, her ex. But she laughed and said in her Southern accent that she couldn't think of a more melodious name—Kathie-Rose Burnham.

Anne had to get out of there. She was going to gag.

She managed to slide along the side of the table while Kathie-Rose held out her hand to show off the diamond. Cameras clicked as Anne glided into the hallway.

It was cooler there. The conference room had been warm with all those bodies and emotional cross-currents. Anne breathed deeply and leaned against the wall, closing her eyes.

Her rest was short-lived. She heard the door opening and Mitch's voice booming out thanks to everyone for coming. Then he stepped into the hallway and saw her.

Anne gave him an awkward smile, then held out her hand.

"Congratulations," she said, trying to sound sincere. He shook her hand and impulsively pulled her into a big bear hug. She smelled the musty odor of his shampoo—something like polished leather—and felt the stubble of his late-day beard against her cheek. His embrace was strong and...

Squeezing her eyes tight she repeated in her mind *don't freaking cry don't freaking cry don't freaking cry.*

"Man, oh, man, I couldn't have pulled this off without you there, Annie. Thanks. You're a rock." When he pulled away, he gave her a friendly chuck under the chin. "Don't know what I'd do without you."

Chapter 18

From Mitch Burnham's book *Business as Warfare*:
> *Face it, you could get slaughtered out there. Nobody's going to give you a helping hand. Sometimes your worst blows come from your so-called friends. There's no one to rely on but yourself.*

4:52 p.m.

"Anne? Everything okay?" Ken stood up as he saw Anne racing around the corner. Was she crying? Man, he hoped that press conference had gone well. It would be just like Burnham to ream her out in front of guests if something went wrong, to prove what a "leader" he was.

He was about to go after her when his cell rang, Cyndi's number flashing in the LED. He hesitated before answering—he'd left her a message with his wishes, after all, and didn't really want to get into a long discussion. But he owed it to her to let her chew him out for wasting her time on the look-see, on the search in general when he wasn't quite ready.

Just after his hello, she launched into her speech. But it was a slightly different version than what he'd expected. She delivered it with her characteristic good cheer, which, for some reason, heightened its impact as the meaning slowly seeped past its presentation style:

"Look, Ken, I don't mind taking you or any client to see properties," she said in a congenial tone. "I don't mind holding your hand through the process and helping you figure out what you want. You're savvy enough to know that for people like me, this is a numbers game. I show enough people properties and eventually I close a deal. I have no doubt I'll close a deal on that M Street property very soon."

"I agree," said Ken, hoping his sheepish tone would communicate his remorse at wasting her time.

"But here's the thing, Ken—I've also seen enough properties and enough clients to know when something is right and they're making a mistake by letting it go. This is a once-in-a-lifetime chance, kiddo. Prime spot at a below-market price because the landlord is hot to move after a drawn-out legal hassle with the previous tenant. Those planets just don't align every day. They don't align at all, in fact. Not in my twenty years of work have I ever seen such a perfect opportunity—"

It was too painful to listen to. He couldn't let her go on.

"I really appreciate all you've done, Cyndi. But I was wrong getting you involved so early. I thought I could reconnoiter the market, get a feel for things and then when I was ready, know what to offer and how to make the best deal. I jumped the gun. I should have started when I had more stashed away."

"Don't say no just yet, Ken. Sleep on it. I don't have to get back to the landlord until tomorrow."

"Things won't change by then, Cyndi. Unless I win the lottery."

"Well, go buy a ticket."

He smiled. "I don't want to lead you or the property owner on. It's better just to kiss this deal good-bye. And put my search on hold until I'm ready."

"When will that be?"

He sighed and did the calculation. "Maybe another six months."

"You're sure?"

"Yes."

"All right. You know my number."

❖❖❖

In the bathroom, Anne splashed water on her face and stared at her reflection feeling like Jane Eyre giving herself the get-real talk about why she was a fool to think Mr. Rochester would want her.

After this stressful day, her already-pale skin was as colorful as cold cream. Her lips, too, had faded to a washed-out gray. And her eyes' dominant color was red. *Very attractive combo.* How did Kathie-Rose stay so fresh-pressed and pinched-pink this late in the day? Maybe if Anne could figure out that secret, she'd snag a guy, too.

With a swift intake of breath, she thought about Ken and the kiss and how she was moving three thousand miles away from all that.

She had to get a grip. She wasn't entering a convent, for crying out loud. She had a plan and she was working it. She was moving to California for a great job. She was going to make good money and probably work her way up to VP of Communications. And she loved California. Right? And she loved what she did. Right? As for romance, she might meet someone there. Or Ken could come visit. Why, the possibilities were endless.

More water on the face.

It's awfully hard to plan a future, Anne, when you didn't know until now what you wanted. Another thing Anne's mother had figured out about her all along. That was why she kept nudging and prodding Anne, asking pointed questions about babies and marriage. She knew.

Anne thought of Mitch as he made that goofy, romantic gesture with the public proposal. That's what Anne wanted. She wanted her very own goofily romantic gesture.

When Anne was at the towel dispenser, Sheila walked in.

"Everything okay?" she asked, looking at Anne's puffy face. Yes, Anne had managed to add swollen to its charms.

"Fine, fine. Just kinda emotional, that's all."

"Oh yeah," Sheila nodded before heading to a stall. "I heard about the press conference. That must have been a blow." She closed the door behind her and Anne was wondering if she'd known about her affair all along. "The male stripper's here if that's any consolation. That's a nice touch," Sheila said from behind the door.

"Good," Anne sniffled.

"I thought you had that press conference mapped out perfectly. I was really struggling to come up with something to top it."

"Yeah," Anne managed to say. "Just when you think you have all the bases covered…"

"Kathie-Rose probably tipped him off," Sheila said. "Obviously, they're pretty close."

Anne didn't say anything.

"Cheer up. It'll all be over soon," Sheila said.

Anne threw the paper towel away and stared in the mirror again. Damn it. She looked like the dictionary picture for "stricken." She forced a smile. That was better. Now she just looked like the dictionary picture for "deranged."

"Did you know about it?" Anne asked Sheila. "The engagement, I mean?"

The toilet flushed and Sheila appeared a second later. At the sink, she peered at her face, not at Anne's reflection. "No, but I wondered." She turned on the spigots and washed her hands. "I mean I wondered if he'd ask her, not if he'd do it like he did today." She laughed as she dried her hands. "Of course, that's typical Mitch, don't you think?"

Anne pretended to laugh but the observation jolted her. Sheila had "wondered." That meant she'd suspected Mitch was headed down a more serious path with Kathie-Rose, more serious than he'd been with Sheila or with other women—women whose initials were A.W. Did Sheila have psychic powers—or was Anne just dense?

"I didn't realize they were an item." Anne laughed again but it sounded too artificial, especially bouncing off the tiles of the bathroom. "I thought he was seeing a bunch of people."

Sheila threw her towel away. "I saw a society page photo of her with him at a fundraiser for the Juvenile Diabetes Foundation. Since his daughter has diabetes, I figured he must be serious about Kathie-Rose to involve her in that part of his life."

If Sheila had slapped Anne, she couldn't have felt any more surprised. She swallowed hard. "His daughter has diabetes?"

"Yeah, poor little thing. It's the only soft spot in that big frozen heart of his. Not a lot of people know. He and Glynda apparently didn't want her to feel different. So they don't broadcast it." Sheila smiled at Anne and touched her arm. "But now you know. Don't you feel special?"

Anything but. Anne felt about the most unspecial person on earth. The man she'd once been in love with had just announced his engagement at a public event to a woman whose attributes made her feel like wallpaper. No, worse than wallpaper. A tiny speck of beige in an ornate wallpaper pattern with lots of curlicues and tiny flowers. And she'd just heard the news that his daughter had a chronic illness from a woman whose relationship with said man lasted less than a quarter of the time Anne's had lasted.

What in heck had Anne talked about with Mitch? Maybe that had been the problem. Anne had talked. He'd just had sex.

"Back to the salt mines," Sheila said, leaving the room. Anne lingered for a few more seconds, composing herself. Eventually, she took a deep breath and followed.

At least Anne had the satisfaction of seeing the end of the stripper event. A man with a less-than-perfect figure wearing a loose thong and bow tie—guess you couldn't get A-list strippers when you called at the last minute—rushed out of Mitch's office, carrying a bundle of clothes in his arms.

"Well, I've never been called that before," he gushed, his head held high as he smashed in the elevator button.

4:58 p.m.

Anne halfheartedly apologized to Mitch—"I thought I'd ordered a singing telegram," she told him—and then she headed back to her desk to regroup. She was tired now, wishing the day would end. The office powwow wasn't until six—it was just like Mitch to extend the day for this kind of thing—so she still had time to think of more screwups. But she was distracted. She kept thinking about Kathie-Rose looking at that gigantic ring on her finger.

Before reaching her desk, Anne's cell phone buzzed in her pocket. When she pulled it out, she was surprised to see her brother's number. This time, however, fear didn't race through her. If he was calling her again today, maybe it was with good news. Maybe his deployment had been postponed or even canceled. Anne punched the connect button expecting to grab a piece of yang after so much yin.

And she was greeted with a harsh question instead of a hello.

"Guess who I just got off the phone with?"

"Donald Rumsfeld? And why are you calling me on my cell?" Anne rounded the corner to her cubicle.

"Your voice mail keeps kicking in on your other phone."

Ah yes. She'd been lax about answering her phone today. She'd even changed the message again: "This is Anne Wyatt. If you leave a message, maybe I'll call you back. Maybe I won't." She didn't think explaining all this to Jack was a good idea, though.

"Mom, that's who I just talked to," he seethed.

Uh-oh. Anne still hadn't told her—

"Ohmygod," she said. "I forgot to talk to her today. But, Jack, I've been so busy. I was going to do it. I would have remembered. Probably after work. You have no idea…"

"Just one thing, Anne. I ask you to do just one effing thing."

Anne looked at Ken who gave her a quick smile and raised his eyebrows in a question: *are you all right?* Sheila was back at her desk but merrily humming to herself. She probably thought this personal call was another ploy. Anne gave Ken a quick "I'm okay" head nod, and headed for the now-empty conference room where she closed the door behind her and slumped into a chair.

"Jack, I'm really, really sorry. I meant to. I was going to. I just— this day has been crazy. I've hardly had time to take a breath. You see, my boss, he decided today…"

"Save it. I don't care what cockamamie scheme your boss is working today. And whatever it is, you had time to go out on your lunch hour. Mom says she ran into you."

Anne sighed. Yes, she'd run into her. And had been so befuddled by her dust cloud of conflicting emotions that she'd let her promise to her brother vanish into the wormhole of selfishness.

"I'm sorry," she repeated quietly. She felt so defeated. She saw herself in an infomercial demonstrating the Magna-Marva Shredder of Life. She was dressed in a Jackie Kennedy suit, pearls at her throat, hair glued into place with a caseload of Aqua Net, gesturing to the shredder with both hands: *Don't you feel the weight lifting off you as it rips every bad thing apart with its magnificent, hyper-sharp blades? Here, ladies and gentlemen, watch it destroy the unkept promises, the oaths of honor, the duty one owes one's family yet never repays… I happen to have a carton-full handy…*

A fat tear dripped onto the laminated table. Damn.

Damn damn damn.

"When she told me she ran into you," Jack continued, "I assumed you talked to her."

"Oh no." Anne sniffled. Another tear fell. Maybe mucking up the conference room table would get her fired. Salt water corroded things, didn't it?

"So I told her I was glad she was taking it so well." A kid screeched in the background and Anne heard his wife Marie scolding their son. Jack was calling from home. He must have been doing a hundred things today. A hundred and one, thanks to Anne.

"I shouldn't have counted on you."

Anne said nothing because she agreed. She was beginning to think nobody should count on her for anything. She couldn't even count on herself.

"Are you there?" Jack asked after the silence stretched for a few seconds.

"Yeah." Her voice sounded congested.

"Shit," Jack said in a soft, uncomfortable voice.

Great. She was the very thing he'd hoped to avoid—a crying woman—when he'd asked her to take on the task of informing their mother. She was the crying female, the weak sister. She sniffled again and sat up straight. *Got to get the ol' sibling spat mojo back. That'd cheer him up.*

"Look, Jack, I would have told her. You should have kept your mouth shut until I had a chance."

Responding to Anne's more confident tone, Jack fired back. "When would that be—after I shipped out?"

"Tonight, you moron. After I got home from work. I was going to go see her in person." *Yeah, right. She'd just made that plan.*

"I get it. You'd get a free meal out of the deal."

"What?!"

"You know—you're always mooching off Mom."

Okay, it was true that she sometimes timed her visits to their mother so they coincided with mealtimes, but she looked at it as a perfect time to bond. After all, wasn't mealtime supposed to be family time?

"I am not now, nor have I ever been, a moocher," she said unconvincingly. As evidence in her case, she offered him a piece of recent history. "I'm the one, remember, who actually moved home when Dad got sick." *Take that,* she thought. Jack had been stationed in Georgia at the beginning of Dad's illness.

"You moved home because you were broke."

She tried to think of a good retort, but the events of the day had moved a large piece of furniture in front of the door to her brain's sibling-comeback closet. Or maybe it was the cigarettes cutting off blood flow to the gray cells.

"It was a sacrifice for me to move back from Monterey. I loved Monterey. It was beautiful. Sunny, perfect, and..." And dreamy. Like her. She shook that feeling and instead dredged up some old-fashioned righteous indignation. "I had friends there. A job. A life."

"No money."

"I never borrowed anything. I always paid my way." She was proud of that. She might have lived on peanut butter and raisins and maxed out credit cards, but she'd paid her way. And often, her roommates' way too.

Silence. Silence during which she tried to remember just what it was she'd been doing in Monterey those years out of college. Art history major—what can you do with that? She'd felt so special majoring in the arts when the rest of her family had been a bunch of action figures. Her parents still had a few of her pen-and-inks hanging around the house. She had a couple in her own apartment. They represented a claim to something, some bit of territory that Jack hadn't staked out, some part of the universe that Anne Wyatt could leave her mark on.

"Anne, I have to get going." Jack cut in.

"Maybe I'll join the Army so I can go gallivanting off to parts unknown," she said. Boy did that sound dumb. Dumb and mean. Score one for Anne.

"I'll have the recruitment papers in the mail this afternoon, baby sis," he said, a laugh in his voice.

She opened her mouth to respond but stopped. Jack was laughing. Wasn't that a good thing? A small, unfamiliar voice whispered in her mind: *Let it go, let him have the last laugh as a gift.*

So she laughed too, a small giggle that gave way to a full-throated chuckle that melded with his into a ripple of hilarity as they both imagined her, Anne Wyatt, in army fatigues and stiletto heels. It was the first pure emotion she'd felt all day and it cut through the muddle of feelings like primary colors on a canvas of muted grays.

When their laughter petered out, she leaned into the table. "I'll talk to Mom, Jack. I'll make sure she's okay. Don't you worry about that for one single second, okay?"

"I'll be able to call and email."

"I know. I'll remind her." And, in a fit of inspiration, she threw in, "I'll go over every weekend."

"From San Francisco? That'll be tough."

"Oh," she managed to say. Go figure—she was spending her day trying to get fired so she could start a new job on the West Coast, and she'd just forgotten about the new job part of the plan. "Whatever. I'll do what I have to do."

He became gruff again, reminding her to look out for Mom, and he was off the phone so fast she stared at it for a few seconds trying to determine if she'd just imagined the whole conversation.

5:03 p.m.

"Smoke break," Anne announced when she returned to her desk.

"Is everything all right?" Ken asked, his brow creased in worry.

She smiled at him, which, for some reason, made her eyes tear up. Maybe it was because here was one kind soul concerned about her welfare.

"A little stressed," she said and looked away.

Sheila just waved her hand as she chatted merrily and loudly to a friend in Japan. Anne knew it was Japan because Sheila kept asking how things were in Japan. Anne didn't think she'd heard the word "Japan" used so much in her life, in fact. Not even in a documentary about the dropping of the atomic bombs. Anne grabbed her cigs and headed for the elevator.

Keeping with her devil-may-care attitude, Anne lit up on the elevator, which proved to be a mistake when Lenny stepped on at the next floor. He asked if he could bum one off her and she nervously made an excuse, telling him it was her last one, while she tried to hide the pack in the waistband of her skirt. She wasn't sure he was fooled. He looked miffed when he left at the second floor.

"I googled that church of yours, Anne, and couldn't find a thing on it," he said without looking at her as the elevator doors closed.

Down on the first floor, Anne stepped outside into the late afternoon shade. The street was busy with traffic so she figured smoking wouldn't damage her lungs any more than the carbon dioxide pouring out of exhaust pipes. She leaned against the gravelly cinder block of the building watching cars go by.

SUVs, minivans, dark private cars, even the occasional limo zoomed and crawled, depending on the flickering signals and skill of the drivers. During one lull, Anne saw a woman in a two-tone, silver-and-blue Volvo drumming her fingers on the steering wheel. She was about Anne's age, her hair a smart, no-fuss cut that hung loosely around her face and curved elegantly at the nape of her neck. Even from Anne's distance, she could see what looked like a heavy, expensive watch glistening on her wrist, and her fringed-lapel suit jacket was upscale if not designer. She wore sunglasses that hid her eyes, and she took a sip from a coffeehouse thermal mug while she waited. Anne couldn't see a wedding band on either hand. In the backseat of the car was a container of rolled-up papers—they could have been posters, drawings, blueprints, anything artistic.

Something about the scene depressed Anne. It was the convergence between beauty and pleasure, she guessed. The woman was beautiful. Her car was beautiful. She probably had things of beauty in that box in the backseat. And yet she was no starving artist. She'd made some money and spent it on things that gave her pleasure.

"Nice time of day, isn't it?" Ken's voice floated to her and she whirled around. He stood, staring at the very same scene, the woman in the Volvo.

"Nice car, too," he added, nodding toward the vehicle. It was a two-tone with a retro-looking wide band of chrome fender separating the colors.

"I was just thinking that." She stared at it. "Can you imagine the designers standing around in the Volvo design office, everybody in white coats, chins resting on their hands, saying, 'sweet' when the design was unveiled?"

She glanced at him as he smiled. Then he spoke softly, as if regretting something, "Sweet because beauty is so narrowly defined in Volvoland that a wide band of chrome represents a bold departure."

"At least they probably got paid well," Anne added.

"Can't begrudge them that," Ken said. "Wish I could figure that out."

She turned to him again. "What do you mean?"

"I mean they're combining creativity with liquidity. They're getting paid for being creative."

"So are you."

"I guess I am."

She thought Ken had come out to offer her comfort. Now she wasn't sure. He seemed as rattled as she was.

"Have you ever seen the opera *La Bohème?*" she asked.

He nodded. "Nice."

"Do artists really ever live like that—in a garret full of joie de vivre?"

He chuckled. "Well, Mimi's 'vivre' got zapped eventually. She dies at the end of the opera."

Anne smiled. "True, true.

"But I know what you mean," he said. "The characters in that opera are happy even though they're sacrificing comfort."

Now she nodded and said nothing, remembering Jack's words about her selfishness.

In the arts, you either don't mind starving or you find a way not to. You either have the passion to live like the characters in *La Bohème,* frozen and hungry in your garret but happy because you're pursuing your dream, or you compromise your dream and make some money in an artistic field slightly off the path of the one you would have chosen. Like the woman in the Volvo, you find a way to make the arts make money for you.

Anne hadn't liked starving but hadn't been willing to compromise. She'd expected a fairy tale or nothing. The doors would magically open or they wouldn't. She hadn't cared enough to make them open. And when they didn't, she'd moved back home to lick her wounds. Jack was right. She'd come home just as much to escape facing her failure as to help out with Dad.

Damn she hated it when he was right.

Do what makes you happy or be happy at what you do. That's what her father used to tell her. He certainly managed to do both. He loved the Army but he didn't always love his postings. He learned to be happy at it. Why couldn't she?

Well, she was doing that. She was going to a new job with more money, a job away from a boss whose gift of heartache overshadowed his gift of jump-starting her new career, and to a city where time passed at the speed of the trolley cars cranking their way up Telegraph Hill. She was going to be happy, dammit. She might not be using her artistic sensibilities like the woman in the Volvo, but she'd be using some skills, hard-earned skills. She was good at what she did, yes she was, and proud of it. She'd become some woman somewhere with money and time and… something. Something that eluded her.

"Everything all right with you?" Ken asked eventually. "Sheila said there was a snafu with the press conference."

She smiled. Yes, a snafu that hadn't gone as planned. "Mitch proposed to Kathie-Rose Kimball during the conference."

"You're joking."

"Nope. Asked her to join him on an adventure all their own."

"Good Lord—the man is shameless. I'm guessing she said yes."

"You got it," she chuckled, despite her earlier confused feelings. She felt something lift off her with Ken's laser-like assessment.

"Any woman who falls for him deserves what she gets."

"What?" As quickly as her mood had changed, it zoomed back, not to sadness or confusion, but to irritation. Where did Ken get off passing judgment on women who fell for Mitch?

"Don't you think that's a bit harsh?" she asked him. "Mitch is a powerful, attractive man. I can see why women would find that sort of thing… compelling. It's only natural."

Now he was the one to laugh. "I wouldn't call it 'natural.' I would call it 'shallow.' From what I've seen, Kathie-Rose Kimball isn't a deep reservoir, if you know what I mean."

"Kathie-Rose is a powerful woman in the news media. She had to have something on the ball to get that job!" Anne couldn't believe she was defending Kathie-Rose. What was wrong with her? But Ken's opinion of Mitch and women who loved him was too glib. "Just because a woman is physically beautiful doesn't mean she's a bimbo… a… a news babe." And yet, until a few seconds ago, Anne had called her that. Go figure.

"Even if we assume you're right, accepting a man's proposal on national television says something unflattering about her." Ken looked into the distance as if searching for the right words. "It's a silly spectacle. And by participating in it, she's as guilty as he is of exploiting the media for personal satisfaction."

"I didn't think of it as a spectacle," Anne countered, again thinking how a few moments ago she did, in fact, think that very thing. "I thought of it as kind of a… goofily romantic gesture." And that, too.

Now Ken guffawed. Anne's face reddened.

"If you were proposing to a woman, what would you do?" she challenged him. "Throw the ring at her and ask her to sign a pre-nup?" She crossed her arms over her chest.

"I certainly wouldn't use my bride-to-be in a publicity stunt." Now it was Ken's turn to darken in anger. "That's not romance. It's commerce."

Anne opened her mouth to offer yet another argument but started coughing instead as she inhaled a blast of exhaust-laden air. Ken came over and patted her on the back.

"The smoking, Anne. I think the surgeon general is right on this one."

She looked up at him, her anger dissipated and she laughed, which only made her cough more. By the time she was done, she felt washed out and cleansed at the same time.

"We should get back in," she said. Then she thought to ask him why he'd stepped out in the first place.

"Just needed a break."

She remembered his downcast look earlier. "Everything okay with you?"

"Nothing serious."

They walked in together. When they got to the elevator, she sensed Ken's nerves. Maybe he thought she'd jump his bones again. Darn if she didn't want to.

Chapter 19

From Mitch Burnham's article "Expect It and Get It"
(*Managers Roundtable* magazine):

You pay your employees well so they should perform well, right? Wrong. They perform well because you will fire them if they don't.

5:10 p.m.

THE HAPPY-GO-LUCKY OPENING MUSIC of *La Bohème* played in Ken's head on the way back up to the office. Spring, *La Bohème,* Anne next to him. He wished she'd impulsively kiss him again.

He'd seen *La Bohème* several times with his parents, and once since moving to DC. The line that always stayed with him was Rodolfo's answer to Mimi about how he lives: *Vivo,* the tenor sang. *I live!*

If it were only that simple.

But wasn't it? His problem was he'd never been willing to live like the bohemians in that opera. He'd grown too accustomed to… things. He couldn't give them up. Look at him even now—he could be saving more from his salary, but he liked the regular dinners out, the taxi rides instead of the metro, the ability to play generous friend by picking up the tab the way he had at lunch.

While Anne slipped into her cubicle, Ken took a detour to the empty office down the hall. Sheila was noisily yakking on the phone, her voice barking through the room like a seal waiting for its trainer. He'd never get anything done here.

But when he arrived at the quiet corner, he just drummed his fingers on the desk. The day was almost over, thank God.

His creativity sapped, he decided to spend the remainder of the day calling printing salesmen back, telling them to just mail him their samples.

Anne spent ten minutes at her desk making phone calls—first, she called her friend Louise to confirm her visit after work. Then she phoned Mitch's publisher and various bookstores in the area where his latest release was displayed. Needless to say, she didn't help his sales.

Sheila, meanwhile, sent an email to subscribers of the Burnham Report that "accidentally" directed them to a white supremacist website with swastikas as the main design theme on the home page. She followed this up by circulating a raunchy—no, pornographic—joke to the entire staff with a note saying "I know we're not supposed to circulate stuff like this but this was so funny I'm sure Mitch won't mind." And, in keeping with her politically incorrect theme, she emailed political messages to the subscriber list as well, neatly focusing the Moveon.org material on the more conservative members and the Pat Buchanan messages on the more liberal base. She culled the appropriate information from subscriber survey results. She was thorough—the very attribute that normally drove Anne crazy was spurring her creativity.

5:20 p.m.

Sheila had gotten hold of one of those spray-string canisters and was running around zapping everybody with it. Anne had been whacked twice already—neon orange. Sheila's favorite ploy was to stand near a doorway waiting for someone to come out and then surprising them. She managed to get Mitch this way once when he stepped out to give something to Robin, who was away from her desk. Anne didn't know if she could compete.

Anne made some more calls—canceling camps, ordering expensive steaks to be sent to every employee (bill faxed to Mitch immediately, of course). But her imagination wasn't as wild as Sheila's. The sky was the limit with her. All you could do was sit back and admire.

5:31 p.m.

Sheila was giving cha-cha lessons to Lenny. Every time he made a mistake, she smacked him on the butt. Anne was beginning to think he liked it. Sheila told him the most open space to dance was the hall in front of Mitch's office. She very loudly counted the beat and sang along to the music. Her voice wasn't half-bad.

Anne responded to several solicitations Mitch had received from charities, telling them Mitch would be glad to serve on their boards. One was an obscure eco-friendly group devoted to the preservation of the tamarisk tree in Southern California. She volunteered Mitch for several committee chairmanships. She also committed the Burnham Group to a pricey table at an upcoming fundraiser for the Legalize Drugs Now movement and signed the release form saying Mitch didn't mind if his photograph was featured in their literature. She drafted press releases on the same and shot them to Mitch through email and Robin.

5:42 p.m.

Anne was having trouble hearing herself think. Sheila was singing "I Could Have Danced All Night" at the top of her lungs, waltzing around the office with Verna from payroll. She must have run out of ideas and was sticking with the dance theme. It made Anne feel good about herself—after all, she'd probably planted the notion in Sheila's head with the conga.

Anne decided to forgo the ruffles and flourishes Sheila was finding so appealing, however, and opted to continue the fundraising theme. She got the vice president for development of Mitch's alma mater on the line and insisted Robin put him through to Mitch. Anne knew the veep would be asking Mitch about his half-mill donation—Anne had told the veep about it before the call was patched through.

While Robin was in the ladies' room, Anne got on her computer, mailed Mitch's calendar to her computer, and deleted it from Robin's, telling the secretary when she returned that "something horrible had happened." Robin fumed and fussed, just as Anne had hoped. Anne would give her back the calendar at the end of the day—no point in punishing Robin.

5:53 p.m.

Sheila was yodeling.

Ken came around the corner, took one look, and went back to wherever he was wisely hiding out.

Mitch stepped out of his office and glared at Sheila.

Anne used that occasion to tell Robin she hadn't been able to fix the calendar yet.

5:55 p.m.

Sheila tried to teach Robin to yodel.

Anne decided to grab her chance and rushed past the Swiss Miss in short shorts, blasting into Mitch's Inner Sanctum like an Arctic jet stream.

She had about five minutes before they were all to gather for their last big meeting of the day, the moment of truth when they'd hear the bad news. Mitch had yet to meet with Anne for a self-evaluation and she was not going to be denied, especially since doing it now would delay the start of the meeting and have him thinking particularly dark thoughts about her at a crucial moment.

"Go right in," Robin said from behind Anne. "Don't let me stop you."

Mitch sat, feet propped up on his desk, files spread out before him. He held one open on his lap and was wearing reading glasses, which he quickly took off when she entered the room. Mitch hated people to see him with reading glasses. He had all his speeches and press conference materials prepared in 16-point type.

"I'm busy right now, Anne." But maybe he remembered her words about his inaccessibility (and how it led to the announcement of his salary cut) because he immediately shifted demeanor, waving her in instead of chasing her away. "Is this important?"

"We never met for our evaluation/interview/whatever meeting," she said. "So I decided to take the initiative and come in on my own."

He closed the file in front of him and sat up straight. To Anne's dismay, she noticed it was Greg's file he was perusing. Feckless Greg—he'd be tough for either her or Sheila to beat in this race to the bottom. All the more reason to plow forward. Courage, she imagined Dan Rather whispering in her ear.

Mitch didn't say anything but leaned his elbows on his desk, staring up at her.

"In fact, I've decided that my weakest attribute—I know you've been asking everyone what theirs was—is my lack of initiative. So today I've decided to take the bull by the horns and strike out in new directions on my own." She paused, waiting for a reaction, but there was none. This made her nervous and her self-confidence began to waver. Mitch wasn't reacting. It was as if she was too late. He fingered Greg's file with one hand and grabbed a pen with another. *Oh no! It was Greg who was going. Of course. All this time she'd been focusing on beating Sheila when Greg was the real menace. He didn't have to struggle to screw up. He was a natural at it.*

But she couldn't stop now. She'd come too far to take yes for an answer. She'd make him change his mind. She squared her shoulders.

"So I called various bookstores around town," she told him. "And you know all those gorgeous displays of your latest book? I've instructed the booksellers to send them back to the publisher. I know you were unhappy with the number of typos in the final. So I took matters into my own hands." Still he didn't move. Darn it—Greg's fate must have been sealed tighter than a vacuum-packed toy.

"I also took it upon myself to order free copies of Peter Jasmine's book for the entire staff and have sent them to him to inscribe. I know you like us all to keep up-to-date on what others in the field are saying." Still nothing. If anything, he looked bored.

"And I canceled the West Virginia team-building camp scheduled for next month because I know you wouldn't want them going forward with that until the white-water-rafting folks confirm the safety precautions are 100-plus percent." This was complete hokum—Mitch didn't check on that sort of thing and she hadn't really canceled the program. But the West Virginia camp was the only one in the next quarter that was booked to capacity, so Mitch should be pretty upset at the prospect of it fading from the schedule. "I'll be instructing Lenny to send out the refunds with the cancellation bonus before I leave for the day."

"And finally," she said, her voice growing weaker as he grew more silent, "I've called your editor in New York and told her that you... that you..."

"Yes, Anne?"

"That you're not interested in writing any more books because you're tired of putting out B.S. guides to the obvious and that the only rule business leaders really need to remember is the Golden Rule, the one about treating others the way they want to be treated."

He drummed his fingers slowly on Greg's file. She wasn't sure but his mouth seemed to tighten just a little. Finally, he spoke.

"Could you send Robin in on your way out?" And he opened the file again, pulling a piece of notepaper from his monogrammed stack, and beginning to pen notes. His head was down; his attention had shifted. It was as if she weren't there, and had never been there. What was going on here? Hadn't he heard her?

She started to speak again, but his hand lifted ever so slightly as if to shoo a fly away.

After Anne left and Robin went in to see him, she heard him giving the secretary brusque orders—call his publisher, call the bookstores in the area—all undoing what Anne had just done. But his voice was completely devoid of emotion as he issued his commands.

Chapter 20

From Mitch Burnham's book *Fair Play, Fair Pay:*
> *Don't coddle your employees' egos. Be miserly with praise and fulsome with criticism. Soon they'll be hanging onto your every word, hungry for the crumbs of kudos you toss their way.*

6:07 p.m.

THE CONFERENCE ROOM LOOKED particularly shabby as they gathered for the big news, a far cry from the boardroom on Donald Trump's *Apprentice* show. Folding chairs used for the afternoon press conference cluttered the corners. A few scraps of crumpled notebook paper littered the floor. Mitch might have directed the janitorial staff to get the table set up, but that's about all they'd done. Maybe some of them had been cut today as well.

The long oval table now in the center of the room was obviously laminate made to look like walnut. Instead of polished wood paneling, the room featured scuffed wallboard painted a bland cream adorned with a couple of framed posters from old art exhibits at the National and a credenza with magazines and reports. Mitch didn't use this room for anything but staff gatherings. His board meetings took place in a posh suite on the top floor that was sleek and classy.

As Anne made her way into the room, her thoughts were as jumbled as the room itself. Mitch seemed unimpressed by her latest antics, even when she'd been waving them directly under his nose. And poor, clueless Greg could be in the line of fire.

All right then, Anne. Grab that spotlight back. Don't let Mitch shine it on Greg. There's still time. Mitch is nothing if not unpredictable. It's the most predictable thing about him. There's still a chance to change his mind.

The other team members straggled in and they all sat on one side of the table, nervous and quiet. Sheila and Anne exchanged a few knowing glances but even they were anxious—who had made the cut? Anne shot a comforting smile at Ken and a nervous zing shot through her as he responded in kind. Once she got the "bad" news from Mitch, she'd be able to be frank with Ken—about moving, about starting a new job, about starting a new relationship.

In a few moments, Robin entered, taking a seat opposite at the long table. She had a leather portfolio before her and several high-quality pens. After asking if anyone wanted coffee in a voice that indicated she wasn't about to serve any, she opened the portfolio and pulled out files with their names on them. These she set before the empty chair next to her.

As if on cue, Donald… er… Mitch opened the door and silently entered. He gave Robin an approving nod, pulled his collar loose, and sat next to his secretary, looking through the files. Anne waited for the piped-in background music, but only the muffled buzz of the ventilation system filled the space.

That is, until Greg began humming. Robin shot him a look of disapproval and he said, "huh?" then went back to humming, adding a nice little ostinato of finger-tapping on the boardroom table. *Shut up, Greg,* Anne thought, but when she stared at his beating fingers to signal he should stop, Greg just bobbed his head like a big Saint Bernard being told he was a good boy. Mitch was wincing.

Okay, if you can't beat 'em… Anne started tapping too, hoping to supersize Greg's irritation and draw Mitch's attention her way.

But then Sheila picked up the beat and soon the three of them were a finger-tapping version of *Stomp*.

"Will you cut it out?" Robin asked. "I already have a headache!"

Anne grabbed her chance. "Yes, we should get on with it. It's already late."

To her disappointment, Mitch agreed!

Closing the last file, he said, "This won't take much time. I just want to get your thoughts about today, how it incentivized you."

The monster! He *was* going to use this nonsense as the basis for an article. Robin was taking notes for it.

Anne's irritation bubbled over, ruining the calm she'd hoped to project.

"Really, Mitch. How crass to exploit the suffering you've caused today!"

Mitch's face shot up. He hadn't been prepared for rebellion. *Good.*

"I think what Anne is saying is that the day was probably more of a counter-incentivizer," Ken said.

Ken was trying to back her up—how sweet. But she didn't want him getting into trouble because of it.

"Counter-incentivizer, morale killer, just plain stupid idea," she said to Mitch, keeping her voice even and controlled. "Letting someone go is one thing. Doing it through an exercise like this is laughable. Just get it over with." She locked gazes with him, daring him to get it over with by pointing his finger at her. She saw him redden and thought a quick victory might be within her grasp.

But no, he looked down the table at Greg.

"Did your morale suffer today?" Mitch asked him.

"Huh?

Anne couldn't let Mitch zero in on Greg. That was dangerous territory.

Goal Number One: Get Greg's name off the list.

Anne smiled beneficently at Greg. "Greg's always a happy warrior. And his work was superlative today. Absolutely stunning. Fast turnaround. Quality craftsmanship. I've never seen him work harder or better, stronger, higher..." *Wasn't that the Olympics slogan?*

Sheila and Ken stared at Greg as they tried to process this unusual praise of their goofy coworker. Greg stared at his nails. It didn't take Sheila long to get with the program, though, and she proceeded to heap her own praise on feckless Greg, who'd started humming again as the proceedings obviously began to bore him.

"Greg!" Mitch shouted to get his attention. "Your colleagues think you're doing a good job. What do you say to that?"

Greg looked like a bobblehead shaken from side to side as he absorbed this question.

"Uh." He looked at Ken, Anne, and Sheila in turn, then back at Mitch. "They been drinking?"

Mitch sighed and looked at his watch.

"He puts things on the website in record time, Mitch," Anne rushed to say. "Much faster than the service we used to use—they'd take days. He's always cheerful. And he's..."

"—loyal," Sheila threw in. "Exceptionally loyal. Something you value, Mitch, above all else."

Eureka! Mitch nodded his head in agreement. *Thank you, Sheel!*

"Yes, he is loyal," Mitch said, looking impatient. "Now that we've established that Greg is the Employee of the Year, let's move on."

Hooray! Greg was safe!

Mitch continued. "The amount of work everyone placed on my desk suggests to me that productivity definitely increased today and I'd like to get at why."

Goal Number Two: Knock Sheila out of the running.

Anne stood up and walked behind Sheila, placing her hands on the woman's scantily clad shoulders.

"Look no further for the source of this productivity, Mitch,"

Anne said, her grip so firm on Sheila's shoulders that the woman couldn't move. "Sheila is magnificent. Second only to Greg, of course. And honest and loyal as the day is long," she threw in for good measure.

"Anne's being kind, Mr. Burnham, I mean, Mitch," Sheila said, trying to shake off Anne's praise as well as her hands. "I'm not honest. I... uh... wasn't sick last month when I called in sick."

"Oh yes, she was," Anne interrupted. "She was at death's door."

"Really, Anne," Sheila cooed, "you're too kind. I don't think this is the time to obfuscate."

Obfuscate? What the hell did she mean by that?

"No, Sheila, you're the one who's too kind. You're always helping everyone. You're a veritable Mother Teresa to the staff, pitching in, going the extra mile. And you have a one-of-a-kind institutional memory. No one knows this place better than you do, including where all the skeletons are buried." *That's right. Go ahead and try to fire Sheila, Mitch. She'd reveal all your secrets.*

"Nonsense, Anne. You're the one who schooled me on the Burnham Group's history. And you're a far more loyal employee than I am. I've let things slip, unfortunately, at cocktail parties and the like. Parties with reporters at them."

"Are you folks talking in code or something?" Greg asked, looking from Anne to Sheila and back again.

Although Anne had her hands on Sheila, Sheila wouldn't let go of her theme. "Anne's always been a good worker bee, the best in our merry little hive."

"No, no, Sheila is the very best you have here," Anne said. "Nothing deters her from accomplishing her tasks. She's like the Pony Freaking Express, riding until she falls off the saddle if that's what will get the job done. No one—and I do mean no one—compares to her dedication and fortitude." Anne slapped her on the back to emphasize the point. Sheila started coughing.

"Sheila comes in early and goes home late. She's a peach, I tell you. Irreplaceable."

"Are you all right?" Ken asked Sheila as she coughed.

"Fine, fine," Sheila sputtered to equilibrium. "Anne's being too sweet—one of her assets, one of many. She's incredibly kind, practically a saint. And, as you can see, one of the manifestations of her kindness is her fulsome generosity of spirit. I certainly cannot measure up at all to her. And I'm not as good as she says. Really. I've messed up lots. Why, just today…"

And like a racehorse let out of the box, Sheila was off! She started a long litany of screwups, each one preceded by an example of how Anne was so much better than she was. She talked so fast and furiously that no one could get a word in edgewise. When Anne attempted to interrupt with protests, she was quickly squelched with a steamrolling "Let me finish now, Anne dear." When Mitch tried, Sheila just held up a finger to indicate "one more thing"—and then went on to list at least fifty without so much as a pause for air.

Some of Sheila's gaffes were so creative that Anne's jaw hung open in admiration. Sheila had missed an important directory deadline, put the wrong date on an open house invite to vendors, and—this was what had Anne doing the mental head slap—she'd met privately with Jim Danforth, the Director of Sales, to complain about the communications department. Everyone knew Mitch believed firmly in not going behind teammates' backs to complain. In *Use It or Lose It*, he'd written, "A man—or woman—should have the courage to face his or her compatriots, to say to their faces what is said to the boss."

As Anne suspected, Mitch's ire ignited as Sheila told this story and he was finally, finally able to break into her monologue when she had to take a breath.

"What did Jim say when you complained to him?" Mitch asked, sharp edge in his voice.

"Why, he would hardly give me the time of day," Sheila said in an "imagine that" kind of voice. Good move—protecting Danforth, drawing Mitch's wrath squarely on her.

No, no. Anne couldn't let Sheila grab his wrath! *That wrath was all hers, dammit! What to do, what to do?*

Anne twisted her mouth to one side, frantically looking for ways to deflect Mitch's death rays away from Sheila. Damn, but that would be hard. Sheila, sitting there in her wild and crazy crop top and short shorts, looked several cards short of a full deck. She'd done some more primping to her hair before coming in the room and it was practically standing straight up, making her look like she'd just had an electric shock therapy session.

That was it! Make Mitch afraid of firing Sheila!

"Sheila's mistakes are all perfectly understandable," Anne rushed to say before Sheila could begin again. "Because Sheila, poor dear, is dealing with a disability of sorts. You probably guessed at it yourself." Anne discreetly pointed to Sheila's hair and outfit. "You see, she's been having some psychological difficulties. I've overheard her talking to a therapist, and you certainly wouldn't do anything to discriminate against the disabled. Letting her go would be tantamount to inviting a lawsuit." She patted Sheila on the shoulder.

Mitch straightened and his face paled. He got it. Regardless of what Sheila had done, Mitch wouldn't risk an employee legal action. A suit based on a disability would knock the wind out of his expert-management sails.

Sheila got Anne's point, too. She turned to glare at her as she processed what had just occurred—Anne had draped Sheila in the immunity cape. Anne couldn't help herself. She grinned at Sheila, raising her eyebrows. *Gotcha.*

But then Sheila changed. Her own eyes narrowed and her lips pressed together in a determined but sour smile.

"Did you think I had a therapist?" Sheila said in a singsong voice. "You must have misunderstood. I was on the phone with my hair *stylist*. Not therapist, Anne." Turning back to Mitch, she continued, "You see, every Monday I make an appointment. But Sasha's such a bastard to deal with that I have to spend hours—and I do mean hours—on the phone describing what I want him to do. That's why the Annual Report dummy was late last week. That damned Sasha. I could just bitch-slap him, the MF."

Oh man. Not only had she recovered the ball, she'd thrown in blue language as a touchdown run. Mitch might use the occasional swear word—as he had this morning after the CNBC report aired—but Anne had never heard anything more foul than a "damn" from Sheila. And even if Mitch cursed, it didn't give them permission to use the same language on him.

Robin was shaking her head, but still taking notes.

Ken was confused and silent.

Greg leaned forward to look at Sheila. "Does he own that unisex shop on Connecticut Avenue? I think I went there once."

Mitch was… appalled. He looked like he'd just witnessed a natural disaster.

Ignoring Greg, Sheila grabbed some of her teased hair. "See?" she asked. "Look at these split ends. I've told him a thousand times to get me a fucking conditioner that'll keep these shit-ass split ends under fucking control. I mean, well…"

"Fuck it, yeah, I know what you mean," Greg said, nodding his head and pulling at his own hair to examine the ends. But his hair was too short so he ended up looking cross-eyed at his fingers instead.

"Sheila, really, I think we get your point," Mitch said, his voice low and unsure. Anne rejoiced. He was buying Anne's line. *Keep acting nutso, Sheila.*

"Look, let's get on with this," Mitch continued. "I have a few questions and then—"

"Wait a minute, wait a minute!" said Anne, waggling her hands in the air as she walked to a nearby bookcase to grab a stack of publications. She threw them on the table in front of Mitch. Pointing a manicured finger at an award-winning Annual Report of two years ago, Anne said triumphantly, "Sheila might be crazy but she's good. This piece was all her doing. Remember how proud you were when we got word we'd won the National Chamber of Commerce Publications Award? Do you remember, Mitch, do you?"

Sheila, meanwhile, was between a rock and a hard place, not knowing whether to insist she wasn't crazy or to protest Anne's praise, which might just make her look crazier.

"And this," Anne said, pulling out a "Burnham Group in the News" folder filled with news clips that mentioned the company, "this is Sheila's work as well. She is one demon with a press release. Writes 'em, emails 'em, follows up. It's all her work, Mitch. All hers. The rest of us are just…" Anne looked around and shrugged. "Orcs to her Saruman."

"Yes, she does outstanding work," Mitch murmured, more comfortable with retaining Sheila for good work than for fear of a lawsuit.

But Sheila was not to be outdone. Standing, she leaned over and pulled out a few brochures and a newsletter. She delivered a similar speech about the magnificence of Anne's work, eliciting the now-standard echoes from Ken and even Greg. She talked about how much she'd learned from Anne, about what a great mentor and leader Anne was.

"And, in conclusion," Sheila said, "I don't think the Burnham Group would ever find anyone anywhere anytime as good as Anne Wyatt. You can't let her go, sir, I mean, Mitch. You should be doubling her salary." She paused. "Or you're really fucked up."

Greg applauded.

Mitch shot him a glowering look. Robin rubbed her temples. Ken glanced from Anne to Sheila, his eyes squinting as if he was trying to figure out if he was hallucinating.

Sheila opened her mouth to start another endless monologue but Anne jumped into the breach before she could. She thought of Jack and her dad and how they'd plow on through to the end of the mission no matter what.

And so she began, planting herself directly in front of Mitch confessing each of her snafus with what she hoped was the right mixture of contrition and lack of regret.

"I told the truth in the Annual Report because I thought honesty is the best policy…

"I told CNBC you'd be cutting your salary…

"I mixed up the press conference times…

"I infected my computer…"

Like Sheila, she'd brook no interruptions, plowing past Mitch's attempts to speed things up by talking loudly and pacing the room so she was no longer looking him in the face.

She not only listed all the screwups. She told him what she'd been thinking about when she was working on them and what her horoscope said this morning and the messages she got from her Magic 8 Ball as she decided what to do.

If it was possible to die of boredom, everyone in the room was on life support by the time she finished.

Greg actually had his eyes closed. Sheila had her head down. Robin was yawning. And Mitch was as motionless as a Buddha.

Ken was the only one to speak. "We've all been on edge today…"

Ken, Ken, don't try to cover for me!

"Wait a minute!" Anne cried. "I'm not done yet. There's more! Lots more." But she didn't have more, or at least no more office hijinks to list. All she had were her personal transgressions, the guilt she felt about letting her brother down, the sorrow she felt over disappointing her father, and the stupidity she felt as she contemplated her affair with the man she now wanted most to impress with her supposed incompetence.

"I don't call my mother enough! I didn't listen to my father when I was younger! I always lie about my age and gender when registering for free online subscriptions! I never remember the words to the national anthem! I missed the week in school we studied multiplication tables and always have to add up the nines! I sometimes do eenie-meenie-minie-moe when I vote! I think I ran over a squirrel once! I killed a bluebird this morning…"

She started pacing again, making Mitch and Robin follow her with their eyes like fans at a tennis match.

"I watch too much television, and not the good PBS stuff but the raunchy reality shows about winning a C-list star's love… I keep books out of the library until it's Amnesty day… I pretend to like contemporary classical music, but really think it's a bore… I always take plastic, not paper… and, I… I… I dress like a nun. Not pizzazzy enough. Until today." Her skirt swung as she walked. *I used to dress pizzazzy. In outfits like this one. Maybe that should be the title of my autobiography:* I Used To.

"You dress fine," Sheila interjected.

Anne twirled around to make her skirt belt bells jingle, and nearly fell as her toe caught a tassel on the hem. It made her look drunk. That was okay.

Ken rushed to grab her elbow, urging her to sit down, but she told him she was okay, standing in back of her empty chair.

"My other problem is…" She paused and looked directly at Mitch. "I seem to have poor taste in men. I fall for hucksters and cheats."

Robin stared and didn't write anything. Mitch stared too, eyes frozen like crystals.

"Are you talking about your friend Rob?" Robin asked.

Ken's head whipped around as a question lit up his eyes.

"Can't anyone get it through their heads that Rob and I are just friends? He could be gay for all I know!"

"Why do women always assume men who don't make a pass at them are gay?" Robin said to herself as she resumed writing. "Maybe he's just not interested."

Mitch remained silent, his eyes narrowing as he watched Anne perform. Good. At last she was annoying him. She remembered a cigarette tucked in her waistband and pulled it out, asking if anyone had a light. Greg did.

"As I was saying—" She blew a puff of smoke.

Robin interrupted. "I don't think this is what Mr. Burnham had in mind, Anne," she said. "And when did you start smoking? Don't you know about the no-smoking rules?"

"Oh, let her smoke." Sheila chimed in. "Didn't you get her memo?"

Anne stopped in her tracks. Why this shift from Sheila?

"It sounds like Anne's been under a lot of stress," Ken said, trying to rescue her again.

"Good point, Ken," Mitch interjected, his voice as emotionless as his eyes. Anne got the impression he had given up and now was just biding time, waiting to see how this played out. It was all part of his information gathering, Anne supposed, for that next big article, that next groundbreaking speech. What would he title it—*Scrambling for the Job? Racing to Stay Out of the Poorhouse?*

Mitch should have been disgusted, not ambivalent, not distracted. Anne's coworkers were lousing things up with their little "explanations" and "saves."

"There's more!" Anne insisted, taking another puff.

Sheila stopped her by standing as well, grabbing her cigarette, and putting it out.

On the conference room table. The room smelled like burning rubber.

"There, there, Anne," Sheila said. "Why don't you sit down, you poor girl? Ken's right. You've been under a lot of stress."

Sheila held onto her arm like a nurse leading an invalid.

"Anne's such a devoted employee that even on a stressful day like today she'd never let anything get between her and the goal, even if it means tremendous sacrifice. Just today, I couldn't help but overhear, Anne dear, that you were struggling with a personal crisis, with your brother getting ready to ship out, yet you still performed admirably."

Anne's face warmed, not just because Sheila was one-upping her, but because she was revealing something so personal—Jack's impending deployment.

Well, I guess I opened the door by talking about all those other personal things.

"Anne, you should have taken a personal-leave day today," Ken said, soft sympathy in his voice. He looked straight at Mitch. "No one with a heart would have held it against you."

Anne saw Mitch look at Ken… and at last, Anne saw Mitch's eyes change! The moment she'd been waiting for, when those baby blues morphed from icy lake to flickering inferno. But it was a fire of resentment that lit them now, and the flame wasn't directed at her. Despite his cultivated image of rock-hearted businessman with his gaze fixed unflinchingly on the bottom line, Mitch didn't like being shown up by another man, even in the sympathy department.

Uh-oh. Goal Number Three: Keep Ken off the list.

Anne rushed to turn Mitch's resentment toward her. "I tried to get in to see you several times today but, as usual, it was impossible."

"That's bullshit!" Mitch roared. "I saw you right before this meeting."

His anger poured over her like honey, warm and comfortable. That's what she wanted.

Ken just looked even more concerned, glancing from her to Mitch as if expecting compassion to zoom her way. When he saw none, his face clouded in disgust.

"Look, any fair evaluation has to take into account the pressure we've all been under. Anne especially."

Mitch scowled. "So you're making excuses for yourself, Montgomery?"

Ken straightened. "None whatsoever. I'm just saying that—"

No, Ken, don't. You don't understand… I'll explain it all soon.

"Stop it!" Anne yelled. "Ken is a marvelous employee and is only trying to be helpful, one of his finest qualities. Greg is stupendous at what he does and always happy doing it. And Sheila is the A-one, best-ever, top-notch Employee of the Century!" Anne moved behind Sheila and grabbed her arms. "Look at her. Just look at her, Mitch. She's the best. She never complains—"

"I complain all the time!" Sheila interjected.

"She always meets deadlines—"

"I'm late half the time!"

"She comes in early and stays late—"

"I pretend to stay late!"

"And you can't let her go because if you do…" Anne twirled her finger by her ear in the universal sign for crazy. Sheila sensed the movement and swiftly turned just in time to see the signal "… you'll regret it."

Shaking free of Anne's grip, Sheila leaned toward Mitch. "I. Am. Not. Crazy," she said. But Anne had to snicker because if there's anything that sounds crazy, it's someone saying they're not crazy in that tone of voice.

Desperate, Sheila looked as if she'd cry. Her face crumpled as she considered defeat. The more she protested, the loonier she'd sound, thus ensuring that Mitch would keep her, for fear of the lawsuit that would result should he let her go. Anne had won, by gum. She'd beat Sheila!

"Mr. Burnham," Sheila said in a soft, even voice. "Anne has some exciting news to share."

Uh-oh. Something was not right here.

Squaring her shoulders, Sheila sat with her hands folded in front of her. She was the old Sheila now, all serious and business-like, in control and on top of every project. Anne was afraid. Anne was very afraid.

"Today we all became aware of a glorious event in Anne's life. It was in the memo you obviously didn't read." Sheila smiled at Anne, but it was as empty of genuine joy as an inflatable snowman. "This afternoon Anne shared the tremendous gift of faith she feels has been bestowed on her through her recent conversion to the Church of the Divine Creator of the Universe and Beyond." She touched Anne lightly on the arm. "Go ahead, Anne, why don't you tell us all about it again?"

When Anne remained silent, Sheila filled the void. She explained the tenets of Anne's new religion—including the smoking—better than Anne could explain them herself. She talked about how "joyful" and "inspiring" it was to see Anne throw herself into this new faith with such abandon and such passion. She was sure, Sheila told Mitch, that this was not a "passing fancy" but a "deep-rooted conviction," and that Anne didn't take it lightly and would brook no attempts to convince her that her faith was, well, problematic for others in the office.

Oh no. Anne saw the path Sheila had just bulldozed as if it stretched like a strip-mined clear-cut through the Appalachian Trail. She knew where this was headed. Sheila was going to raise the specter of Anne going after Mitch for *religious* discrimination if he let her go. This had PR Disaster written all over it and Sheila knew it. Oh, Sheila was smart, she was. Very, very smart.

But Anne was smarter.

"That's all over," Anne said coldly. "Didn't I tell you? I found out the church's leader is a misogynist."

Robin sucked in her breath. "Oh my. Just like all those priests?"

Sheila was not deterred. "But it doesn't matter, Anne, that you gave it up. The important thing is that you did believe. And that you felt called to the faith *at a critical point in your employment at the Burnham Group.*" Sheila looked at Mitch as she said this. "So Mitch could never let you go—not knowing that it could be perceived as a slap in the face against your religious beliefs, against, why, anyone's religious beliefs. It's a matter of principle."

Grrrrr.

"Whatever my beliefs are, or were, that doesn't alter the fact that you are seeing a shrink."

Eyes closed to thin lines, Sheila glowered at Anne. "And you are a religious fanatic."

"Maniac."

"Zealot."

"Stop it!" Mitch said. He looked at Sheila, then at Anne, as if they were two naughty daughters. "This is enough about you two." He looked at his watch, then at Ken. Sighing, he continued, "Back to you, Montgomery. What do you think your problem areas are?"

In a flash, the spotlight was yanked from the two women and zoomed onto Ken. Surprised to be called on so soon after the performances that had gone before, Ken fumbled. "I… I'm not sure… I don't like to take risks." He shrugged, as if disinterested. "I think I meet deadlines. I try my best. I guess… I guess sometimes my energy level is not as high as it should be." He held a hand up as if to say, "Okay, there's a flaw, are you happy?"

To this, Mitch nodded enthusiastically. "Exactly," he said, and it took several seconds for Anne to realize that there was a wee bit too much affirmation in that word. "Sometimes I wonder if your heart is really in it, Ken. What say you, Greg?" Mitch looked over at Greg who was studying a brochure as if seeing it for the first time. After an instant, the young man looked up, searched his memory for the question, retrieved it, was happy he remembered, and smiled.

"Yeah," Greg said. "Sometimes Ken is kind of down."

"Down?" Ken's voice was incredulous, as well it should have been. "Maybe today, sure. But today was different because of this goofy exercise. Everyone was on edge and mistakes were made—mistakes I took it upon myself to correct."

What? Ken corrected mistakes? Oh no. Oh yes. Oh crap.

"Well, Ken, the whole point of today was to see how we all worked under pressure," Mitch said, irritated again. Ken was getting under his skin.

Something was wrong here. The only "discouraging word" being directed at an employee was now being directed at Ken. But Ken was the innocent. Ken should not be showing up on Mitch's "you're fired" screen at all. If anyone should have been there well before this exercise, it should have been Greg. And Anne and Sheila had both taken care to sing his praises to protect him. Had they not done enough for Ken? Frantic, Anne slid back down into her seat and leaned into the table.

"Mitch, Ken is a professional. The rest of us are zygotes," Anne said, spreading her arm to include Greg and Sheila. Sheila nodded. She got it. Greg just pouted, bewilderment on his face. "Malingers, ne'er-do-wells, brownnosers, slackers, you name it, we've done it. Ken is innocent!"

Sheila slammed the table with her hand in agreement. "Ken's an angel. Blame me for the bad coffee. I made it."

"No you didn't," Anne said, turning to her. "I made it this afternoon."

"I made another pot," Sheila said.

"Psycho!" Anne hissed.

"Missionary!"

"You're both crazy!" Robin chimed in.

"We're not talking about bad coffee here," Mitch said, the flat hint of condescension coloring his voice. "We're talking about who deserves to stay and who doesn't."

"Ken deserves it," Sheila interjected.

"Amen," Anne shouted, immediately regretting the religious connotation.

"Hallelujah," Greg chipped in, glad to play along.

Mitch sighed. "Okay, okay. Let's move on. This is taking too much time."

"He has an appointment," Robin chimed in, looking at her watch.

Mitch asked them to list each other's assets but since he'd heard more than enough from Sheila and Anne, he focused on the men. Ken praised each of them, admitting he knew little about Greg's work except that it… was there.

Greg's sputtered through some "you knows" and "likes" before hitting on his formula: Ken is da bomb, Sheila is straight, and Anne is combustible.

Afraid Greg wasn't doing enough to help himself, Anne grabbed the spotlight again. She looked at them all and announced in stentorian tones, "Every single person at this table deserves to retain their job except me." She let it linger in the air just in case Mitch missed the point. "They are all devoted to the Burnham Group. They follow the rules. They do their work on time. They're punctual and neat and good at what they do. And they're honest. They all deserve—"

"—to stay except me," Sheila interjected. She moved forward, her hands together as if in prayer. "Let me go. I don't deserve to be here. I'm awful, I suck, my work is fucked up, I'm a bitch, I treat everyone like bastards, I don't give a shit."

"Enough with the cursing already," Robin said. "It doesn't sound natural, for crying out loud."

"Sheila's wrong," Anne said, taking her cue and going for the direct approach. "I deserve it. I deserve to be let go. Not her. Not Greg. And certainly not Ken."

"No, Mitch," Sheila said, "fire *me.*"

"No, me."

"Me."

"Me!"

"Me!"

"Me! Me! *Me!*" A sobbing shout shot from Anne's mouth. "For the love of God, Mitch, fire *me!* You can't let Sheila go—not when you know that the two of you at one time were—"

Sheila gasped.

"Anne," Mitch began. "I hardly think that's fair."

Fair? Mitch Burnham was going to tell Anne what wasn't fair? A man who took and discarded lovers as if trading in cars? A man who fooled the world with psychobabble business advice? A man who used a marriage proposal as a publicity stunt? And as for Sheila, she'd revealed something personal about Anne—her brother's deployment. Hadn't that nullified their personal code of honor?

Ash white, Sheila bolted up. "I quit!" she shouted. Her voice shook as she continued. "I've taken a new job. I was just trying to get the severance pay. I…" She trailed off, sucked in her lower lip, looked at Anne with a glance that screamed "traitor," and left the room.

Anne needed the shredder. She'd hurt a good woman. What in the hell was the matter with her?

Robin's low, gravelly voice filled the void. "I wouldn't be throwing any stones at glass houses, Anne."

The room fell silent. Mitch looked to the door where Sheila had left and turned back again, shaking his head. Slowly, he closed the folders and put them away in the leather portfolio. Taking her cue from him, Robin capped her pen and sat primly, hands one over the other, waiting for his verdict.

He cleared his throat. He sighed. He placed his hands together, steeple style.

A defeated sigh escaped Anne's lips as well. He was doing his bad-news routine. What did this tell her? It told her that this decision was preordained, that whoever was being let go had probably been on the black list this morning when he'd called them all in, and that only a spectacular performance or a devastating one would have altered the scenario. The bastard. The pompous, manipulative, conniving bastard. Something inside Anne was weeping. Something inside her felt shredded.

"I know this has been a difficult day," Mitch said slowly. "And, to be honest, a lot of my decision isn't based on performance as much as it is on company needs. When I gave you this challenge, I wanted to see how you'd perform under pressure." So Anne had been right—this was just a lab experiment he'd write up and broadcast to the world. It might even get him another book deal. It might put him on top again. What a moron she had been. No, a guinea pig.

"Some of you performed admirably," he was saying. Then, at Anne, "And some less so." Then, at Greg, "And some the same as always."

"I am many things," he continued. "But I am not a fool." He paused to let this pronouncement sink in. "Any games that went on today only confirm that I have a clever and creative staff working under me. And all I need to do is channel that creative energy into our objectives."

He straightened. "The communications office has some redundancy in it. Some skills that are duplicated when the tasks don't require two staffers with those skill sets. So when I thought of making a cut, my first thought was in fixing that redundancy."

Redundancy. Anne was redundant with Sheila, but Sheila had just quit.

Anne was not really there. She had left this scene. She felt Ken glance at her occasionally. What must he be thinking? He must have known what was going on, what Anne had been about to say and what Robin had meant with her "glass houses" comment. Forget about explaining her wacky behavior to him. Now she'd have to explain this.

"I must admit," Mitch went on, "that initially it was very painful to consider this particular cut. This employee is valuable, has done superior work, and is a capable worker. But today's exercise has helped me understand cutting this position is the right way to go because this particular employee performed at sub-par all day. Missed deadlines. Hurried work. Long lunch. Extended absences from the desk."

This could be Anne. There could still be hope. Somehow, though, she wasn't feeling the victorious excitement she'd expected at this moment. She just wanted to get it over with, collect her check, make lengthy and complicated explanations to Ken, and leave.

"So at the end of the day, the company's needs and this person's performance added up to the same conclusion." He scanned them one by one, his hand raising ever so slowly, the index finger pointing, pointing, pointing…

"Ken Montgomery, you're fired."

Snow in August couldn't have shocked Anne more. Of all the people Mitch could let go, Ken was always the least likely. He was their only graphic designer. Something was fishy here, something Anne didn't know, that Sheila didn't know…

"What?!" Anne breathed out. Ken gripped the sides of his chair, stunned and speechless.

"It's unfair." Anne whimpered. "I was working hard for it! I deserve it."

"I knew it," Robin said under her breath.

"Is there a hidden camera in here?" Greg asked, looking around.

Ken slowly rose. He stretched forward and shook Mitch's hand.

"Thanks. I appreciate your taking me on when you did." And with quiet dignity, he left the room. They watched him go, his proud straight back a silent rebuke to the rest of them. Anne felt like a child, a bad child who deserved to stand in the corner.

Mitch stood, followed by Robin. She scooped up the folders and he put a pen in his jacket pocket.

"Wait, wait!" Anne cried before he could turn to leave. "I don't understand. Why Ken? He's our only graphic designer! Why not me? Or Sheila?"

Mitch smiled. "Greg does design work, too," Mitch said simply. "And we can't afford two on staff. It's a redundancy, like I said."

"Greg doesn't do squat!" Anne responded. Greg, to his credit, was nodding in agreement. "I mean, he's nice, he's creative, but he's not—"

"Good at work," Greg added seriously.

Mitch looked at Greg as if he were a big dog constantly getting in the way. "He came here with a very good recommendation," he said darkly. "From Calvin Theopoulus, his uncle."

"Oh yeah," Greg said.

So that was it. It all made sense now. If Mitch had fired Cal's nephew, he'd have had all hell to pay.

"But still, Mitch, what about me? I..." Pushing her chair in, Anne followed him toward the door. "I need to talk to you. Alone."

Mitch sighed heavily, tired of this scene. "In my office. I have about five minutes."

Chapter 21

From Mitch Burnham's book, *Use It or Lose It:*
> *Life isn't fair. Why should you expect the workplace to be any different? You want your employees to give their best? Pay them well and then keep them guessing.*

6:42 p.m.

"WHAT?" MITCH'S VOICE BARKED out. He threw folders on his desk and didn't even look at Anne.

"I just want to tell you that I… I'm leaving, too. Like Sheila."

He took off his Nehru jacket and went to the door. "Robin, can you send this to the cleaner?" In a few seconds, she was at the door taking the coat from him.

"I've accepted a job at St. Bartholomew's Children's Hospital." Anne stood in front of his desk, but he kept moving around. "In San Francisco."

He opened the door to his executive washroom and turned on the water. Quickly, he splashed his face, then grabbed his toothbrush and began brushing.

"Did you hear me?" Anne asked him.

He nodded his head, toothpaste foam oozing out of the corners of his mouth.

"In six weeks," she said.

He nodded again, scrutinized himself in the mirror, and wiped his face with a towel.

"I figured." He walked back in the room and grabbed a black blazer from a closet in the corner.

"What do you mean you figured?"

As he shrugged into his jacket, he didn't look at Anne. "You heard me in there. I'm no fool." He pulled the cuffs of his shirt down and out of the jacket sleeve. "Although at first I thought maybe…" He smiled and shook his head.

"Maybe what?" Her heart beat fast and her face warmed.

He looked straight at Anne. "I thought for a little while you were, you know, rattled by the engagement news."

The arrogant…

"You what?!" She laughed, but it didn't cover her embarrassment. The engagement news had rattled her, but not for the reasons he assumed, not because she was in any way still in love with him. No, it had bothered her because she couldn't stand the thought that she once *had* been in love with this pompous jerk. What did that say about her?

Mitch went back to the washroom and combed his hair. He changed the subject. "You can't leave. I was counting on you to supervise Greg." He pointed the comb in the direction of Greg's office. "And with Sheila going…"

"Listen, if you think for one second that your engagement act bothered me—well, you have that all wrong." Damned if she would let Mitch think he was even close to being right on that score. Anne wagged a finger at him. "That stunt wasn't romance. It was commerce," she said, repeating Ken's earlier words.

"I'll double your salary," he said softly, ignoring her comments while he squirted hair gel into his palms and worked it through his gray locks.

"What?"

"You heard me. I'll double it. If Sheila's going, I have the money. Another redundancy gone." He turned to her and smiled. "You know I've always thought you were invaluable."

Double the salary—that was hard to say no to. Maybe she should consider it… *No, no, stop it! Don't be sucked in!*

It was so easy to say yes to Mitch. The tone of his voice could ooze reasonableness. How could something so phony seem so genuine? She stared at his eyes, looking for something to bring her back to reality. Those bright eyes, devoid of fully realized emotion, only capable of telegraphing primal needs. It didn't matter who was standing here. He would have said the same thing to them.

"I don't think you view anyone as invaluable," Anne said.

He stiffened as if tapped by a hot poker. "Oh no," he said. "You were more than rattled by the engagement, weren't you?" He came over to her and put his hands on her shoulders, which only made her skin crawl and her temperature rise.

"Anne," he said softly into her hair, breathing deeply. "You were so special to me. I'll never forget you." His scent teased her, an understated piney fragrance, something from the soap he used, a special blend, something mixed with thyme and rosemary from an expensive French bath shop in Georgetown. Now it made her want to gag. How could she have loved… this? "You made those months bearable, when I thought I'd never recover from Glynda, when—"

"Stop it!" She pushed him away, anger clouding her vision. "I didn't help you recover from Glynda. That was Sheila. I was the one you were with when you were still legally married!" Good Lord—the man was an absolute monster. He should come with warning labels!

He looked confused—he was trying to remember, sorting the dates all out, disappointed with himself that he hadn't kept his lovers straight!

She was numb with rage. She wanted to simultaneously run from the room and kill him. What had ever made her think he was worthy of her?

He was undeterred. He took her rejection and correction in

stride and moved behind his desk where he retrieved his car keys from a corner.

"More vacation," he said, his voice business-like. "Bigger contribution to your 401(k)."

"I don't have a 401(k) plan."

"Then we'll start one."

"I don't want—"

"You can set your own hours. Flex time. Some work from home if you'd like. You still have that apartment in Kensington?"

"Crystal City." Kensington was probably where Sheila lived.

"Anne, you must know you're the most valuable member of the communications team." He said it with a hint of disdain, probably to cover his earlier gaffe in confusing her with Sheila in his March of Lovers Past. He paused, keys in hand, to look at her, head tilted up, smile teasing his lips. "Your ability to pick up the skill set to work here after previously handling…" He waved the air.

"Art," she spat out, disgusted.

"It impressed me. Really impressed me. You're bright. Talented. Creative. Artistic." He said this last word with a sense of pride, now that he was remembering her background. "When I recruited you, I saw all those things, and I encouraged them, shaped them, took you from starry-eyed dreamer to goal-oriented PR specialist. That should count for something."

She got it. He was trying to make her feel guilty. *Sorry, Mitch. My give-a-damn's busted as far as you're concerned.* She remained silent.

"Just think about it, Anne. Don't make any snap decisions. Think about it." With that, he headed for the door. "I have to go. But you sleep on it and let me know in the morning, okay? And if this other place—"

"St. Bartholomew's."

"St. Bartholomew's—if they're offering you more than what's on the table, we can negotiate." He stopped at the door and half turned toward her. "Look, I know you're upset. I don't want you doing anything rash, throwing all this away," he said, gesturing toward the office, "just because you're a little ruffled by today's events."

He left. Anne heard him giving Robin some last-minute instructions and then his voice was there no more.

6:48 p.m.

"There are boxes in the supply closet," Sheila said to Ken. She was packing up her things in one. Numbly, he followed her lead and found one for his few personal items. Back at his desk, he placed a mug, drawing pencils, a calendar, and other odds and ends in the box. What had just happened? Anne and Sheila both had deliberately been making mistakes. Anne hadn't been distracted by this crazy day—or her attraction to him—she'd been working a plan as wild as Mitch's own. He shook his head, trying to get his mind around it all, deflated that the few things he'd assumed today were completely false. He hadn't been safe. And Anne might not have been that into him, after all. *Way to go, Ken, letting your ego lead you on that one. For all you know, she could have been using you as part of her scheme.*

At least he'd had the good sense to tell Cyndi not to move ahead with the Georgetown storefront, he thought. He hadn't screwed up on that assumption.

He stopped and stared. There was something else gnawing a hole in his heart and mind—the implication that Anne had had a thing with Mitch. Sympathy and anger burned simultaneously. Mitch? He was a charlatan! A poseur!

A... successful millionaire. A doer, not a dreamer. A man of action.

Action—what had Anne said in the meeting? Oh yes, she'd been "working hard for it," for the layoff. Despite his disappointment, Ken admired Anne for trying to trick Mitch. It took guts. But why did she want the layoff? Was she pursuing some dream, like he was?

If so, she'd had the willpower to go after it full bore today, no matter what the consequences. She'd taken a risk.

"Damn," he muttered under his breath as he resumed packing. He went through desk drawers. He sat at his computer, scouring programs for any personal items he might have left, emailing himself files of designs he wanted to keep for his portfolio. He grabbed an accordion-style folder from a bottom drawer full of printed copies of items he'd designed. His hand brushed his leather case as he did so. He couldn't help himself. He pulled out the drawing of Anne. Who was she really?

He heard Sheila on the phone, talking to somebody about starting her job earlier than she'd expected. Sheila had fallen for Mitch's line of crap as well, and she was no pushover. How did he do it? A hundred mysteries Ken would never solve. At least he could try to solve one: What job did Anne have lined up?

At that moment, Anne came around the corner from Mitch's office.

"I'm so sorry," she said, standing outside his cubicle. He didn't turn toward her. "I just don't understand it. You shouldn't be the one let go. It should be me."

"Don't worry about it," he said, not looking at Anne, afraid his disappointment would show.

Sheila sniffled. "I don't understand you, Anne. We had a deal."

"I'm sorry," Anne repeated to her. "I don't know what came over me."

Courage, Ken wanted to say.

"Blind ambition." Sheila threw items into her cardboard box. "I thought you were a better person than that. I thought you were…" She stopped and looked at Anne. Her eyes were red. "When I first came to work here, I thought you were a really cold fish. But today, I realized we could have been friends." She sighed. "My first assessment of you was accurate." She went back to packing.

That was harsh. Ken remembered their kiss. Anne was hardly a cold fish.

"I just don't know what came over me," Anne continued. "I was desperate. Desperate to get out of here."

Desperate, Ken thought. *Maybe that was what led to her impulsiveness with me.*

Sheila snorted. "You knew you were getting out of here! You have another job—three thousand miles away from this place!"

Three thousand miles away? Of course. California. Where she'd worked before, where she'd gone to school. She knew she was moving far away and yet she'd...

What? Led him on? *Get a grip. It was one kiss.*

One connection.

"I know that, but somehow it began to feel..." Anne struggled to find words. "It began to feel like more than just the severance pay. It began to feel like I had to do this to break free."

"Break free of Mitch, you mean." Sheila threw a mug in her box and Ken heard something crack.

"No, no, of this." Anne swept her hand around. "His business advice crap. His whole corporate gobbledygook. His adventure camps. His—"

"Not *his*, Anne. *Him.* You were trying to break free of *him.*" Sheila threw her purse on top of the box. "Don't think I don't know what that's like."

"No, no, that's not it. I can't stand the guy. He creeps me out. I don't know what I was thinking when, when..."

Anne noticed Ken's gaze and turned to him, her eyes wide with pleading.

"I really feel awful, Ken," Anne said. "I... maybe we can talk?"

"Where exactly are you moving, Anne?" He couldn't keep the accusatory tone from his voice.

"San Francisco."

"Something in the arts, I presume." San Francisco was a great arts town. At least she was going back to what she loved.

But she shook her head. "PR for a children's hospital. St. Bart's... St. Bartholomew's."

His eyes narrowed. Could Sheila be right—was Anne just trying to get as far away as possible from Mitch? Anne's eyes were wild with a new desperation. "Look, I'm going to go back and talk to Mitch about keeping you on. I'll tell him again everything I did—even the things I forgot to mention. Everything. There was the Annual Report copy, the ad, the books, the employee newsletter—" She started the list again.

"Hey, the newsletter was mine!" Sheila said. "I wondered why you told him you'd done that."

"Mitch thought it was mine," Anne murmured.

"So did I," Ken said. He snorted out a quick self-deprecating laugh.

Both Sheila and Anne did an about-face toward Ken. Sheila spoke first.

"How'd you know about that?"

"I saw it," he said. The corner of his mouth twisted up in an ironical smile. "And I fixed it."

"That's right. You said that in the meeting," said Anne, remembering. "What else did you do? I could tell Mitch that's why you were away from your desk."

"The Annual Report President's Message. A few other things." Those seemed two ice ages away now. "Didn't really redo all of them. Just left him notes that I had them."

"My stuff, too?" Sheila asked.

No, he hadn't. He'd been intent on saving Anne. His silence answered Sheila's question.

"I'm sorry, Sheila," he mumbled. "I only caught a few things..."

But she wasn't listening. She threw in the last of her items and picked up her box. Tossing her hair over her shoulder, she stood as proudly as a cadet and turned to leave.

"I'm glad I'm out of here," she said to no one in particular.

"Sorry." Anne mumbled to the air behind her at the same time Ken muttered the word.

Sheila headed for the elevator. Anne rushed after her, her voice carrying back to Ken.

"I'd like to keep in touch. I'd like to hear how your new job is going. I'd like…"

He heard the elevator whoosh open and close again. Sheila must have left in stony silence. Ken felt sorry for both of them. And for himself. How humiliating to be laid off after only six months on the job. He should have gone for the gold like Anne and Sheila. Then it wouldn't smart so much.

He resumed his packing, methodically taking things out of the box and placing them back in again to fit more snugly—a mug, a pen set, some drafting tools, the files with samples, the Santa tie.

What to do now? Find a job, that was the first item on the agenda. He didn't want to be delving into his savings for living expenses. The severance pay wouldn't provide much cushion, despite Mitch's grand claims about how terrific it was. That reminded him—Mitch had said the fired employee could pick it up at the end of the day. He'd stop down to see Lenny on his way out. As he thought through these plans, Anne reappeared, the tinkle of the bells on her skirt announcing her arrival.

"Why'd you fix my stuff, Ken?" she asked softly. "Did you fix it because…"

No, no, he wasn't about to add unrequited attraction to his list of humiliations today. "You seemed distracted. I didn't want you in trouble because of it."

"Why didn't you just tell me when you saw the mistakes?" Anne asked. "Why didn't you just point them out?"

"I tried," he said "But you were always on the go. And it didn't take long to fix the problems." He wanted to leave but she persisted with the questioning.

"Was it because… did you feel… I mean… did our thing in the elevator?" She looked at him with puppy-dog eyes and he suspected she'd like to hear that yes, he did have a thing for her. *Sorry, Anne. I've got some pride. Don't feel like having my ego used for a punching bag any more than it already has been today.*

"If you want to know the truth, I thought you might be distracted partly because you decided to pursue *me*." He picked up the box and grabbed his leather portfolio.

Now her pleading stare turned to annoyance, warming her cheeks. "I had a thing for you?"

He shifted the weight of the box and began walking toward the elevator. She followed, calling after him. "You were the one secretly drawing pictures of me!"

He stopped, turned, and stared for a second. She'd looked at his portfolio. What had she been doing snooping through his things? Damn. He jammed the elevator button with his thumb.

"You were the one jumping me in the elevator," he said coldly.

"That was just… the… the buzz… from lunch!" she said, standing next to him, hands clenching at her sides.

His own hand slipped on the portfolio and it fell from his grasp. They both bent to pick it up and as they did so, their faces nearly collided. He smelled the faint odor of her musky perfume and brushed his hand over hers. He saw her eyelids lower, her head bend, and his own desire rushed so fast through his body that his breath trembled.

But he pulled away and stood as he thought of what she'd just said.

"Buzz from lunch. Right!" She was attracted to him for sure, but it was cold comfort. She was leaving, moving thousands of miles away. *Thanks, Anne.*

Recovering, she stood as well.

"Look, this was a stupid plan of mine. As stupid as Mitch's scheme in the first place. But if I had been better at it, I'd be going and you'd be staying. I'm sorry I wasn't better at being bad." She smiled. Just a little. That Mona Lisa grin.

It was enough to melt the corners at least of his ice-hot irritation. But not enough to stay.

The elevator dinged. He got on.

"We could stay in touch," she said.

"You're moving three thousand miles away."

"They have these things now—they're called phones… email… airplanes…"

The elevator closed as he shifted the box again. The movement triggered the Santa tie's ridiculous song. He zoomed downward to the electronic tune of a Christmas carol.

As soon as the doors closed, she missed him. She knew that, once he left this building, their chances of getting together decreased exponentially. She could call him, sure, but why would he want to invest time in her when she was moving, taking another job thousands of miles away? Why should he want to be with her when she'd withheld this information from him as he attempted to light a fire between them? She remembered his kiss, how warm and open it was, and how much she'd wanted to repeat it just now when they'd both bent to retrieve his portfolio.

"Loser," she said to herself in the empty hallway. He'd now seen her for who she was—a silly, selfish, shallow woman.

His sandalwood scent's mystery lingered faintly over the petroleum-product smell of office carpet and furniture. Somewhere in an unseen office, a phone chirped and stopped. She stood in front of the closed elevators waiting for something to happen, for a door to open and someone to walk off who could tell her what to do.

She couldn't breathe. She couldn't think. She couldn't anything. She stood there for what seemed like an hour. In reality only a minute passed by.

What was she going to do?

It should have been clear. When she'd stood in Mitch's office, she should have been able to say, "Eff You, Mitch Burnham, take this job and shove it." *I should I should I should* but—but twice her salary? More vacation? It started to suck her in again. She should look at it dispassionately, as if someone besides Mitch had made the offer. Would she be so quick to turn it down then?

She could stay in the area, see Mom more—keep her company while Jack was away, see her sister-in-law, and get to know her nephew better. She could even try to reconnect with Ken now that they'd skipped all that glow-of-courtship stuff and gotten right down to the disillusionment and disappointment part of a relationship. That was so much more efficient—he'd thank her for it eventually, right?

She shook her head to clear it and walked back to her cubicle.

She had misjudged everyone and everything. She'd thought Mitch was a dunderhead, when he had been on to her and Sheila all along. He was no fool, he'd said. And he was right. He was no fool even if he was a slime and a cad and a scoundrel. It was only a matter of time before Kathie-Rose was bawling her eyes out on *Dr. Phil,* telling the world what a cheating louse she'd married.

Anne had thought Ken was timid when he was good-hearted. She had thought Sheila was a Burnham drone when she was…

Ohmygod. When she was just like Anne!

The thought ignited a panic alarm in Anne's brain as she did a flashback to her years at Burnham. She hadn't been a drone, had she? People hadn't seen her that way. No, they couldn't have! She started a mental catalog of differences between Sheila and herself. Sheila was buttoned-down and straitlaced, nose to the grindstone and humorless. Whereas Anne was funny and sarcastic and clever and witty and…

So was Sheila!

But Anne was loyal and hardworking and…

So was Sheila!

Okay, but Anne was adrift and empty and needy and had had an affair with…

Just. Like. Sheila!!!!!! Ohmygod.

No, no… but Sheila wasn't artistic. Anne had been an art major. Sheila had gone to Tufts, she'd said. She'd majored in political science. So they were both working outside their fields. Only Sheila would soon be working in hers, taking a pay cut and a step down the career ladder just so she could start over. Finally, there was the difference between the two. Sheila was taking a chance. Anne was… not!

She felt like sobbing.

7:05 p.m.

Ken picked up his check from Lenny—probably made out that morning—and hailed a taxi. And to think he avoided taking his car into work to save on gas money. Lugging all this junk was too awkward for a subway ride. On the way home, he thought again of Anne's crazy courage in going after the layoff. He needed some of that bravado. He was too risk averse, dammit. Maybe getting let go from the Burnham Group was just the kind of kick in the pants he needed. If he wanted to be able to jump on the next opportunity that presented itself, he had to bite the bullet and ramp up his moneymaking capabilities. He knew how to do that. If it involved eating some crow, so be it.

His cell phone buzzed. He gave it a quick glance. Felicia. Good. Might as well take care of this right now.

❖ ❖ ❖

Anne's eyes blurred as she made her way to her car. She turned the CD player on full blast. No pop or country music right now. She needed *Sturm und Drang*. The Grieg piano concerto ripped and roared in the car, its crashing chords shutting out everything. She kept envisioning the day as if it was one of the many documents she'd shredded. She wished she could rid herself of its lingering bad taste and see its fine, confetti-like strips whirring through the blades of time.

The job in San Francisco was losing its sparkle. Must get it back. It was a children's hospital. It wouldn't be like the Burnham Group at all. Just because they used the Burnham techniques during orientation didn't mean they were the same. They couldn't be more different!

But maybe she should sacrifice that job, stay with Mom…

Uh-oh. Sacrifice as avoidance again. What had her brother said—she'd moved home from California because she was broke, not because she'd wanted to help out with Dad.

Well, you know what? He was right. She'd jumped at the chance to come home. She'd used Dad's illness to keep from confronting her miserable existence. She'd been going nowhere. She'd had no prospects. But she'd helped out once she'd arrived. She'd been there.

She was going crazy. Was there a mental health facility nearby? Perhaps she could drop in on her way home for a quick check.

She wished she knew what she wanted. Her father used to tell her that sometimes you don't know what you want until you end up somewhere you don't want to be. The key, he said, was to avoid that as much as possible, to think through what you like about your life and what you don't like, and where you want to be five years from now.

He told her that her senior year in college when he and Mom came out for graduation. At the time, she'd rolled her eyes and shrugged it off as just worn-out Dad advice, the kind of stuff parents feel obligated to tell you at big moments like a college commencement.

Now she wondered if it wasn't a more targeted message. He'd asked what she was planning on doing after graduation, and she'd told him about moving in with some other artist friends. She'd had her first temporary gallery gig in Carmel set up and she was excited about it, but she'd told him there was no guarantee it would lead to a permanent job. And it hadn't. And then he'd asked her if she wanted to move to New York or Los Angeles or even back to DC.

What an odd question, she'd thought at the time. She had said no, she was quite happy in Monterey; she'd enjoyed it there her four years in school. He said he thought there was probably a bigger art scene in bigger cities and then he'd given her that piece of advice.

He knew, of course, that she was just playing around, that she still wasn't quite serious about what she wanted to do, that she was drifting, waiting for a strong tide to push her one way or another. And darned if he hadn't been that tide pulling her back to DC in the end.

Traffic snarled to a stop and she looked out the window. She'd just crossed the glistening Potomac with the boxy, sterile Kennedy Center hugging its edge, the domes of important buildings in the distance, the shy, pale yellow green of eager trees ready to bloom dipping near the shore. Apartment buildings and condos rose around her and, at a crosswalk, a group of people hurried past.

They looked so full of purpose. And she felt as empty as the office when the elevator had closed on Ken Montgomery.

Chapter 22

From "I Told You So," an article by Mitch Burnham
in *Business Month* magazine:

> *Over and over I hear from managers who just don't
> get it. They listen to their employees. They give them special
> perks. How many times do I have to say it? Your employees
> aren't your best friends. You want a friend? Get a dog.*

7:55 p.m.

ANNE SAT IN LOUISE'S living room, and Louise was trying to
comfort Anne. She had talked a little about her husband at first
and Anne had provided the appropriate words of disdain and encouragement. But then Anne had ended up eating up all the time
with a description of her day, ending with the phone call from the
hospital human resources drone right before lunch. The women's
roles were reversed. Louise was offering Anne tea and sympathy,
when Anne had originally come to visit Louise as an errand of
friendly mercy.

"To be honest with you, Anne, I never understood the allure
of the St. Benedict's job." Louise handed her a cup of herbal tea
and went back to cleaning up the sheet music scattered around
the small room. She and Paul owned a rancher, and this room was
barely large enough to hold an upright piano angled in the corner, a
modest-sized sofa, a recliner, and a television. Bright plastic toys

were scattered on the wall-to-wall carpeting, and muted light glowed through the western-exposed picture window, creating a sense of miracles about to happen. Her children, Louise had explained when Anne arrived, were at a friend's house for a party. Paul was not coming home tonight.

Louise turned to the window, staring out over the suburban neighborhood. Dusky light blanched her already-pale skin to a translucent glow, and Anne wanted to tell her she was beautiful and she hoped she'd never ever doubted it. Louise wore a broomstick skirt of yellows and reds and a ruby T-shirt to match. Her frizzy hair was held off her face by a gold scarf of shifting hues. Louise was sometimes very unsure of her looks, with her long nose and pointy chin. But in this light, this painter's light, she was a Madonna, a saint, an aristocrat waiting to be captured on canvas.

"Your new job sounds similar to what you do now. And as long as you've been at the Burnham Group, you've complained about it," Louise explained, not looking at Anne.

"No, I haven't." And the jobs couldn't be more dissimilar. St. Bartholomew's cured kids.

Turning toward Anne, Louise smiled. "Yes you have. I can't remember the number of times you've said that you could do the work in your sleep, blah blah blah."

Blah blah blah? She was blah-blah-blahing Anne? Anne sat up, her face warming as she listened to the scold. She did remember telling Louise those things, but they were complaints born of frustration with Mitch, like referred pain that keeps you from realizing the true source of the irritation.

"When you told me about this new job, St. Benedict's—"

"St. Bartholomew's," Anne corrected her.

"—St. Bartholomew's, I figured you'd find the work interesting at first because it's new. But as I thought about it, well, it would probably be the same kind of work."

So Anne's friend had analyzed her job prospects for her? When had this occurred—as she served porridge to her toddler, or as she scoured the bathroom, or sat up waiting for Paul to come home?

"Not really," Anne said, suddenly feeling like she had to defend the job in San Francisco. Louise didn't know anything about communications work. She didn't realize how different venues meant different challenges.

Louise came over to the sofa and sat beside Anne. "Okay, tell me what you do at the Burnham Group."

Anne listed her duties, from media relations manager to publications guru to speech writer to employee communications liaison.

"Now tell me your duties at St. Bart's."

"Bartholomew's. They prefer St. Bartholomew's," Anne said, with condescension dripping from her voice. "And I know what you're getting at. But at St. Bart's... Bartholomew's... I will be handling important stuff, stuff that makes a difference in people's lives..." That's how she'd felt when she'd interviewed for the job. She remembered a quick burst of excitement at the thought of working in a building where lives were saved—children's lives. What could be more important?

"Like sending out a press release announcing the new chief of staff?"

Anne reddened. "Like..." And she stumbled, flipping through the mental file of possibilities. Yes, the press releases announcing new appointments, the Annual Report headaches, the brochures touting new and better services, the employee newsletter with its requisite cheery tone—they all paraded before her like a Burnham Group newsreel.

Louise read Anne's mind. "You'll just be typing more interesting things in your MS Word files. You won't actually be healing the kids."

Anne heaved a sigh. "What are you saying—I should just stay at Burnham and take the money Mitch offered me?"

"It's a lot of money, Anne." She looked at a crack in the wall near the window. "That's nothing to sneeze at, believe you me." Poor Louise. She was probably thinking of how she was going to make ends meet on some miserly child support check she'd be lucky to get every other month.

"It's not just the money." Anne shifted in her seat and put her tea on a coffee table scattered with magazines, coloring books, and paper airplanes. "It's my boss. I don't like... being around him anymore."

Louise's head moved back an inch. "Has he been coming on to you? That's illegal! You should get a lawyer. I could recommend one when I see one myself."

Anne had never told Louise about the Mitch affair. When Anne had been in the throes of it, she hadn't had a lot of contact with girlfriends. Mitch was the sun she'd orbited around. And there had been something sexy about keeping it secret.

Now it was just the sort of thing Louise would want to hear—a sad tale of a man betraying his wife *and* his mistress. A sort of misery-loves-company thing. And Anne was tired of lying so she did confess, skimming over the story, not filling in a lot of details and acting as remorseful as she felt.

Louise, however, had antennae sharpened by heartache, and she zoomed in with laser-like precision with her questions.

"So he was still married when this was going on?"

"Well, technically, yes."

"Technically?" Louise stood and went to the window again. Anne realized it was an automatic movement. She probably watched her children there, or looked for Paul returning from work.

"They were legally separated."

"And no children?"

"Well, one child. A girl." Anne didn't know why she threw that in. "He went back to her, to his wife," she explained. "But then he got divorced later. And now he's getting remarried."

Louise crossed her arms and stared at Anne. "So that's why you can't stay there? Because he's getting remarried?"

"No! I don't care about the new gal. Really, I don't!" How could she make that clear to everyone? She really didn't care about Mitch and Kathie-Rose. It felt good not to care about them. She'd just wanted Mitch to… hurt… today. As much as he'd hurt her. And that simply wasn't going to happen. Ever. It was a fool's errand. Mitch was no fool. But she was one if she expected anything like remorse from him. She was letting that go, and it felt good. "I can't stay there because he's a jerk and I'd go nuts." Anne explained how Sheila, too, fell under Mitch's spell and was moving on because she felt it was a humiliation to stay there. She left out the part where she'd nearly blurted out the news of Sheila's affair at the board meeting.

The Sheila story seemed to turn off Louise's judgment button. She was all about joining Anne's diss-fest of Mitch, now that she saw him as prime-cut gigolo, something a step beyond her own chuck-roast gigolo husband, Paul. As she went on about what a creep Mitch must be, though, Anne couldn't escape the feeling she was really talking about Paul, venting all the horrible things she couldn't bring herself to articulate about her husband because she had, after all, married the guy and had two children with him.

"All right," she said at last. "I see your point about not wanting to stay there. That puts the St. Bart's job in perspective."

"I thought you just told me the St. Bart's job was no good." Anne was starting to crave a cigarette. Damn, it had been a mistake to smoke today.

"Well yeah, if your current job was better. But your current job doesn't sound too hot."

"He *is* offering twice my current salary. I could get a bigger place, maybe even buy a condo or something, build up some equity." Anne snapped her fingers. "No, I know! I could save the extra money. Put it all in a money market or mutual fund or stocks or something. And retire in five years."

"Hardly likely. We took a hit when the market went bust a few years ago." She stopped, realizing she was using first-person plural. "Yeah, you could save the money. It would be a nice nest egg for one."

Anne mentally calculated what she could save in five years' time, but as soon as she thought "five years," she envisioned a prison sentence. She gagged. She couldn't do another five years working for Mitch Burnham. She just couldn't. Even if he were to drop off the face of the earth tomorrow and someone else ran the company, she still couldn't face it. Couldn't walk over that threshold and know that everyone—Robin, Lenny, Ken, Sue, the copy-machine guard dog, the human resources she-witch, and all the others—had probably had her pegged as a Mitch conquest for years now.

No, wait—Ken wouldn't be there. That seemed to make it worse, not better.

She heard the distant sound of children's laughter and Louise moved to the open door. Her kids were coming home. She swung wide the screen door and bent forward to greet them. Anne heard a woman's voice calling to Louise.

"I thought I'd walk them home with mine, Lou," she said amiably.

"Thanks, Ginger!" Louise's eyes grew wide and her mouth opened into a joyful smile as two sweaty, tired children toddled into the house holding balloons and party bags. "Now what do you have there? Did Kyle like her presents?"

They nodded and giggled and babbled in a strange, lispy language Anne had trouble understanding. But Louise got it just fine. She knelt at the door, wiping chocolate from her son's mouth and reclipping a barrette in her daughter's hair, listening with rapt attention to their gibberish. She looked like those people Anne had passed in the crosswalk—all filled with purpose and meaning. Even in the midst of heartbreak she had the mojo that Anne seemed to lack.

Louise told Anne to wait a second and led the kids into the bathroom down the hall where Anne could hear her washing faces and hands and congratulating her son—*what a big boy you are!*—after the toilet flushed.

While she waited, Anne looked around at the living room. It was more Louise's space than Paul's. Her sense of beauty permeated the room. Dried flowers hung on a wall near the front door. An antique plate was propped up on a shelf above the piano. A framed photograph of Louise dancing hung between living and dining rooms. It was such a humble place, but it was Louise's. Maybe she'd be able to keep it.

"Have you thought of alimony?" Anne asked when her friend returned.

Louise burst out laughing, the quick staccato of her chuckle echoing in the room and lifting Anne's spirits. "Spousal support is what it's called these days. And I doubt Paul will have much to spare." She sat on the sofa and nodded toward the hall. "They're in their rooms coloring. But they're so jazzed on sugar right now, I doubt we'll be able to talk much longer without interruption." Already Anne heard a stream of babble coming from one of the rooms, growing louder by the second.

"What are you going to do?"

Sipping her own mug of tea, Louise shrugged. "I'll get by. I'll find a cheaper place. Probably get a part-time job. I hear Nordstrom is hiring for the summer."

"But you've put a lot into this place," Anne said. Her heart was breaking for her even as she remained calm. "Maybe I could help. After all, if I keep my job and get all that extra money… I could loan you some until you get on your feet."

Louise nearly spit out her tea laughing. "Get on my feet? That won't be until they're in college." She nodded again toward the kids' rooms and then patted Anne's knee. "Besides, I'm not going to let you use me as an excuse to stay at Burnham. Uh-uh. Find another patsy."

"How about your parents? Can they help you?" Anne knew they lived somewhere in rural Virginia now, a sparsely populated area that Louise enjoyed visiting.

She shook her head fiercely at this suggestion. "I'd hate that." Finishing her tea, she stood and took the cups into the kitchen. It was clear that Anne should leave soon. Louise stood by the piano when she returned, leaning on its top edge. "They'd want me to move back home. That's how they'd offer to help. They don't have a lot of money to spare anyway ever since they bought their new place."

Anne stood. "Would that be so bad—moving back home? It could be a great place to raise your kids, out in the country, away from the crowds. Didn't you tell me you were concerned about the schools around here?"

Louise smiled. "Yeah. Paul would bring home some horror stories."

"You could get them away from that. You could be a big fish in a small pond, Lou. Start a dancing class. Get some part-time work." Anne grabbed her purse and walked toward the door.

"But living with my parents…" Louise gave a mock shudder. "Not that they're monsters, mind you. It's just I'm grown-up now and they'll still treat me like a kid. You know what it's like."

Yeah, in a different way Anne did. Her mother didn't treat her like a kid. She wished Anne wasn't like one anymore.

"But didn't you tell me they have some sort of apartment over their garage? And they were kidding you about having the grandkids come and stay there when they got older?"

"Anne, that apartment is unfinished. And I think they *were* half-joking." Louise took her arm off the piano's ledge. "I can't believe you're seriously urging me to move back in with my parents."

"It's just an idea. Don't push it away. It could help you save money. Be home with the kids. And if you fixed up that apartment, you'd have a space all your own. That's not bad, Lou." Anne was making it sound so good, in fact, that she wondered if Louise's parents would let her use it instead.

"It's only big enough for one person," Louise said. "Well, maybe two if you divide the front room…" She was thinking about it.

"You could put the kids in there. In the small room."

"Listen to you," she laughed. "You haven't even seen it and you're redesigning it for me!"

Turning toward the door, Anne opened her purse to grab her car keys. There she saw the gold foil–wrapped box—the gift she'd bought for Louise while shopping at Union Station. She'd forgotten! Sheepishly, she handed it to her.

"I got this for you," Anne said, "to cheer you up." She walked over and handed it to Louise.

Eyes twinkling, Louise took the gift. Ripping open the box with the unabashed glee of a child, she pulled the filigreed medallion from its cottony cushion, her face lighting up in a broad smile.

"Anne, I love it! I saw something like this a week ago but couldn't afford…" She stopped, on the verge of tears, and gave Anne a big hug. "It's perfect. And perfectly timed."

At last, Anne had done something right today, something that put her talent at the service of compassion. It felt so good, she wanted to thank Louise. Damn, she started to tear up as well.

"I'll call you," Anne said. Louise nodded and pushed a strand of hair from her face, the light behind her already moving to shadow, the room now bathed in milky gray, as cool and restful as Louise's soul.

"Here you go." Wendell Montgomery handed his nephew Ken a scotch and water. Ken had sped up Interstate 95 rehearsing in his mind how he'd ask his father for his job back. Every time he thought of his humble-pie speech, though, it sounded in his head as if he were really saying, "You were right, Dad. I'm a loser."

At least he'd had the satisfaction of blowing Felicia off for good. When she'd called to ask why he was late for their cocktail meeting, he'd revealed he knew Arthur Howard wouldn't be there, and he would be working this problem on his own. She'd sputtered and simpered and tried to make it sound like she had been trying to reach him, but he knew she was blowing smoke and he didn't stay on the line. Chapter closed.

The conversation with Felicia had unexpectedly settled something else, though. He'd fallen for her at one point in his life. Why should it then bother him that a woman like Anne had fallen for Mitch? If she'd been a sucker for the powerful boss, so had he.

He accepted the scotch from his uncle and took a long sip. He needn't have worried about facing his father. His dad was in New York on business.

"So you really want to come back to work at the firm?" Wendell Montgomery leaned against the edge of his oak-carved desk, his own drink in one hand. The office whispered wealth and power in ways Mitch Burnham's never could. Muted colors, antique rug, leather chairs, and floor-to-ceiling bookshelves filled not with tomes on how to "use it or lose it," but biographies of great leaders, histories, photo books of old Baltimore—all of this created a comfortable hum of importance, making the Burnham Group feel like a cheap knockoff in comparison.

"Well, I kind of need a job…" That didn't sound exactly right. Oh hell, nothing would. Ken launched into an explanation that was as brutally frank as it was ridiculous. When he described Mitch's one-day-to-save-yourself exercise, Wendell let out a snort of disgust and shook his head. But, as was typical in the Montgomery family, he refrained from spending too much time discussing something that didn't deserve attention.

"You were doing their graphic design work?" he asked instead.

"Yes. Advertising layouts, annual reports, and more." Ken took another sip. "I have a strong portfolio."

"I can check with our communications folks to see about openings. I'm sure your father would be happy to make a space for you."

"Actually, I was hoping to come back into the financial side of things." Ken looked up at his uncle with a half smile. "More money."

Wendell walked to the windows overlooking Baltimore's glittering harbor. He stood for a few seconds admiring the view before responding. That was another Montgomery trait, Ken realized—the long pause.

"Are you experiencing some difficulties?"

Ken laughed. "No, no. I'm fine. No debts to speak of. I've just been saving money at a prodigious rate and would like to continue." He then spilled out his dreams, including a description of the storefront in Georgetown he'd seen that day, interrupted by pithy questions from his uncle at various points during the story. He spoke so long that the umber glow of dusk had faded from the sky by the time he was done. His uncle turned on his desk lamp and sat in a chair opposite his nephew, placing his empty glass on a table beside him.

"I don't understand why you don't just pursue that plan," he told Ken, referring to the gallery proposal that Ken cherished. "It sounds like you've found exactly the right spot. And, frankly, if your heart isn't in a job here, it's not a good idea to take on clients…"

Now it was Ken's turn to stand. He couldn't hide his frustration. "I was good when I was here. And I'm more focused now. Besides, the timing isn't right for the gallery! I don't have the money I need to safely attack the plan."

"So we'll be your temporary employment agency?" There was amusement, not irritation in his uncle's voice.

"I… I'll be completely committed while I work here. You can count on it."

His uncle paused, thinking. Finally, he spoke again.

"Why not ask your father for help?"

Ken ran his fingers through his hair. He didn't feel like getting into that.

There was no need. His uncle broached it for him.

"Look, Ken, I think you harbor some misunderstandings about your father. He supports you—"

"—as long as I do what he wants," Ken spit out, regretting immediately how bitter it sounded.

"That's unfair." Wendell stood and both men looked at the view, as the lights of the city sparkled on in the shadowy dusk. "What your father wants is for you to go after what *you* want."

"Then why did he lure me into the firm after college?"

"He didn't 'lure' you." Wendell chuckled. "He offered you a job when it was apparent you had no other plans. He just didn't want you drifting."

Ken sighed. Drifting—that's what he was doing now. He put his hands in his pockets and rocked on his heels. "Dad thinks all this art stuff is nothing more than play. Not real work. Not like the work he does."

Wendell's voice held an edge. "If it's not just play, then prove it, man. Stop acting as if it is!"

Surprised, Ken turned to his normally reserved uncle, seeing a steely sense of injustice in his eyes.

He thinks I'm being too hard on Dad. Am I?

To soften his hard words, Wendell put his hand on his nephew's arm.

"What I mean is your father is proud of you. He wants to see you succeed at whatever you choose as your ultimate career path. He would happily support this plan you've talked about, Ken. It's a solid business investment. You've worked it all out. Your reluctance to move forward without the necessary capital is proof of your sense of responsibility and maturity." He pulled away and stared at the view. "And there's another thing—you know we'd be happy to take you back on board, especially with a commitment to focus entirely on the job. But if you came back, I think your father would prefer it to be… permanent. In other words, he'd be disappointed to see you jump again to something else, instead of settling in and letting him mentor you."

"He told you that?"

"No. These are my assumptions."

Assumptions or not, Ken knew they were true. How selfish he was, thinking that going back to work for Montgomery Financial would be his grudging gift to them. Why should they want an employee whose heart wasn't really in the job? Damn.

"Don't misunderstand me, Ken. We'd take you back in a heartbeat. Your father would be extremely happy, I'm sure."

Happy like a father greeting the return of the prodigal son. But this son had no intention of staying. Once he had enough cash, Ken would be leaving once again. That wasn't fair. His father didn't deserve that.

Ken knew there was a limit to what his uncle would reveal about his father's opinions of his son. But in that instant, Ken saw his father's reactions and comments through a different filter. No longer did he see them as judgmental and critical. They were merely the sometimes less-than-subtle nudgings of a loving parent, pushing Ken to get on with things, to move from dilettante to professional. To stop dreaming. To start doing.

"Look," Wendell said. "Why don't you email me your business plan? I'll look it over, maybe offer some advice, possibly come up with terms of a loan…" He went on to detail the structure of such a deal, percentage rates, payback schedules, and more. When he was finished, he said, "Well, what do you think?"

Now it was Ken's turn to pause. But not for long.

"I think it sounds great." Ken shook his uncle's hand. "But if I'm sharing my plans, I should do it with Dad."

8:45 p.m.

Anne was drained and dead tired, but she headed over to her mom's after leaving Louise's house and did exactly as Jack had predicted— she mooched a meal.

Her mother had pulled out leftover meatloaf and potatoes for her daughter. Anne's skirt was feeling mighty tight by the time she was finished.

"I can't believe you wore that to work," Mrs. Wyatt said, leaning against the kitchen counter. She was already in her bathrobe, ready for an early bedtime.

"I didn't start the day in it."

"Well, I like it. Makes you look softer," Anne's mother said, wiping a smudge from the edge of the sink. The kitchen was spotless. Ever since Anne had gone away to college, her mother had amped up her cleaning. No more clutter anywhere. Not a stray crumb to be seen, not a plate nor pot out of place.

"So, did you hand in your notice?"

Anne didn't spill the whole story to her mother, but she did tell her of her own efforts to get the ax and they shared a few good belly laughs over it. Her mother clucked her tongue when Anne told her Ken was the one who drew the short straw.

"He looked like a nice fellow."

"You would say that about anyone I was out with short of a lunatic."

She turned and started wiping the already-spotless counter with a damp washcloth. "Well, you have Rob anyway."

"Yeah, thanks for mentioning him when I was out with Ken." Anne scraped her plate and put it in the dishwasher.

"So you *were* out on a date with this Ken?"

Yes. No. Not that it mattered. So Anne changed the subject from Ken back to Rob, telling her mother how he was moving overseas and it suddenly felt so comfortable in her bright kitchen and Anne was so tired of keeping things bottled up in her chest that she confided in her mother her misgivings about the move to San Francisco. She even started to cry.

Yes, she ended up crying with her mother's arm around her shoulders, a little girl again coming home with a boo-boo for Mommy to kiss and make better. And damned if Anne didn't feel better, as if she had been carrying the weight of everything on her slim shoulders and it could leave her now that she'd confessed to Mom. Anne didn't tell her about Mitch—there were some worries she didn't want *her* to be burdened with—but she did tell her how confused she was because she didn't want to go back to the Burnham Group and she didn't want to leave the area now that Jack was shipping out. She hadn't intended to cry, hadn't even felt it coming, but as soon as she'd started telling her mother about what Louise had said, how the St. Bart's job was just different stuff in her MS Word file, Anne gave in to that inner child that needed comforting.

"Aw, honey, you know I'll be fine. You can visit me," her mother said, stroking Anne's short hair. "And I'll come see you too." She sat next to Anne and folded her hands over her daughter's.

"It isn't just that," Anne said, confused, wishing her father were there to give her some of that advice she'd never bothered to listen to. She resolved to scour her memory that very evening for every pearl of wisdom he'd ever dropped in her lap and write them down. "It's the job. I don't know if I want it anymore. The new job."

Anne's mother patted her daughter's hand some more and didn't say anything. The house was hush silent. Not even a ticking clock in the distance or a meowing cat. When Anne had lived there, she'd always had something blasting into the space—television, radio, CD player.

Eventually her mother got up and handed her a tissue. Then she resumed her place across from Anne. As Anne blew her nose, she studied her mother. Her face was twisted up with worry, her eyes scrunched and her brow creased, and Anne knew what she was thinking. She was thinking she wished Dad were there too. But she squared her shoulders as if to say she was up to filling his shoes and she put her hands over her daughter's again.

"We always wondered if you missed your art studies. Your father was worried about that when you moved back home. When you got the job at the Burnham Group, he figured you were changing direction. So did I."

Yeah, she'd changed direction all right. She'd chosen the road best left untaken.

"Have you thought about going back to it—looking for jobs in the arts? There are certainly enough museums and galleries around here." She said it softly and timidly, as if she was afraid to broach the subject with her daughter. Anne didn't blame her. She'd never taken kindly to Mom's suggestions. It was something girls were hardwired to do—run in the opposite direction of motherly advice.

"I'm nearly thirty, Mom. I haven't done anything like that in years. And even then, I just kind of dabbled." She spat out the last word, disgusted with herself.

"Yes, I know. It would be hard. Like starting over."

"How would I support myself? I have an apartment. A cat."

"Success follows you when you're doing what makes you happy. Your father used to say that."

"I thought he always told me to choose between doing what makes me happy and being happy at what I do."

Anne's mother laughed and pulled her hands away.

"Yeah, I guess he said that, too. The point is, Anne, if going back into the arts is what you really want to do, then get serious about it and do it. I know you don't want your mother's help, but I could see if I know anyone, if any of my friends know anyone. Your father and I made a lot of friends over the years, a lot of connections."

"They're all military people."

"Not all of them. They're government mostly, yes. But you'd be surprised."

"I don't know, I don't know." Anne stood and went to the sink, where she splashed water on her face. "I have to think about it."

"When do you have to let your boss know if you'll stay?" Mrs. Wyatt twisted around toward Anne.

"At this point, whenever I damned well please. He's got no staff in the communications department without me." Hmm… that made Anne feel good, that Mitch was now high and dry.

Mrs. Wyatt stood. "Anne, you know I don't like to butt into your business…"

Except to nudge her toward marriage and parenthood, of course, but Anne let it pass.

"… but I don't think it would be, well, healthy, for you to keep working there."

Anne's head shot up and she stared. What did this mean? *Mom knew.*

Her mother continued talking, very quietly, and it amazed Anne how she was able to say so much without admitting she knew her daughter had had an affair with her boss. Of course she knew. Mothers sensed those things.

"I was sad to hear you got a job thousands of miles away. But I was happy for you too. I didn't think it was good for you to keep working at the Burnham Group. It changed you. When I saw you today, I thought…"

She didn't need to finish. Anne knew what she'd thought. She'd seen Anne in her peasant outfit with a different guy and she'd thought she was finally done with Mitch, and that was leaving her free to move beyond her placeholder boyfriend Rob. When did she get so perceptive?

Suddenly, Anne wanted to tell her mother all about Mitch. It would have been great to unload that burden as well, to confide her heartache, her pain, her disappointed hopes. Anne started to say something, to say her mother was right because…

But she stopped herself as she gazed at her mother's worried eyes. She didn't need one more ounce of sorrow placed on her shoulders. Not one more. Anne thanked her for the dinner and promised to call her the next day. And then she gave her mother a big, warm hug and headed home to her empty apartment with her empty heart.

Chapter 23

From Anne Wyatt's childhood diary:
When I grow up, I hope I live in a place where I never have to worry about saying good-bye.

6:00 a.m. the next day

ANNE DIDN'T SLEEP WELL. Her dreams were half dreams that trotted around and taunted her into a state of frenzied worry. At night, everything was painted in stark contrast. Louise's words about St. Bart's provided the undercurrent. What she put in her MS Word files would just be a little more interesting. Another Burnham Group, in other words, dressed up in a white lab coat. Instead of promoting gobbledygook team-building exercises, she'd be living them.

In the middle of this can of worries, a dream glided by. A man in a white lab coat, standing at the altar waiting for her. She, on the other hand, waited at the back of the church in a floating, gypsy-like dress similar to the outfits she used to wear. She was waiting for the wedding march music before starting down the aisle. The groom was smiling at her, waiting, waiting. His smile faded to irritation as she remained where she was. He looked at his watch and scowled. Panic gripped her. No music. All she could hear was some of the music she'd tortured folks with the day before.

When she finally awoke close to six, sun streamed through her gauzy curtains. She didn't know if she should call Robin and tell her she wouldn't be in, or if the secretary would just assume no one would be there after yesterday's debacle. Unable to resist the temptation of responsibility, Anne reached for the phone and left a message on Robin's voice mail.

"It's Anne Wyatt. Tell Mitch I'll call him later."

She'd been leaving messages right and left since coming home the night before. She'd left a long one for Sheila on her cell phone's voice mail, torrents of sorrys and breast-beating apologies. She'd left another for Jack, telling him she'd talked to Mom and would make sure she was okay, and asking if they could get together before he shipped out. She'd left yet another on Calvin Theopoulus's work voice mail, apologizing for her behavior. And she'd tried to leave one for Ken but when it clicked over to voice mail indicating he was on the phone, she couldn't think of what to say. She'd hung up.

She still didn't have a plan, to go or to stay. She had only a sense of the moment. Maybe if she went through the motions, inspiration would strike. She jumped in the shower, washed, and dried her hair. The day was so beckoning that she opened a window to let its cottony promise scent her room. It dissipated the gloom of the night before, intoxicating her with a sense of possibilities. She didn't feel nearly thirty frigging years old today. She felt twenty, on the verge. Inspired by this optimism, she reached in the back of her closet for a simple sundress in an Indian print. It was the only piece of clothing she'd kept from her college years. She added bold jewelry she'd worn just as infrequently and found yesterday's espadrilles to place on her feet. She was crawling back into her skin.

On the ride into town, she played the radio loud over the white noise of the blasting breeze. Not classical music today, but an offbeat radio station that played oldies and new hits and country all mixed up. Paul Simon's "Diamonds on the Soles of Her Shoes" came on as she pulled into a DC garage, followed by Barenaked Ladies' "If I Had a Million Dollars." It ignited a smile.

She made a quick stop to pick up two mochaccinos and croissants and a few minutes later, she was waiting on a bench, watching life and workers pass by. Maybe he wouldn't come. Maybe he would. She'd take what came either way.

When she was a little girl dreaming of possibilities, what she wanted most in life was love and happiness. She hadn't known then that she'd be required to fill in multiple-choice forms to define those terms. Marriage, family, career, or all of the above? Downtown, suburbs, condo, townhome, apartment? Husband, lover, good friend? Business, art, nonprofit, mindless job?

When she'd been in college, her dreams were no more specific. Once, when Jack asked her what she wanted to be when she graduated, she'd jokingly answered, "A star." She hadn't had a clue. She'd just wanted to keep playing at life. She hadn't thought of choices.

The air stirred softly, picking up momentum, blowing the hem of her dress and teasing her lips into a smile.

Take it, the breeze whispered. Take the step.

She stared at the reflecting pool. The buzz and bubble of government workers gurgled by. "*Feels Like Today.*" She heard that song wafting through the air from a faraway boom box. Or maybe she only heard it in her mind.

Ken was the lucky one. He'd been pushed out into the world like a bird from its nest.

She needed a push, too! Staring into the bright morning sky, her eyes watered.

They watered so much that her cheeks glistened with tears within a few seconds.

Her leg started twitching nervously as she searched for a tissue. Damn sunlight. Why hadn't she brought her sunglasses?

Louise's words jumped into her head like a squirrel in front of a moving truck. *You'll just have more interesting things to type...*

And she heard her own words to Louise—*why don't you move back home?*

Back home? That was such a retreat. Back to a life of Mom wondering who she was seeing, what she was doing, worrying if she was happy. She knew what Louise meant when she'd shuddered. No matter how great your parents were, they'd always see you as a kid.

Isn't that what she still was?

Closing her eyes against the sunlight, she let her future drift before the red curtain of her eyelids, a future without the Burnham Group, without another job…

She saw herself giving up her apartment and moving back home. Oddly enough, there was the real sacrifice. The real hard work. *Going home.* She saw herself getting that job at Nordstrom that Louise mentioned just so she could pick up a part-time course to polish up her art history knowledge. She saw herself traipsing to interviews, letting her mother use her "connections" to set up lunches and brunches. She saw herself picking up temporary gallery jobs just to get a foot in the door, struggling like she'd never struggled before to make the dream she'd never fully developed become reality. She saw herself working at the Renwick and eventually becoming the Woman in the Volvo, contented and purposeful.

She saw herself calling Ken and seeing if he'd take a second look at her.

And in this dream, she was smiling, happy to make the sacrifices she needed to make in order to get where she wanted to go, happy to ask her mother to treat her like an adult because she'd be acting like one after thirty years. There was no need for a shredder in this dream. It was all gung ho, down the path to glory.

She pulled out her cell phone. Her heart beat wildly, a hundred galloping horses tugging her along. She punched in one digit, then another…

She had a moment of backsliding. Maybe she shouldn't be so rash.

She held her breath. She pushed the other numbers…

7:34 a.m.

His eyes bleary from lack of sleep, Ken yawned as he waited in front of the M Street property. He'd called Cyndi as soon as he'd left his uncle's office the night before, leaving a desperate message for her to hold off on contacting the landlord and to call, no matter what hour, as soon as she got in. While he'd waited, he'd spent the time going over his business plan with a fresh eye, seeing it as his father would see it, knowing the questions he'd ask, the vulnerabilities he'd identify. It had been past midnight when Cyndi had returned his call, fresh from a Kennedy Center concert. No, she hadn't talked to the landlord about Ken's turndown. But she had set up a time to meet the man at the property in the morning, to go over issues for other possible tenants.

Thus this morning's meeting. He looked at his watch. As usual, Cyndi was running late. He sipped at the coffee he'd bought on the way into town. Not as good as the coffee from… that place on the other side of the river.

He was a new man. He didn't know who that person was who'd worked at the Burnham Group yesterday.

He saw Cyndi's figure approaching and he raised his hand to wave. She was talking to a burly man in a sports jacket. As she approached, he caught the sunshine from her infectious smile. After quick introductions, she pulled out the keys and unlocked the door.

"Ready?" she asked as they headed into the space.

"I'm all about taking chances today."

8:25 a.m.

Robin picked up on the third ring. She must have just gotten in. When Anne asked for Mitch, the secretary said he wasn't there.

"He had to go out of town unexpectedly," Robin said, the sound of papers moving around in the background as she searched for a note. "He said to tell you that you could reach him on his cell. Do you have that number?"

Anne shivered. Just talking to Robin brought back the scents and sounds of the office, the fluorescent lighting, the sterile, climate-controlled air. Mitch. Gobbledygook.

Her resolve strengthened.

"I won't need it," she told Robin. "You can tell him I've thought it over and it's a no."

"What's a no?"

"I won't be staying," Anne continued. "He offered me a deal and I'm not going to take it. I'll be by to clean out my desk in a little while." Great timing—she'd be able to get in and out without the possibility of running into Mitch. Although she was sure seeing him would only bolster her decision to go, a meeting with him would just be unpleasant. She didn't want unpleasantness to shadow this otherwise beautiful day.

"So you're giving notice?"

"Yes. But I'll be taking my unused vacation days instead of hanging around for two weeks. You know how Mitch feels about staff who hand in their resignations." They should leave sooner rather than later, he'd written in an article, before poisoning the rest of the team. Speaking of resignations, she'd yet to officially send hers to Mitch. "I'll send him my resignation through email." It would be short and sweet, with no flourishes.

Standing, she flipped the phone closed. She'd call St. Bart's this afternoon and give them the news she wouldn't be coming, and then she had to cancel her temporary housing.

She looked into the distance and saw workers and tourists starting to fill the green. With a sigh, she decided she'd waited long enough. It was no surprise he wasn't there after the stunt she'd pulled yesterday.

Maybe she'd try to call him later. She'd never left a message, after all. At the very least, she could apologize again. It warmed her, thinking of the possibility of talking to him at least one more time. For now, she'd head into the Burnham Group and begin the cleanup.

"Anne?"

A faint familiar voice. Maybe someone else, looking for another Anne. She'd just scanned the crowds and not seen...

"Anne, wait up! Sorry I'm late!"

She turned and saw him, ambling down one of the gravel paths, wearing jeans and a faded polo shirt, his face lit by happiness, looking different from his buttoned-down office persona, looking... as real as she felt.

Ken.

She smiled and waved, holding up the bakery bag. Her eyes welled as sunshine flooded her gaze.

The wind was a lover's breath on her cheek, warm and intimate and well known. It pushed cherry cloud blossoms through the air, a thousand little angels announcing spring.

A flash of blue caught her eye as a bird soared from branch to branch.

"I'm so glad you came," she said, walking toward him, ready to fall into a comfortable embrace.

The End

Fire ♥ Me

Readers who would like to learn more about what happens to Anne and Ken can go to www.LibbyMalin.com and sign up for a free extra chapter!

Acknowledgments

This book has had a long journey from idea to printed page with many twists, turns, and bumps along the way. Throughout the process, several people have served as cheerleaders, helpers, and just good listeners.

Thanks first and foremost to my incredibly supportive family, especially my husband, Matthew (who keeps waiting for the day he can retire as my "pool boy"). Thanks to the rest of my family fan club—my three terrific children, my sister and her family (especially Sarah for her advice about things artistic), and my in-laws, starting with Leslie, to whom this book is dedicated (and she knows why). Thanks, too, to my very dear writing friends, Jerri Corgiat and Karen Brichoux, whose talent is as boundless as their capacity to serve as sounding boards, comforters, and counselors while we navigate through this crazy business together.

Thanks, too, to Deb Werksman at Sourcebooks, whose faith in this project made all the difference; to Bruce Bortz, who launched me and has helped me build a foundation of self-confidence; to my agent, Holly Root, for her cheerful guidance and "never say die" attitude at a critical point in this project's life; and, last but definitely not least, to Hollywood's Amy L. Byer, whose perseverance, creativity, and simple kindness helped light the fire of *Fire Me*'s success.

About the Author

Although writing was always her first love, Libby Malin earned both bachelor's and master's degrees from the Peabody Conservatory of Music and also attended the summer American School of Music in Fontainebleau, France.

After graduating from Peabody, she worked as a Spanish gypsy, a Russian courtier, a Middle-Eastern slave, a Japanese geisha, a Chinese peasant, and a French courtesan—that is, she sang as a union chorister in both Baltimore and Washington Operas, where she regularly had the thrill of walking through the stage doors of the Kennedy Center Opera House before being costumed and wigged for performance. She also sang with small opera and choral companies in the region.

She eventually turned to writing full-time, finding work in a public relations office and then as a freelancer for various trade organizations and small newspapers.

Her debut women's fiction book, *Loves Me, Loves Me Not,* was hailed as a "whimsical look at the vagaries of dating…" by *Publishers Weekly,* called "charming" by the *Washington Post,* and dubbed a "clever debut (offering) quite a few surprises…" by *Booklist.*

Writing as Libby Sternberg, she is the author of four YA mysteries, the first of which was an Edgar finalist and a Young Adult Top 40 Fiction Pick by the Pennsylvania School Librarians Association. Her YAs have been called "taut, vivid, and stirring" (*Library Journal*), "simply a delight to read" (*Romantic Times Book Club*), "lively and captivating" (VOYA), and "an entertaining original" (*Romance*

Reviews Today). Her first historical YA, released in 2008, was chosen as one of that year's "Books of Note" by the Tri-State YA Book Review Committee of PA/NJ/DE.

For many years, she and her family lived in Vermont, where she worked as an education reform advocate, contributed occasional commentaries to Vermont Public Radio, and was a member of the Vermont Commission on Women.

A native of Baltimore, Maryland, she now lives in Lancaster, Pennsylvania. She is married and has three children.